According to Carley Love

CURTISS ANN MATLOCK

SWEET OLIVE STUDIO PRESS

ACCORDING TO CARLEY LOVE

Copyright © 2023 by Curtiss Ann Matlock

Sweet Olive Studio Press

ISBN 978-0-9856144-7-8 (paperback)

Cover Design by Tammy Seidick Design

Interior formatting by Rosebud

Praise for Curtiss Ann Matlock

"...a Bradburyesque vision with drugstore soda fountains, old-timey radio shows filling the airwaves and a cast of characters who wouldn't be out of place in Lake Wobegon....Matlock conjures a sweet spell accented by tart drama, as refreshing and delightful as a lemony sweet tea."

— PUBLISHERS WEEKLY ON THE
BESTSELLER *CHIN UP, HONEY*

"Once again, Matlock delivers a gentle, glowing tale that is as sweet and sunny as its small-town setting. Readers will be delighted by this deft mix of romance and...slice-of-life drama."

— PUBLISHERS WEEKLY ON *AT THE
CORNER OF LOVE AND HEARTACHE*

"Ms. Matlock masterfully takes readers into a world full of quirky characters and small-town simplicity where they will wish they can stay."

— ROMANTIC TIMES BOOKREVIEWS ON
COLD TEA ON A HOT DAY

*Love at first sight is easy to understand; it's when two people have
been looking at each other for a lifetime that it becomes a miracle.*
~ Amy Bloom

A happy marriage is the union of two good forgivers.
~ Ruth Bell Graham

*Behind all your stories is always your mother's story, because hers is
where yours begins.*
~ Mitch Albom

For Jimi and Mama

~

The Journal

CARLEY LOVE WELLS came upon the journal in an old, faded green Belk-Tyler shirt box. Taped to the front cover was a ripple-edged black and white snapshot.

Lifting the journal to eye-level, she got a bead on the photograph through dark-rimmed reading glasses.

Two figures sat on the brick stoop from a bygone era: a middle-aged woman with upswept hair with her arm around a teenaged girl with dark curls to her shoulders. They gazed out from the cloudy photo, the woman with a faint smile and up-lifted chin, the girl straight, sober, eyebrows furrowed. "Reba Love" was written in flowing dark ink above the woman and "June Marie Love" above the girl.

"Mama," she whispered, her lips forming a trembling smile.

Carley Love caressed the image with her fingertips. Her gaze drifted downward into the shirt box. Sitting cross-legged on the floor, she sifted through the musty items: faded snapshots, two small, falling-apart albums of sepia-toned photographs of many unknown people, an ancient

Bayer aspirin tin containing one powdery tablet, a dried-up Sheaffer fountain pen, discarded old buttons, and a collection of acrid vintage matchbooks.

She set the box aside, dabbed her eyes with a tissue, used the same to clean her glasses, and straightened her legs and wiggled her red-painted toes.

The call of a mourning dove brought her gaze upward toward the bedroom window. It was open. Beyond the screen, out in the stretch of yard, the bare pecan tree limbs formed dark silhouettes against the fading turquoise sky.

Pushing to her feet with stiff motions and a soft groan, she padded barefoot across the room and opened wide the double doors. The faint pungent scent from the nearby creek and fall leaves wafted inside.

The spotted dog lying in the doorway to the hall gave a faint whine.

"Well, come on...here, girl."

The dog rose to her feet, swished her silky tail, but did not cross the threshold.

Carley Love shook her head at the dog, then stepped gingerly onto the brick porch and across it to a rose bush at the edge. Golden late-afternoon light bathed the green leaves and the few blossoms of fall.

"Oh, Mama, bless my heart, here I am, talkin' to myself and groanin' when I move, headin' into middle-age in your footsteps. I remember the rose bush, Mama. *I* dug it from Granny's and *I* planted it here. Puffin' and sweatin'...while you sat there in the lawn chair givin' needless *di*-rection."

She broke a blossom from the bush and put it to her nose, inhaling the sweetness. "I miss you, Mama."

Returning to the bedroom, she stopped at the mirror

above the dresser and tucked the rose behind her ear, a splotch of magenta against her pale hair.

A buzzing sound brought her turning toward the window, where a little green tree frog had appeared on the screen. The buzzing sounded again. Her gaze shifted to the nightstand. Three quick strides and she grabbed up the cell phone.

Jackson.

Reading the name in green letters on the screen, she melted down to the edge of the bed. The phone buzzed again before she answered.

"Hello." Her voice came out raspy.

"Carle'Love?" Jackson's deep voice came faintly. "Can you hear me?"

She cleared her throat, took up the watery glass of sweet tea from the nightstand, and sipped. "Yes. The connection is noisy, but I hear you."

"You sounded far away." When she said nothing to this, he continued, "I tried the house phone before. I've called three times."

"I shut the ringer off on the house phone. I was gettin' mostly robo calls." She paused and stated, "But I'm right here, where I was when you left."

The response to this comment was crackling static.

Then he said, "I'm awfully sorry about Memaw."

She looked down at her painted toenails. "Thank you," she said in a polite tone.

Static sounded again before his deep voice came slowly, "I told Royce today that I was comin' to the funeral, but it occurred to me that maybe I should make sure it's okay with you."

Her response to this was to lift her eyes toward the

ceiling and breathe deeply. Straightening her spine, she said, "Of course you should come. No matter about us, you will always be Royce's daddy, and he's lost his grandmother. And I know Mama would appreciate the respect."

Then—"She loved you, Jackson. She loved you and would want you to be there."

Again silence, before he said in a low voice, "I loved her, too."

She closed her eyes and swallowed. "Jackson...Mama told me that you visited her. When I was at work. I'm glad you could do that." The words came hard and with an echo of offering.

He said, "Yeah, well...I'll see you tomorrow then. And... Care'lina—are you okay?"

"I'm okay as best I can be, Jackson. Goodbye."

She clicked off the call, drew back her hand to throw the phone at the wall, but tossed it instead atop the ivory chenille bedspread. She took a deep breath and sat gazing downward.

She blinked, looked at the memorabilia scattered on the floor, then lowered herself once more into the midst of it all. Slipping on her reading glasses, she hauled the worn shirt box onto her lap. From it, she chose three photographs and set them aside atop a growing pile.

Again taking up the journal, she peered closely at the photo taped to the front cover. Her eyes grew soft. She then examined the entire journal, turned it over, saw a Goodwill sticker and smiled. With a tentative motion, as if expecting something unlikely to pop out, she opened the cover and stared at the page with its few sentences written in pencil.

If all is not lost...where is it?

You know you are getting old when you watch an event on the History Channel and can say that you were there.

If you want long friendships, develop a short memory.

She chuckled, even as tears welled up. She turned the page. There, written in flowing cursive with a black ball-point ink pen that skipped, was:

My name is June Marie Love Murray Crocker. I was born in Pasquotank County, in eastern North Carolina. For the better part of my first sixteen years, my mother, Reba Love Downie Murray, and I lived with my grandmother Myrtle Love Downie, who came from Quakers and changed over to Christian Scientist in her later years. At the age of six, I had appendicitis and Grandmother refused to call in a doctor but prayed over me and called it good. My mother snuck me out a window to get me to the hospital, a move that saved my life. Those were my people.

Carley Love turned the page. The next was empty.

Frowning, she fanned the pages. They were blank. Inside the back cover, she discovered a pocket. She ran her fingers into it. It was empty.

"Oh, good grief, Mama, is this all?"

Gripping the journal, she pushed to her feet. The rose tumbled from behind her ear and hit the floor in a scattering of magenta petals.

"Well," she said, "that's about the size of my life."

She stalked from the room, bare feet padding hard on

the oak floor. The dog followed at her heels down the hallway to the master bedroom where thin sunlight fell through opened French doors. The dog curled on her cushion in the corner and Carley Love sat at the small desk, pulled the chain on the lamp, opened the journal, and took up a pen. She reread her mother's words, turned the page, smoothed it, and began to write.

~

MONDAY, October 16, 2006

3:30 p.m.

Well, those were my people, too. June Marie Love was my mother, and she died the past Wednesday. Her funeral is tomorrow. And my ex-husband is coming.

The thought that pops into my head—not trying to be funny—is that both my mother and my marriage are now burnt to ashes.

I can see Mama, hear her laughing over that. She had such a delightful laugh. And a unique sense of humor. Oddball was the term Mama used, and she was absurdly proud of it. She cultivated it.

Oh, Mama I miss you.

And Mama I am so much like you. I've seen that in me more and more. I used to hate it, but now I'm glad about a lot of it. I sure am glad I've inherited the same unfailing humorous bent. It gets you through, doesn't it?

Now here I sit, laughing and crying at the same time, talking to Mama and God and who knows on these pages.

I tell you, making up a memory board for Mama is proving harder than I had imagined it would be. Every time I open a drawer of the old oak dresser, memories of all the people and places of my blood come to me in the scents of the home place: damp one-hundred-year-old wood, pressed roses, and the scent of Granny Reba Love—Chanel No.5 and Camel cigarettes that she smoked like a chimney all day long. That smell seems heavy in Mama's room. No doubt Granny Reba came to escort Mama up to heaven. Mama died in her own bed. I am so glad.

Of course now Freckles will not come into the room. She sees or feels what I cannot—Mama just beyond the veil, as they say.

So many things we cannot see in this earthly life. We walk by faith, not by sight, bound for Glory, as Mama used to sing. She is there now, and I've been moved up to the next in line.

This journal is surely a surprise. I cannot imagine my mother entertaining the smidgen of an idea to keep a journal. She flat out wouldn't write letters, and the etiquette of a thank-you note escaped her completely. It is further surprising that this journal is beautifully bound, genuine leather covered, and embossed with the word Journal, I guess in case you tended to forget what it was. There is a Goodwill Store sticker on the back. Mama loved her thrift store shopping. She would come home with armloads of novels and things like a cock-eyed lamp or plastic wall plaque with a funny saying.

I remember Mama telling me that story about Granny Reba Love taking her out the window. I was about ten years old when I first heard that story and thought it all so heroic on Granny Reba's part. Now I wonder at it. Why in the world didn't Granny Reba just bring Mama down the stairs and out the door? I remember Big Granny as a wisp of a brittle woman. Granny Reba could have pushed her like a feather.

I suspect Granny Reba loved the drama of sneaking out the window. That's one thing about we Love women—we are all drama queens. And funny as all get-out.

I do wish I had asked my mother more about the incident. But when you are young, you aren't interested, and later time, responsibility, and emotion cause constant distraction. Besides, sometimes Mama and I didn't want to talk to each other, we didn't want to hear what the other had to say because so much of it was about disappointment.

Even so, I know my mother loved me beyond all reason. I was the miracle 'late' child of Mama's middle-age. Mama had wanted to name me after Granny Reba Love, but Daddy wouldn't have it. He and Granny did not get on.

Anyway, here I am, Carolina Love. Love is a family name. Mama's name is June Marie Love, two middle names, which irritated her all her life, because invariably she got called June Marie, and she didn't like that. I think it is beautiful.

I am so very glad to be remembering all this on these pages. Maybe Mama didn't need to write much, but I think I do. Maybe I'm making up for her not writing, which is the silliest thing in the world. Maybe it's just that when a woman loses her mother, she loses a big part of who she is, or was.

I suppose I am processing everything. I know I'm processing a lot of guilt about not carrying Mama up home to be buried alongside Granny Reba in the cemetery with a host of other Love women—and where there's not a single soul who knew her anymore—and choosing cremation here.

But I am having a small service. It's the last thing I can do to honor my mother.

Pastor Conroy is going to speak, and once I started planning a funeral, people started saying they were coming —Ronni, of course, and a number of people from the church, and my boss Miss Lila and the girls from the office. And then Sully said he and Brenda will make the trip down from Charlotte.

And now Jackson is coming.

I don't know what to say to it.

I am still mad at him. This evening his calling me Care'lina like he does sometimes—the only one to ever call me by my given name—tore clear through me because I remembered about him coming to see Mama but not me.

It is upsetting to still be mad. I want to be over it. Anger hurts so horribly. The anger of man does not serve the purpose of God, as is said. I well know mad does not get a person anything but worn out. It is fruitless and painful and generally so *undignified* all the way around.

But there it is, like chewing gum swallowed and stuck in my throat.

Anyway, I did okay speaking to him. I did not say or sound like I wanted to hit him upside the head with a shovel. I am well trained. Mama always said that when one could not be polite, then be *very* polite.

I almost said that I wanted him to come tomorrow, but thank goodness stopped myself. I do want him to come, but I *don't want* to want him to come.

But, okay, on this page that no one will ever read, I can admit that I am glad he is coming. It is necessary, maybe like the lancing of a boil that hurts horribly but brings about good healing.

And certainly Jackson was an enormous part of my mother's life. The plain fact is that when Jackson married me, he got Mama in the bargain. The people who think they can run away and get married and leave their family behind are fooling themselves. No matter how far from home we go, we bring with us all of our family heritage and culture. Our family is borne in our blood and in memory and habit and responsibility.

Well, I have not slept but a few hours a night in weeks, and it shows. My eyes are like two burnt holes in a blanket. Making myself up tomorrow will require a big effort. When a woman is going to see her ex-husband, she wants to look so good that he will be sorry to have lost her.

The Funeral

＄＄＄

WHEN RONNI ARRIVED, Carley Love was dressed, except for putting on her shoes. She sat at the kitchen table with a cup of coffee and watched the dancing of dust motes in the ethereal golden light. Every now and again, she gave evidence of memories swirling in her mind, as she smiled, or chuckled, or teared up. Several times, she shook her head and whispered, "Mama, you were somethin'," and, ruefully, "Mama, here I am."

Ronni entered the back door without knocking. "It's just me...well, hello, Freckles, don't knock me down."

She pet the dog and set the tote bag she carried on the counter. Carley Love rose and went into her friend's open arms. The two women embraced long and hard, broke apart and smiled at each other.

"My aunt sent chicken salad and my sister a pecan pie." Ronnie pulled the items from the tote bag and opened the refrigerator. "Girlfriend, you are filled up in here."

"Ladies from the church brought a load of food yesterday, and Lila had cold cuts and veggie plates delivered from

Winn-Dixie, and two neighbors stopped in this mornin'. Everyone has been so kind," Carley Love looked up from slipping on her heeled sandals.

"Honey, don't seem so surprised. You are loved. I don't know how often you have cooked food for others."

Carley Love shrugged. "I guess it will be feast or famine, dependin' on who comes here after the service. My brother Sully already said that directly after he and Brenda are headin' to Tallahassee to visit one of Brenda's cousins."

"Really? He's not stayin' to go through your mama's things?"

"He said the only thing he wants is Aunt Ida's painting of the old Quaker meeting house. Don't let me forget it."

"Okay." Ronni shook her head, as if mystified.

Carley Love, adjusting the straps on her heels, said, "He's eighteen years older than me. We never were close. We were like only children really, and his wife Brenda didn't care for Mama or me. To be fair, we never much cared for her, either. Sully left home a long time ago and never returned. We aren't like your family," she added, teasing in her tone.

"Huh, you might appreciate that. At least your brother isn't all up in your business, as my people are."

"That is called love, honey."

Ronni pulled a bottle from the tote bag. "Well, here's my offering, cheap blackberry wine."

Carley Love cast the woman a disapproving eye.

Ronni said. "It's not too strong, and experts agree that a glass at night is good for relaxation...and Jesus did turn water into wine, sugar, it was *not* grape juice." She closed the refrigerator door with a shove.

Carley Love stood, tested her heels, gave a satisfied sigh,

and looked downward, smoothing her dress. She wore a black raw silk sheath with a matching long jacket.

Taking a wide-brimmed black sun hat from the table, she placed it on her head and moved to look into the oval wall mirror.

"So Jackson is comin' to the funeral?" Ronni said.

"Yes." Carley Love adjusted the hat and turned back and forth, studying her image.

"I love it," said Ronni. "Stunning, and black is your color. You'll wow Jackson."

Carley Love cut her eyes to her friend, then returned her gaze to the mirror.

"And Trey is coming?" Ronni's eyebrow raised.

"He said he was." She pressed her lips together as she continued considering the hat.

"He's interested in you."

"Trey?"

"Yes, Trey."

Ronni moved forward, and the women's gazes met in the mirror.

Carley Love turned from the mirror. "Oh, Trey is simply being kind and supportive, as my attorney and friend and all. He's the church's attorney, too, which makes him part of the church crowd, you know—and he's at least five years younger than I am."

"Ah...that's common. Everyone knows it." Ronni gave a dismissing wave.

Carley Love snatched the hat from her head, saying, "I can't do the hat. It's too dramatic and pokes my head."

She stood in the stream of sunlight, gazing down into her opened purse in a lost manner.

Ronni studied her for long seconds. Stepping to her own

purse on the counter, she pulled out a cosmetic bag. She told Carley Love that she was too pale and went to work on her friend's face with the swift skill of the professional makeup artist that she was.

∾

THE SMALL GROUP of people gathered in the visitation room of the funeral home talked easily among themselves. Carley Love made rounds to chat, until Ronni came to her side and whispered that she didn't have to hostess like at a social tea. "You're mourning. These people came to comfort *you*."

"Well, it comforts me to welcome people," Carley Love responded. Her gaze went to the front door. "I don't know what to say to Jackson when he comes."

"You will. You always do," said Ronni.

"Oh, there's Sully and Brenda." Carley Love crossed to the door to welcome her brother and his wife. Brenda even hugged her before stating, "I'm goin' to leave you two to it. I'll be back later, darlin'," she said to her husband, and left.

Ronni, who had come to be introduced, stared at the woman moving swiftly out the door. Carley Love made the introductions to her brother, then led him to the memory board, where her son, Royce, had pretty much rooted himself, fascinated with the old photographs. She stood watching her brother and her son, as if drinking in the sight of them together.

Trey Cummings and Jackson were the last to arrive. Trey entered in long strides and exchanged greetings with a number of others in the room as he made his way to Carley

Love at the memory board. Jackson slipped in and stood for some moments looking around.

"Hello, Trey," said Ronni, bringing Carley Love turning to see him, looking upward at his taller height.

"Trey! Thank you for comin'."

With a glance of acknowledgement to Ronni, he said, "Hello, Carley," took her extended hands and bent to kiss her cheek.

Surprise crossed her features, and she smiled up at him.

A movement behind his shoulder caught her eye. Trey moved to the side, and there was Jackson. She let go of Trey's hands.

"Hello, Care'lina," he said, his eyes directly on hers.

"Hello, Jackson. Thank you for comin'."

They gazed into each others eyes for long seconds, until Ronni drawled, "Hi, Jackson. How are you doin'?"

He looked at her a moment and said, "Hello, Ronni. I'm fair to middlin', I guess. How 'bout yourself?"

"Oh, I'm just shy of amazin'."

His gaze moved on to Trey. The two men greeted each other politely and shook hands.

Shifting his stance so as to be directly in front of Carley Love, he said, "I guess I'm off the hook for pullin' the plug on Memaw."

To that, Carley Love burst out with a laugh loud enough that heads turned their way.

Ronni and Trey shot her questioning looks, and Carley Love explained that her mother had made a living will with Jackson as the one with authority over all medical decisions. "Mama used to like to say, 'My son-in-law will pull the plug on me.'" A chuckle traced her tone with the last.

"That sounds just like your mama," said Ronni in a warm voice.

"Well," Carley Love looked pointedly at Jackson, "I guess as it turned out, it's a good thing you weren't needed, since you weren't here to pull the plug."

The grin instantly faded from his face.

Carley Love ducked her head, and at that moment, Mr. Morgan, the funeral director, came to say all was ready for the service to begin. He led Carley Love, with Ronni beside her, to the front row of chairs. Trey came right behind them, and Carley sat between them and stared at the small black urn on the table and the name plaque reading, June Marie Love Crocker.

Mr. Morgan in his dark grey suit blocked her view. He bent and whispered to Trey. Trey moved down a seat, and Royce slipped into his place next to Carley Love. She grabbed her son's hand and squeezed it. He smiled at her and put his arm around the back of her seat.

Minutes later Mr. Morgan came again, this time with Jackson beside him. With more whispering and shifting, Trey moved to the next row, Royce moved down and Jackson took his place beside Carley Love. The entire time all this shifting went on, Carley Love's eyes widened and her mouth frowned. Her gaze lingered on Jackson's hand adjusting his pant leg. When his arm started to go around the back of her seat, she looked at him. He slowly pulled his arm back down to his side and straightened his coat sleeve.

Carley Love faced forward, her eyes focused on her mother's urn, name plaque, and flowers. She pulled a tissue from her sleeve and shifted her gaze to Pastor Conroy, who appeared at the narrow podium, opened his Bible, and began to speak.

AFTER THE SERVICE and the departing of the majority of visitors, Mr. Morgan brought her mother's urn to her in a tote bag. She stood holding it, while Ronni and Sully and Royce held forth on burial versus cremation.

Carley Love opened the tote bag and gazed down into it.

Brenda arrived and Sully asked about the painting he wanted. "Did you bring it with you, sis? I guess me and Brenda need to get on the road."

Carley Love saw Brenda standing near the door.

"Oh. Yes, yes, I have it in the car," she said, but stood without moving.

Jackson's hand reached out and took the tote bag from her. "I'll get the painting for him. Are you ready to go?"

"Yes," she said.

Jackson walked Carley Love and Ronni to the Escalade, set the tote bag in the back seat and retrieved the painting for Sully, who bid them all good-bye.

"I'll call you, sis," he said at the last, his gaze coming to hers and hesitancy causing him to pause, while his wife stared at him from where she stood at the open door of their Altima. "I appreciate all you did for Mom, you know."

Carley Love stepped to him and went up on tip-toe to kiss his cheek. "Thank you for comin'," she told him, her tone warm with emotion. "I really appreciate it...and I know Mama does, too." She grinned.

He nodded, was about to say more but settled for patting her shoulder, turned and walked away.

Jackson helped her up behind the wheel and closed the door after her.

She regarded him through the driver's window. "You are welcome to come to the house. There's plenty of food. Royce's comin'...Trey and a few others."

Jackson shook his head and glanced to the side, saying, "Thank you, but I've got to work."

She nodded and pressed her lips together.

He returned his gaze to her. "Can I come see you tomorra', though, Carle'Love? Can we talk?"

Her lips parted, faint surprise swept her face and was gone. She said, "Okay. Call me tomorrow."

She jammed on her sunglasses and started the engine. She left the parking lot at a fast pace.

When she turned right, she looked into the rearview mirror and saw Jackson's truck turn left on the street and head away.

"Hey!" Ronni put her hand to the dashboard.

Realizing her speed, Carley Love slowed.

"I'M COMIN', Mama!" Carley Love hollered into the night. She threw back the covers, jumped from the bed, and raced out of the room.

She was halfway across the shadowy hallway when she came fully awake. She looked down to see Freckles right beside her, peering up.

"Just your human being silly," she told the dog in a breathless whisper.

She went, shaking, to the doorway of her mother's room and stared inside. Moonlight poured through the windows and over the ivory bedspread and made a pattern on the wall. She crossed to the dresser and gently laid her hand on the square black box now sitting there.

"Well, Mama, I guess I will hear you call me 'till the day I die."

Blinking away tears, she pattered, dog following, to the kitchen. Opening the refrigerator, she gazed into the illuminated interior for long minutes. The shelves were packed full of dishes and food wrapped in plastic.

"Ronni Ann Boudreaux, dearest friend, bless your organizational heart."

Then she spied the wine bottle. Carley Love rolled her eyes and chuckled. Bending, she searched up and down each and every shelf. Lastly she pulled out the deli drawer.

"Ah-hah!" She lifted out the pecan pie—missing only one slice. She shut the refrigerator door with her foot, carried the pie to the counter, cut a generous slice, and ate it by hand in the glow of the light over the sink. She gave Freckles, who sat expectantly nearby, the last bite of crust.

She noticed the banker's lamp atop of the desk in the alcove of the kitchen had been left on, and walked over to turn it off. A note was stuck to the green lampshade. *I paid your electric bill with your credit card. R.*

"And thank you for keepin' me with lights, Ronni," she murmured.

She noticed her friend had also neatly sorted and stacked the mail she hadn't attended to in days, or weeks. One envelope was set aside from the others. It bore the very official-looking address of the county circuit court.

Slowly she lifted the envelope. Lips pressed together, she used a letter opener to slice the flap and gingerly unfolded the contents.

In the matter of the marriage of...District Court...State of Alabama

She scanned the text and then flipped to the following page, her eyes falling to the line requiring her signature.

She suddenly let go the papers. They drifted onto the desk as she turned, stopped, crossed her arms, and rubbed her shoulders. She looked unseeing around the room, then walked slowly into the living room and on through the house to the bedroom. The dog followed.

Freckles went straight to her cushion. Carley Love retrieved robe and slippers from the closet. She then opened wide the doors to Jackson's side of the closet and stood long seconds contemplating the few items—shirts and slacks, a sport coat—left hanging on the rod.

Shutting the doors with a swift motion, she went to the bedside chest and drew a small black jewelry box from the drawer. She opened it and regarded the set of wedding rings inside.

She closed the box, returned it to the drawer, and stalked back through to the kitchen, the dog hurrying to follow.

She jerked open the refrigerator door and drew out the bottle of wine. She squinted at the label. Blackberry. With a screw-off cap. She fetched the a gaily-striped stemmed Fiestaware glass from the cabinet and poured it half full of the dark, shiny liquid. After a moment of hesitation, she took a gulp, and coughed and gave a shiver.

She sipped the wine, went to the back door and opened it. Faint sweet scents came to her. A night bird called. A frog peeped.

Turning back inside, she again hurried through to her bedroom, where she snatched up the journal, a pen, and a blanket. Returning to the porch, she wrapped in the blanket and settled onto the lounge chair. Freckles hopped up and curled on her feet. She pet her for long moments. Then she opened the journal on her lap and began to write by the dim light falling from the kitchen window.

~

WEDNESDAY, October 18

1:55 a.m.

Well, the funeral is over, and Mama now sits atop her dresser. There's an audacious statement that would please her.

Mama's urn is a small black plastic box. Mr. Morgan brought it to me in a tote bag with the funeral home logo on it. I could not believe it weighed so much. Mama wasn't but itty-bitty when she died. I didn't purchase a fancy urn because I keep thinking I want to take Mama's ashes up home to bury by Granny Reba Love. But that little box did look overwhelmed sitting there between two enormous bouquets of flowers—one from Sully and his Brenda and the other from Jackson and Royce. In the front of it was the small vase of three roses I brought from Mama's bush out back. Fanning out on the floor were other bouquets and plants. People's kindness just fills my heart.

And I am relieved I kept hold of good sense and decorum and didn't cut Jackson out of the few photographs of us together that I used for the memory board.

Really, you can't look back at thirty-five years and cut out the hurtful parts. I don't think, in my honest moments, that I would want to. I believe, eventually, those hard moments make us. *Eventually* being the key word.

And I smile now to think of how delighted both Royce and Sully were with the memory board. Sully could identify people with Mama and Daddy in the early photographs. It was good for Royce to hear about his people. Good to see, Sully, too, and to see he is happy and well. We are not close, but we wish the best for each other. That is enough.

Trey Cummings came to the funeral, too. Ronni says he is interested in me, but I don't think so. He was a friend and attorney to both me and Jackson, made our wills, before he became my divorce attorney. He might have represented Jackson instead of me, but I happened to contact him first. And not to sound petty, but I was glad Trey was with me when Jackson arrived.

It turned out not to be too awkward. I said hello and thank you for coming. By then I had said the same thing to everyone so that the words just flowed out of my mouth.

His eyes were so beautiful blue-green. His blue shirt set them off, as has always been the case—and do you know it was the blue shirt that I gave him last Christmas. I don't think he has a shirt that I didn't buy for him.

And he mentioned, of all things, how he didn't have to pull the plug on Memaw. Mama would have loved it. I wonder if she saw. She would have been aggravated with my sharp comment about him not being around to pull the plug. Jackson looked like I had slapped him with that, and I am ashamed of such sarcasm right there at my own mother's funeral.

Now get this: Jackson had on his wedding band. That surprised me. As did him coming to sit beside me.

When I think of it now, though, I appreciate him coming and paying such respect to Mama, and to me. To all that has been. He had a right to sit there as her son like that after all the years he helped care for Mama, as if she were his own.

I forgot to tell Pastor Conroy to call Mama by her preferred June Love, so he just kept saying June Marie throughout his entire spiel. I could just see Mama having a fit over that. Otherwise, she would have been pleased with his sermon because he gave an upbeat word about death being a passage from our temporary earthly life and how she loved her family, and didn't go on too long about it.

I invited Jackson to come to the house afterward for dinner, but he declined, saying he had something to do. That cut through me, but I did not let on.

He said he wanted to come talk to me tomorrow, which is today. I think it is to my credit that I did not spew my first thought, which was: You should have wanted to talk more before you up and left.

Now that I found the papers from the court, though, I know what Jackson wants to talk about. He wants me to sign those papers.

Well here I am, ending my marriage of thirty-five years to the man I have been with since I was sixteen years of age. In the space of a few weeks I have experienced the death of my marriage, the death of my mother, the death of all the life I have ever known.

Lord, what am I going to do?

The Divorce

CARLEY LOVE SMOOTHED her silk blouse, checked her image closely in the mirror, wiped beneath her eyes and touched up her lipstick.

"You look fine, girl. You do not look one bit like you fell into drunken sleep on the porch—thank you, Lord."

Her gaze went to the clock. It read twelve-ten.

She cut two slices of pecan pie and poured two glasses of cold sweet tea, took it all on a tray to the porch and sat it on the round glass-topped table. The deep green sweet olive shrub at the porch corner overflowed with fragrant tiny blossoms. She dashed into the kitchen, returned with scissors, and cut sprigs, sniffed them and smiled. She tucked the sprigs into a vase of water and placed them in the middle of the small table.

Then she sat on her chaise to wait. In less than five minutes, precisely at twelve-thirty, Jackson's black pickup truck rolled up the long driveway. Patches of sunlight falling through the live oak trees glimmered on its shiny dark surface.

The dog barked, and as soon as Jackson got out of the truck and rounded the hood, Freckles leaped from the porch and raced to him, wagging her entire body in eager greeting. Jackson bent to pet her. The dog turned circles and Jackson gently roughed her fur tail to neck. The dog turned circles again and licked him all over the chin.

At last Jackson straightened and came slowly up the walkway with the dog dancing beside him. Carley Love's steady gaze moved over his thick and greying brown hair and down across his broad shoulders.

Reaching the bottom step of the porch, his gaze met hers, and he smiled. She smiled in return.

"Hello," he said.

"Hello. I have cold tea and pecan pie."

"Thanks."

He came up onto the porch and across to lower himself into the large dark wicker porch chair, reaching immediately for the plate of pie. She took her own plate and settled on her chaise.

After a couple of bites, he pointed at the pie with his fork, saying, "You didn't make this."

"No. Ronni's sister made it."

"Yours is better," he said.

"I use maple syrup and honey. This is made with corn syrup." Her lips twitched with a small smile that she hid in looking downward and forking her pie.

They spoke of the weather and how the dog had gained weight.

Those subjects exhausted, awkward silence stretched.

Finally Jackson broke it. "So why didn't Pastor Talbot preach your mother's funeral?"

Carley Love regarded him. "I changed over to the Baptists."

He gazed at her. "Oh."

Again silence stretched. It was the loud silence of unasked questions. Jackson fed a last piece of piecrust to the dog. Carley Love opened her mouth to speak, closed it and looked out at the trees.

"I'm real sorry about Memaw," Jackson offered.

Her eyes swung to meet his. "Well, I'm glad she's not sufferin' anymore. Truly glad. I know she is in heaven, just as Pastor Conroy said. She's at peace now."

He frowned. "Did she suffer a lot?"

"She wasn't in pain, not like that. But it wasn't pretty the last month." She sipped from her glass. "You know, a lot of Mama's life she suffered."

They sat some moments in quiet understanding.

After a moment, Carley Love continued, "These last weeks, Mama declined fast into strugglin' to breathe. The doctor said it had been happenin' right along, but I guess I was busy...distracted, and didn't see it. And Mama never meant anyone to see.

"But toward the end anyone could see her strugglin' to breath and anxiety gnawin' away at her, and the drugs just seemed to make it all worse." Her words came at a fast tempo. She stroked her hair back from her face and wiggled her toes, her blue eyes as if seeing back in time. "Her anxiety was hard to watch...her hands moved all the time, rubbin' over the chair arm, pluckin' at the bedcovers. Nothin' I did seemed to help for very long or very much. There was so little that I could do..."

Her lips trembled. "It was difficult...and you had left

me...I was all alone." The last was a wail. She buried her face in her hands.

Jackson was beside her, pulling her against him. "I'm sorry, Care'lina. I'm so sorry," he murmured into her hair.

She sobbed against him and banged her fist on his muscles, but he didn't let her go. At last she slumped against him, soaking his shirt with her tears, while he held her and stroked her hair.

When her sobs had faded, she slowly pushed from him, rose and went into the house. She blew her nose and checked her image in the wall mirror, wiping away mascara smudges.

Five minutes later, she returned to find him once more sitting in his chair. He looked at her with an anxious expression. He opened his mouth to speak, then closed it.

She lowered herself onto the chaise, saying, "I'm sorry. I didn't mean to blame you or anything. I guess I just needed to let out the grief. It seems to come at odd moments.

"And I know you are sorry, Jackson. I know. Anyway, it really is over and done." She took up her glass of tea. "Mama was peaceful her last couple of days. She never did need any drugs at the end. She just went into a coma and after a day just quit breathing. Quiet and peaceful as that, she was gone.

"You know, right when it happened, I saw in my mind Granny Reba Love holdin' out her arms to her, welcomin' her. And I swear I smelled Granny Reba's Chanel. You remember it, how that was her fragrance?—strong as Granny standin' right there."

His eyes on hers, he nodded. "I remember."

She looked away, off into the distance. "They are together again now, Granny Reba and Mama and Daddy and all of 'em," she added with a trembling but true smile. "And after watchin' Mama, I will never again be afraid of dyin'. It isn't anything more than what they say—flyin' away to the other side."

She bent her head, staring unseeing at the floor. "The dyin' is easy. It's the livin' part that is hard and fearful."

"I can sure agree with that."

His deep tone was such to draw her attention. They looked each other in the eyes for long seconds, and then Carley Love turned her head to study the yard. She sat perfectly still, while Jackson sipped his cold tea and wiped the bottom of the glass on his denim-clad thigh.

He broke the silence. "I kept money goin' into the account. I hoped to help by that."

"It did," she replied. "Thank you. We had all we needed. I didn't have to worry about workin' or bills or anything."

"The money's yours, too," he said.

Carley Love looked at his hand holding his glass, then shifted her eyes to the nearby shrub. "The sweet olive is bloomin'. I love its scent."

"Yeah...it's nice."

She sat up straighter and spoke firmly. "I have the divorce petition from the court. It came in those last weeks when Mama took her downward turn. I didn't deal with any of my mail then. I saw it last night, though. I think all I have to do is sign and file the papers. I'll phone Trey about it soon...but not today.

"I don't feel like dealin' with anything right now. Lila has given me off as long as I need. I'll attend to it soon, though. Or Trey will likely do it. I think we should leave the settlement to Trey and your attorney to work out, and I believe we'll have to come in front of a judge. I really don't know." She stroked fingers across her forehead.

Jackson sat his glass on the table and leaned forward, braced his forearms on his thighs, and rubbed his palms together, saying, "I got the papers, too...but...I don't want a divorce, Care'lina."

She slowly blinked. "Really?" Her tone was flat.

"Look..." He rubbed his palms together again. "I know I screwed up."

Her gaze went to his hands. She said nothing.

He said, "I just got all crazy. It was just...well, we weren't gettin' along, and there was this stuff at work..." He paused, inhaled a ragged breath, and came out with, "I was crazy and stupid—I admit it. And then I didn't know how to undo it. But...I miss you, Carle'Love. I miss...*us*."

He regarded her with shimmering eyes.

Returning his gaze, she tilted her head. For a moment she appeared about to speak, and then she looked away, squinting at the bright sunlight for long seconds.

Swinging back to him, she came out with, "Well, I tell you what, Jackson Paul Wells, the truth is that in the first months, I imagined you comin' back and sayin' this very thing—that you knew you had made a mistake and wanted me back." She leaned slightly forward. "But in the past couple of tough months those imaginings dried up. Pain and anger just burned all my feelin's up. There's nothin' left."

She looked down at her wiggling toes, then out at the sunlit bare pecan trees.

After long seconds, he said, "Memaw's dyin'...well, it's made me see, really *see*.

"I am sorry, Carle'Love. I know I was wrong and I will be sorry for the rest of my life." He paused, his jaw working,

"But I still love you. I never stopped lovin' you. What I did had nothin' to do with not lovin' you."

He stared at her unrelenting profile, as she continued to focus on the trees.

Finally, she returned her eyes to him and asked, not unkindly, "Do you really think you can just come in here and say sorry, and we can take up again?"

Before he replied, she was on her feet and hurried again into the kitchen. At the sink, she thrust her wrists under a hard stream of cold water. Raising up on tiptoe, she looked out the window and could see Jackson's legs where he sat in the chair, his knees bouncing up and down.

She slumped over her arms, with the water still running on her wrists.

At last she shut off the faucet. Still over the sink, eyes closed, her lips moved with silent words.

Straightening, she took her time drying her skin, patting the damp towel to her face.

She checked again to see Jackson was still there. Her eyebrows knotted. Then her eyes rolled heavenward. "Well, Lord?"

She closed her eyes a moment, then straightened her shoulders, pushed out the screen door and returned to take up her place on the chaise, sitting with a straight spine.

"Why did you leave, Jackson?"

His response to this was to breath deeply, clear his throat, and straighten in his chair. "Well, we hadn't been gettin' along...and on top of that, there was work. I wanted that promotion, and when I didn't get it...do you even remember me tellin' you about that?"

"I remember."

He rubbed his palms on the thighs of his jeans. "I really

expected that promotion, and when I didn't get it...well, it just seemed like all I could see were my failings. My failings in not gettin' to where I wanted to be in my job, my failings as a husband, since we kept arguin'." He shifted in his seat. "It seemed like my time was runnin' out. And I guess I got to thinkin' how we had always been married and I never got to be just me, on my own. I thought...well, I thought space to be on my own...just get myself figured out. I never planned to leave."

She stared at him, her left ear cocked slightly toward him.

"I know I was stupid and crazy, and I'm real sorry to have hurt you. I really am." His voice cracked.

"I never meant to leave, Carle'Love. It just happened. And when it did, I couldn't face comin' home havin' failed yet again. Then you had Memaw, and I didn't want to intrude.

"It was like when she died, everything that was important became crystal clear to me. I saw my own mortality. And I knew I was makin' a big mistake for the rest of my life. I knew that I just had to make things right."

Carley Love's eyes turned tender, and her gaze drifted down to the splayed hands that rubbed on his thighs.

He swallowed, then said, "We have had a lot of *good* years together, Carle'Love. It seems like all those years should count for somethin'—for a bunch more than one foolish mistake."

She gave a bare nod, shifted her gaze out to the yard and then down to the dog who lay sprawled on the porch between them.

Jackson leaned forward. "I want a chance to make it up to you, Carle'Love. I have figured out some stuff, and I want a chance for us to find what we had and...and a chance to see...if maybe you could love me anyway."

His eyes were fixed steadily on hers.

She opened her mouth, then closed it. After several seconds, she came out with, "I don't know what to say, Jackson. I don't know what I feel. Except that I'm exhausted. I really have nothin' to give right now."

She paused, then added, "I need my own space right now, as you said. I think you can understand that."

His response to this was an accepting nod, and then, with hope, "Does that mean we can talk, though?"

"We *are* talkin'," she responded.

RONNI'S VOICE over the phone had a strident tone. "So your divorce is on hold."

"Yes, I guess it is." She paused. "And Jackson is still wearin' his wedding band."

"Uh-huh," said Ronni. "Well, you didn't agree to anything did you?"

"Like what?" Carley Love's eyebrows arched. "I agreed to have supper with him on Friday night. He wanted to meet tomorrow night, but I chose Friday. I've got to have some space." She waved the air in front of her as she spoke.

"Just be careful. Jackson might have realized what it's gonna cost him, and he is backin' up, goin' to find a way to short you."

"Well...I don't think so. Jackson has always been generous. He's continued depositing his salary into our account all these months he's been gone."

Carley Love thought for a moment. "I wonder how he is

livin', actually. He takes so little, and he hasn't touched the investments, either. I wonder if he is sleepin' in his truck." She knotted her brows.

Ronni said, "It has been my experience that all of us have an ugly side, honey. My Uncle Carter, the sweet one everyone of us love, got so mad at Aunt Louise that he went in her closet and cut up all her clothes. And he was the one who had wanted the divorce! And at the risk of saying somethin' difficult, Jackson may be sleepin' with someone."

Carley Love gazed out the kitchen window. "I don't think...that's not like him. And he does have friends."

"Have you asked him?"

"Well, no. It didn't occur to me. We didn't really discuss anything more than to make the dinner date."

"You might want to ask him. Just sayin'. Although I think you should go away for a few weeks. Let him stew, while you take time for you."

To this, Carley Love shook her head with a sad laugh. "Where would I go? The idea of findin' somewhere and packin' is enough to put me under."

Her voice rose. "I do not know how I got into this situation. Well, *I* didn't do it—*he* did!" Her tone broke with tears. "And now my life has become a television soap opera, like *Love of Life* that Mama and Granny Reba used to watch."

Ronni said, "Huh...I don't remember that one. Mama always watched *The Bold and the Beautiful*. She would tape it, and we'd watch together in the evenings. Gosh, I haven't thought of that in a long time. And *The Young and The Restless*. My sister still watches that."

"You are a generation younger than me." She wiped tears from her cheek. "Lordy, I feel old."

"Oh, stop it. You are not old. You are a vital woman."

"I am *fifty-two*, and I have entered menopause, Ronni. My periods have stopped." Her chin quivered. A tear slipped from the corner of her eye. "I am in menopause and my husband has left me."

"You have entered too-much-emotional-pain, that's what you have entered," came Ronni's quick and firm reply. "It's all the stress. No one can care for their mother like you have and not get worn down. You must have lost ten pounds these past weeks."

"Eight. I've lost eight pounds in the past month."

"That is too much for you. We'll have to shake the sheets to find you."

"I have felt old since he left me, Ronni." Tears again trickled down her cheeks. "I'm just so tired, I can't think anything straight. He did hug me before he left, but it was so awkward. I think I'm afraid of it all. I don't want to hurt any more."

Her voice grew husky. "But I couldn't sign the papers, Ronni. I got a pen to do it, but I couldn't. I couldn't breathe each time I tried."

"Then you are not ready," Ronni said. "You are worn out, honey. You just need some rest."

"What comes to me is how easily people can say they are sorry. We really all do things for which we are sorry. I have a ton of things for which I am sorry. But this is a good lesson to me, because I have learned that those words don't magically change or heal what has happened. It is actions that do that. As the old saying goes: actions speak louder than words. He left me. And he could do it again—he did today!"

"Did you want him to stay? And do what? Do you want to sleep with him?"

"No. Well...Oh, I don't know what I want!"

Ronni soothed, "That's to be expected, honey. It truly is. You've had some sizable heartaches."

As if not hearing, Carley Love said, "I guess I want Jackson to fix it all. He has always fixed things for us. He fixed anything around this house before I even knew it broke. Now I want him to fix this with us. I want him to somehow make it go away...make it not to have happened.

"But he can't, so I'm mad at him." Her hand formed a fist and hit the counter.

"Oh, honey, let it be," Ronni said. "Give it all to God right now and let go. I'll bring you out a chicken salad sandwich and another bottle of wine tonight," she added.

"I do not need another bottle of wine. I haven't drank all of that one you left. I do not need to get to be a wino on top of everythin' else."

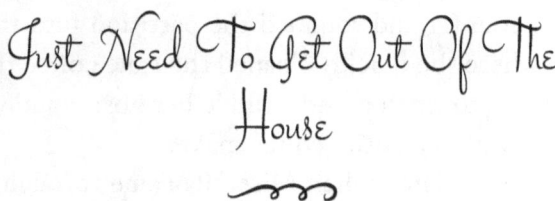

Just Need To Get Out Of The House

AS SHE OPENED the heavy bevelled glass door to Ackerman and Company Real Estate office, the bell above rang out. The reception desk was empty, the room silent. She stood, hesitating. There came the sound of footsteps and Miss Lila appeared from the hallway.

"Why, Carley." Miss Lila's sharp dark eyes surveyed her.

"I know you said to take time off, Miss Lila, but I...well, I just needed to get out of my house. I thought maybe you could use me."

"I understand." Lila Ackerman was a petite and elegant woman who, after almost thirty years of living in the south, still had the inflection of Chicago in her clipped speech. She regarded Carley Love. "And really, we are dead today, as usual on a Thursday at this time of year. If you handle the reception desk, I can go get a pedicure and do a few errands. Norma Fay is up in Montgomery until Monday and Doreen isn't due in until noon." She turned in the direction of her office, then paused to add, "Make some coffee,

Carley. None of us can make it like you do, and fill my travel mug."

"Yes, ma'am."

Carley Love plopped her purse on the desk behind the reception counter and rounded the partition into the small kitchen, where she quickly cleaned the stale coffee from the pot—pausing to smell it and wrinkle her nose—and went on to quickly wipe the entire coffee maker.

Ten minutes later, when Miss Lila came through, Carley Love presented her boss with her tall Yeti mug.

Miss Lila handed her a small stack of files. "Take care of these. You can leave when Doreen gets in, but I'll count on you tomorrow at nine. I have two appointments in the morning." She was already headed for the door. "Carley, take off your sunglasses."

"Yes, ma'am."

~

THURSDAY, October 19

11:15 a.m.

I decided to come to work. I sure am glad Miss Lila could use me. I felt like I might go plumb to pieces if I didn't get out of the house. It echoes with a lot of things that I just don't want to think about.

No one has come into the office, and only two people have called—Miss Lila's landscaper and a possible new client asking for Doreen.

I put away the files Miss Lila gave me and found a big stack atop the cabinet, so filing hasn't been done since I've been out. Then I tidied Miss Lila's desk, watered plants, restocked Cokes and water in the refrigerator, and thoroughly cleaned the break room. It was nasty.

If anyone comes in now, I can quick close this journal and shove it out of sight. I cannot believe I brought it with me. Writing in it really is a stress reliever.

I am trying to figure out my life mess. At least find what I am good at, since I'm looking at supporting myself. Miss Lila, who is flat out stingy with compliments (as well as money), says I'm the best receptionist she has ever had because of my smile and gracious manner. I am proud of how I make people feel welcome when they come in the door of Ackerman and Company, and I do keep things running smoothly around here.

It is hard to believe that I have been working for Miss Lila for nearly two years. Sometimes good things come from procrastination, because if I hadn't put off paying our property taxes until about the last minute, I wouldn't have met Miss Lila at the tax office. She was sitting beside me and having a discussion with another lady across from her, complaining about how her receptionist had run off to California to be on Wheel of Fortune, made a bundle and never came back. Another woman said how much she liked that show, and I put in about Mama being really good at it. The next thing all we ladies was talking. By the time my number was called to the tax window, I had accepted Miss Lila's offer of a temporary part-time receptionist job. Just sort of amazing how things turn up when we aren't even expecting it.

Early on I began courses toward being an agent, but Mama's health and other things got in the way.

Maybe one of those other things was my lack of ambition for facts and laws and such.

Thinking of how my future is now up in the air, though, I might need to put forth more effort to have ambition for something that will actually pay a living wage. You just don't get much money from cordiality and grace and helping people, shameful as that is to say on the human race.

~

THE SOUND of the front door opening startled her out of deep concentration. She had been making a list of possible employment endeavors. There were only three items.

Seeing Doreen come through the door, she slammed shut the journal and pushed it forward beneath the counter.

"Hello, Doreen." She covered the journal with part of the desk calendar.

"Hi, honey. I am surprised to see you here. I thought you were takin' time off to rest." Not waiting for a reply, Doreen continued, "You had a nice service for your Mama. Just lovely. I have never been to a service where someone had been cremated. More and more people are doin' that these days—but not in my church or my family," she added with a chuckle. "My mother always said that cremation meant we couldn't rise up from the grave. Of course, I know we have people burned up in buildin's and blown to bits, like in wars. It isn't their fault they don't get to get buried whole. But do they get to rise up? I can't bear the thought of bein' cremated. What if you weren't dead and you woke up in a furnace?" As she spoke, she set her enormous purse on the counter and dug through it.

Carley Love watched the younger woman bring a cell phone from the depths, realized she had an opening to speak, but Doreen cut her off.

"Ah-ha!" Doreen said, flashing the glittery pink phone, her long silver-sparkly fingernails bright against her dark fingers. "Praise God I did not lose it! I could not remember if I brought it. I was in such a rush not to be late again 'cause Miss Lila threatened to fire me, if I'm late again." Her voice turned hushed and she glanced in the direction of Miss Lila's office. "Her car isn't here, is she gone?"

"Yes."

The younger woman smiled brightly. "And with Norma Fay out, it's just us chickens. Have you noticed that Norma Fay has become something of a phantom the past month? I think somethin' is up with her."

"Her mother needs care," Carley Love injected as the other woman took a breath. "You had a call. A Mr. Hebert asking for you." She handed up the memo.

"Oh. Yes. My cousin said she knew a man just transferred into the area from Baton Rouge. Bet that's him." Then, heading around the partition into the little kitchen, "I need some coffee. Did you make it?"

"Yes, but it's from nine."

Carley Love glanced at the clock, seeing both hands straight up. A flash of light from outside—the reflection of a car pulling up—caught her eye.

A tall man alighted from the black Lexus. Sunlight hit his light brown hair as he came to the office in long, quick strides.

Carley Love rose to her feet behind the desk.

"Hi," he said as he poked his head in the door.

"Hi, Trey. How are you?"

"Better than I deserve," came his instant reply with a grin as he crossed the short distance to the reception counter.

They smiled at each other.

He said, "I saw your car and thought maybe you would let me take you to lunch."

"Oh...I..."

"Hey, Trey," said Doreen coming around the partition, bearing her large cup that read Sista D. "You go on, girl-friend." She waved her hand in a shooing motion.

"Okay...thanks."

Trey held open the door of the sporty Lexus and Carley Love folded herself down into the seat.

Just as Trey closed the car door, her cell phone rang.

She looked at the screen. It was Jackson calling.

As Trey opened the driver door, she pressed the button to silence the phone.

Trey slipped his long frame into the driver seat and smiled at her. "How about Antonio's?"

"Oh, that sounds lovely."

She looked at his tanned hand on the shifting knob and up his arm to his profile. She felt her cell phone vibrate in her purse. She focused her gaze out the windshield.

STILL THURSDAY, 3:30 p.m.

Well, here is how needing to get out of the house turned into going on a date this afternoon:

I went to lunch with Trey, to Antonio's. I did not even think until I returned to get my car and this diary—which I had forgotten!—that I had gone on a date with another man while I am technically still married to Jackson. I called Ronni and asked her about it, and she said it was a date, because Trey paid for it.

Further, I have to say that I sensed a difference with Trey right off the bat. His brown eyes were right on mine, and he gave me the warmest smile.

Trey has the most stunning smile, perfect teeth. Generally speaking, good teeth are a sign that a person enjoyed a prosperous family growing up. Jackson has beautiful teeth, too. Thankfully in my adulthood I could get mine fixed.

Well, Trey is just really good looking, gray hairs at the temple and all that. Yes, I was flattered that he asked me to lunch and tickled to go, and Doreen did about push me out. So I went.

Now, in my defense, I am a separated woman, who is nearly legally divorced, and I thought maybe Trey wanted to tell me something about the divorce, and that I should tell him about the papers having come and me not signing. It did not start out being a date, at least to me.

This sort of thing is sure new to me.

My actions *should* have told me I was on the edge. Right as I was getting into Trey's car, Jackson called me. And I chose to reject a call from my husband, while I went out to lunch with my divorce attorney. Just like a soap opera.

It was quite the experience. He held the door to that sporty Lexus, and just the way he was acting made me feel like a princess.

So we talked about a bunch of stuff, like the fine weather, the good food (the best pasta salad I have ever had) how I come from North Carolina, and Trey once lived on a boat, before I finally brought up about receiving the divorce papers and how Jackson wanted to talk about us getting back together.

Trey did not seem surprised. He said that such situations are not uncommon, especially with long-term marriages. And he made a point of saying that he could recall only one or two couples of his experience that he has heard who succeeded at putting their marriage back together. He made this statement: "By the time couples go to all the trouble of divorce, things are pretty well burned up between them."

Those words made me think of Mama's ashes and also what I had said to Jackson.

This dismal information caused a great sinking inside me at that moment, and really still does. But at the same time, in that intimate atmosphere across the table with a white cloth and delicious food, I wondered what it would be like to kiss Trey, and I imagined getting naked with him —and it scared me to pieces. When one marries young, there isn't a lot of opportunity for experience. I have only been naked and intimate with one man in my life, and that is Jackson Paul Wells.

It is striking to realize my sheltered life, and to wonder how I got to this point.

It helps to get it written out in this journal. I'm going to have to make sure I take this journal with me everywhere, with my whole mess of a life now in it, I sure don't want anyone to read it—and that may have already happened, because I forgot and left it at the receptionist desk and found it moved when I went to get it.

I wonder if Doreen looked in it. I think she is the nosey sort who would read someone's private words. If something is going on around town, just ask Doreen. She knows and likes to talk of it. Yes, I think it likely she would read someone's diary given the chance.

I would not do that, read someone's diary, not even if it was open.

But do any of us know for sure? Would I read it if it were open?

Maybe I would, but I do know it is <u>not right</u>. I would not keep reading.

But what if I could see Jackson's diary?

Silly thought, as he would never write one.

But what if he did? I admit, if I saw his diary, I might have to read it to find out why he left and what exactly has gone on these past months.

The Effects Of Talking

FRIDAY, October 20

2:00 p.m.

Jackson just called, making certain I was still meeting him at the Bayou Shack, or did I want him to pick me up. I told him firmly that I would drive. That was what he wanted to know yesterday, too, when I finally answered his call.

Maybe I have started wanting to get back with Jackson. And that idea scares me so badly that I can't look at it.

I worked a few hours at the office this morning and managed to stay calm and pleasant. Then when I came home, I fell on the couch with Freckles and went to sleep for an hour and it took me ages to get awake after. When I went for my shower, Granny Reba Love's Bible practically shouted at me from where it has been gathering dust beside my bed. It fell right open to Philippians 4, which Granny had marked with a purple ink pen, and which tells us to stand firm in the Lord—that means don't get lost in a hissy-fit—and to take pleasure in the Lord and let our gentle spirit, *graciousness*, *unselfishness*, be known to all people, and to not be anxious for anything, but to *pray*.

Well, maybe the trying counts. Heaven knows I do try to remember to be gracious and to pray.

Granny Reba Love made it through by herself in her later years. I never thought of that before.

I have been so busy with Mama these last months that this is the first time I'm truly realizing that if I divorce, I am going to have to give up this house, because I will have to exist on a stringent budget of time and money. Those facts of life are to be considered. How in the world does a woman do that in her fifties?

Granny Reba did it. She became the manager of The Ladies Style Shop, and she also wrote for the society page of the Bell City Daily News. She must have been around fifty when she started at the shop.

Well, at least I have good clothes to start with. I learned that from Granny Reba—buy the best and they last.

CLOTHES COVER THE BED, before Carley Love finally settling on slim jeans, a soft rose-colored silk blouse, and tall heeled boots. She surveyed herself in the full-length mirror and squared her shoulders with confidence. Then she lowered the thermostat and stood under a vent blowing cool air for a full minute, before taking a great deal of time and effort with her makeup. She was leaning forward and studying her eyes in the mirror when Ronni called.

"How are you doin', girlfriend?" Ronni asked.

"I'm okay."

"Are you still meetin' Jackson?"

"Yes."

"You are drivin' yourself, so then you can leave when you want, right?"

"Yes, ma'am, I am." Then—"Thank you for carin', Ronni. I wish I could go home and cry to Mama. Not that Mama would do anything, but I miss her so much." Her tone turned husky.

"I care, honey. But I do have to say your mess is why I don't want to get involved with a man. All they are good for is heavy lifting."

"You have brothers for that...and a daughter and sisters and cousins and aunts and uncles to help you," Carley Love said. "It is way different when you are alone. It is lonely."

"Well, just give yourself time, honey-bunny," Ronni said earnestly. "Don't go runnin' back to Jackson out of a fit of loneliness. That will only make things worse. You need time to settle down and figure out what you really want to do with you life. Oh, glory, that's my brother beeping in, and I need to take it. Call me when you get home."

Carley Love clicked off. She stood a moment, frowning in thought. Moving to the bedside chest, she retrieved the ring box. She opened it, stared at the rings for long seconds, snapped the lid closed and returned the box to the drawer.

Hearing a vehicle arrive, she hurried to look out the living room window and saw Royce's big truck coming to a stop.

"Hi, honey," she called from the kitchen doorway.

Her son tossed her a wave as he strode to the garage. "I'll be there in a minute."

Returning to the kitchen, she saw him through the window take two tires to his pickup truck and toss each into the truck bed. She checked the clock, then her purse, then watched her son again come up the walk toward the house. When she opened the door, Freckles raced ahead.

"So how's your day?" She scanned his face.

"Too hot for fall." He flopped into a chair. Freckles came and laid against his boot and he stroked the dog's head.

"It's supposed cool down tonight."

"I'm ready."

Studying his face, Carley Love slowly lowered herself to her usual place on the chaise. She smiled. "What's up?"

"Well..." A slow grin swept his face and his eyes sparkled. "I've met someone, Mama."

"Oh?"

As she listened to her son tell of meeting a special woman, she leaned forward, her manner saying without speaking, *Tell me...tell me all.*

When at last he stood to go, she gave him a long hug, saying, "I love you...I'm so happy for you."

"Love you, too," he said shyly and casting her his bright, beautiful smile as he drew back and looked down at her. "You're awfully dressed up. Where are you off to?"

"Oh...just meetin' a friend for dinner. You go on. I'm late now."

He sprinted from the porch, saying, "I am, too!"

She watched his big tall truck roll down the drive, her brows faintly knotted. Then she saw the time and flew into motion to put the dog inside, snatch her purse and get into the Escalade, calling Jackson as she went, telling him she was on her way.

~

THE SIGN ARCHED above the long, low porch of the building that sat beneath moss-draped live oaks: *The Bayou Shack*. The graveled parking area was decorated with lights strung from live oak to live oak and filled with vehicles parked wherever they could find room. Carley Love took the place of a departing pickup truck near the entry.

She alighted from the Escalade, stopped, got back up in the driver's seat, closed the door and sat with her arm on the opened window. She stared out the windshield. She closed her eyes for long seconds. Opening her eyes, she took a deep breath and again alighted. Eagerness came to her motions as she slammed the vehicle door and her strides picked up pace. The eagerness spread to her face as she mounted the steps to the restaurant.

The front double doors were propped wide. A hostess greeted her. She gave Jackson's name, and the young woman led her into the dimly lit dining room, through it, and onto the rear wide deck overlooking the shadowy marsh stretching toward the red setting sun.

Jackson rose from a table at the railing. A hopeful smile eased over his face. Hers started small and then grew.

He extended his hand as if to take her to him, but she moved to sit, so he quickly held her chair.

She told him it was a lovely night for the deck. He agreed. He had already ordered her sweet tea with lemon slices. She thanked him.

The waiter, a burly young man with thick, curly dark hair pulled back in a ponytail, stopped at the table and offered menus. Jackson raised an eye at her. She replied that she knew what she wanted and ordered the shrimp and blackened grouper in the manner of someone who has done it a hundred times before. Jackson likewise ordered a t-bone.

Then they were alone and staring at each other over the candle in the middle of the table.

"Has Royce talked to you?" Carley Love said.

"About what?"

"A new girlfriend."

"No...he talks to me about cars and business and to you about clothing stains and relationships." Jackson grinned.

"Well, he told me that he has met someone," she said, with the emphasis of opening her cloth napkin.

"That's good, I guess." Jackson took up his glass of cold tea.

"Her name is Simona. And she is Romanian."

"Huh. Well, it has turned common to meet foreigners in these parts these days." Humor laced his tone. "We get a lot of pilots from all over the world training at the Naval air station. Does she speak English?"

"I asked the same thing," said Carley Love, chuckling. "He said yes, that she's been in this country since childhood. Atlanta, I think...I'm not sure." Then, "She's a model."

"Our boy does have an eye for a pretty woman."

Their gazes met with understanding.

It was Carley Love who broke away, reaching for her glass. "He said mostly she models her feet and hands, but that she does some fashion modeling. That's how they met—she was over to Destin doin' a photo shoot on the beach. Some months ago, must have been summer. They met at a beach party."

The burley waiter brought salads and a basket of hushpuppies. He asked if they might like wine. "We have a sauvignon blanc that goes well with seafood and steak."

Jackson looked at Carley Love.

"No, thank you just the same," she said to the waiter.

Jackson said, "You can top off my tea."

She took a hush puppy and passed the basket to Jackson without him asking, and continued talking about their son.

"I sure hope this isn't some sophisticated young woman just out for a good time with an attractive country boy. He's been so deeply hurt before, Jackson."

"We can't protect him, Carle'Love," Jackson said, gesturing toward her with a hush-puppy he spread thick with butter. "He's a grown man."

"I know that," she replied in a tone that indicated unhappiness with the idea. Then she added wistfully, "I hope she is the good Christian woman I've been prayin' for him to have."

The next instant her eyes widened. "This is a little shameful to say and reveals my lacking, but I'm not quite certain where Romania is. And maybe she isn't Christian."

Jackson grinned and said in a philosophical tone, "We will have to wait and see."

"Well, I'm goin' to read up...to be prepared," Carley Love said. "When we meet her, I don't want Royce to be embarrassed of his mother for not knowin' things."

"Honey, our son would never be embarrassed of you."

She met his warm gaze and smiled.

The subject of their son exhausted, they fell to quietly finishing their salads and making small talk about the lingering warm fall. Carley Love mentioned planning to get the fireplace chimney cleaned, and Jackson said instantly that he would handle it. He then asked how the Escalade was running, and she said, "Fine."

The waiter returned, easily handling a large tray with his muscular arms. They ate mostly in silence punctuated by an occasional comment about the good food, the warm weather, a couple of restaurant improvements. She asked about his work, and he replied that it was okay. He asked if she was back at the office, and she said she was, although the slow season had begun. The restaurant manager stopped at their table, commented that it had been some time since he had seen them and he appreciated them coming. Without giving time for an explanation on their part, he continued his round through the room.

Jackson looked across at her and said, "I thank you for comin', too, Care'lina."

She looked back at him, opened her mouth as if to speak, but then did not. His gaze searched hers. Shadows entered her eyes, and she dropped her gaze to the table.

Silence stretched between them. She watched him carefully place his knife and fork across his empty plate.

She said, "I still haven't signed the divorce papers, Jackson. I was going to, even after what you said when we talked...but it seems that I can't, at least not right now."

She paused and studied the table. He watched her, waiting.

Her eyes came up to his. "I am really confused. I have no idea of what I want, nor where I am half the time." The last came out with flat honesty.

Jackson nodded. "I sure know what you mean. Except I'm all through that and know what I want now. Like I told you, I want us to get back together, Carle'Love."

"Why did you leave me, Jackson? What did I do?"

"It was nothin' you did," he responded instantly.

The night had grown dark around them. Warm light from the flame of the candle on the table flickered on their faces.

Jackson said, "It was all me. I guess, really, I was tryin' to get away from myself. Which is an impossibility, so—" He breathed deeply and sat back in his chair. "—I just went bat-shit crazy.

"Can you understand that?" His face was intent.

"I think so."

He leaned forward again, braced his arms on the table. His voice was intense and low. Occasionally his lips even quirked into a grin as he haltingly spoke of how young they married and and how he had always loved her from the time he first laid eyes on her. They shared memories in sparse words and fleeting smiles.

He spoke of his work and what had transpired to humiliate him and how this had affected him. His eyes got darker and sadder, and entreated her to understand.

She leaned forward, as well, saying, "Honey, I know. I told you then to quit, and..."

He gave her a look and she stopped speaking and watched his eyes in the candlelight drift downward to the table.

"When you said you wanted a divorce..." His voice came raspy, and he paused to clear his throat. "...well, I got really angry."

"But you said you agreed. You said you wanted to do it, too. And you had..."

He held up his hand. "I know. I know I did. Okay, the night *we* decided on divorce. Now, please just listen, Carle'Love, and let me get this out."

"Okay."

He said, "I felt angry at you, at my job, at the whole world...and mostly crazy angry at myself. I went out and got wasted with a group from work. Really wasted." His gaze met hers and then dropped as he said, "And...I...I think I slept with someone."

Carley Love's response to this was to come up straight in her chair. "You *think* you slept with someone?"

He shifted in his seat. "Well, I don't remember any of the details, but I woke up with someone." His eyes focused somewhere around her chin.

She opened her mouth and closed it.

"It wasn't planned, Care'lina. It didn't mean anything. I was drunk and I made a stupid mistake."

"Was this a friend? Someone you've known for a long time? Do *I* know her?"

"I know her," he admitted. "I've known her for some time, but it isn't like we are good friends. I think you've met her."

"You *think* I've met her like you *think* you slept with her?" Her expression and tone demanded an answer.

Jackson said clearly, "She's the secretary from work, Anita. You met her once or twice at Christmas parties."

He paused and leaned toward her over the table. "I have to tell you because I can't have any secrets between us. I don't want anyone to tell you later."

Tears began to run down her cheeks. She brushed them aside and slid back her chair.

"Don't...please listen..." His voice rose, causing people from a nearby table to look in their direction.

"I can't." She jumped up to hurry from the table. He

quickly followed, reaching for her and caught her wrist, but she shook him away.

He stood watching as she wound between tables and away from him.

~

FRIDAY, 10:00 p.m.

Well, Jackson had an affair.

The words just keep repeating in my head, and like shouting from a megaphone.

Any time I might have thought of him having an affair, and when Ronni brought up the idea, I would dismiss it as totally not something he would do. But then, I never thought him the sort to up and leave our marriage. He was always the rock-solid sort.

I keep playing tonight's scene over in my mind, looking for something, I don't know what. Maybe for what else I have missed. Obviously I have missed a whole bunch of stuff.

I feel lost and angry and guilty and inadequate in a million ways.

Oh, Lord, I was so glad when I saw him tonight. I *was*. I started right in to tell him about Royce and how it looks like he may have found the right woman. It was easy to talk about that. It always has been. As parents, we have always been on the same page. We both love our son with all our hearts, and we both know that. There is no question about it.

But each other—it is so much harder to talk about us.

That's probably a sign of the trouble between us—we

can't hardly talk about our relationship without us both getting irritated. And then the doubts come.

He explained more about losing the promotion at his work, and how management brought in some young wiz-kid from up north. And making the humiliation worse, he had to train the guy, too.

I remember it. I remember the whole situation hitting him hard. I also remember telling him at the time that it would be okay with me if he wanted to quit and take some time off to find something else, to follow some dreams, and he had acted like I was crazy for saying that.

What comes to me now, and what I wish to have said, is that who he should have left was the job and not his wife.

He said more, but I really don't know what it was. I just had to get away—which occurs to me that I fell to doing just what Jackson had done—running away.

Oh, Lord, please help me. I hurt so bad

IN SWEAT PANTS, baggy shirt, and slippers, she shuffled to the kitchen and retrieved the last third of the Mississippi Mud cake from the funeral food and a box of vanilla wafers. Sitting cross-legged on the couch, the only light coming from the television screen flickering with an old rerun of *The Waltons*, she alternately ate the cake and fed the wafers to Freckles, who sat beside her.

Her phone vibrated and she checked the screen. It was Jackson calling.

She stared unseeing at the television and ate her cake.

Her phone vibrated. It was a text. Jackson: *Are you home okay?*

She finished the cake and went to the kitchen, where she got a container of vanilla ice cream from the freezer. Back on the couch, she gave Freckles several wafers and dug her spoon into the ice cream container

"This is the life, Freckles. When you're by yourself, you can eat from the container."

After a moment, she added, "And carry on a conversation with your dog."

Her phone buzzed. She frowned, avoided looking, then her gaze slid to the phone. It was Ronni. She stared at the screen. When it quit ringing, she took up the phone and texted: *I'm okay. I will talk to you tomorrow. I'm tired now.*

A text came in return: *Xxxooo*

Her phone buzzed twice, ten minutes apart. Each time it was Jackson.

The third time, she took up the phone and answered, saying, "I'm home and okay. Or as okay as I can be at this point. I'm digesting that my husband thinks he had an affair, but since he can't be sure of that, I don't know how he can be sure of anything."

"It wasn't an affair, Carle'Love." Jackson shot back. "It was a stupid mistake. That's all. I wish I'd never told you."

"That would have been a better choice."

"And what would you have said if it came out somewhere down the road?"

"I'm gonna tell you somethin', Jackson Paul Wells. Some things are better left unsaid. A person who has an affair, if it means nothin', should never tell their spouse. They should bear the burden themselves."

"I have found that fact out," came his loud reply.

At this, Carley Love was momentarily silent. Then she breathed deeply and stated, "You felt guilty, and you wanted to alleviate your own guilt, so you had to share it with me, and now I've got that pain. What do you want me to say to that? That I forgive you and it is all okay?"

Silence.

"Well, I wish I could. I know you are sorry, Jackson. I know it, and I wish I could be like Jesus and forgive instantly, but I just am not anywhere near that.

"Right now I-need-my-space," she added, using his wording, tears streaming down her face. "I've been married just as long as you. Don't you think maybe I got tired of it once in a while, too? But-*I*-did-not-leave."

She clicked off and threw the phone across the room to land in Jackson's leather recliner.

The Marriage

CARLEY LOVE WAS up before the sun, still wearing the sweat pants and baggy shirt from the day before. After half a cup of coffee, she went to the bathroom to brush her teeth. Instead of doing that, she took up the hand towel and cleaned the mirror, polishing it to sparkling. From there, she began to clean the entire bathroom and on into the bedroom. She polished every bit of glass, chrome, and wood on her way through the hall and into the kitchen.

She had her head in the oven, scrubbing hard to George Strait singing "Fool Hearted Memory" when she heard Ronni's voice say, "Oh, dear Lord! Oh, honey, no!"

The next instant hands seized her shoulders and jerked her backward.

She fell hard on her bottom. Peering upward through strands of hair, she gaped at Ronni gazing at her with wide dark eyes.

"Oh," Ronni said then, her expression relaxing as she saw Carley Love's yellow-gloved hand clutching a rag. "I thought you were attemptin' suicide."

"It is an electric oven." Carley Love blew at strands of hair fallen over her face.

"Well, I didn't know." Ronni moved across the kitchen to lower the volume on the stereo speaker.

Carley Love picked herself up off the floor. Then she bent and wiped the oven glass, grabbed a dry cloth and polished it.

"I brought you a Chick-fil-A salad." Ronni reached out to smooth Carley Love's uncombed hair back from her face. "You are a mess, girlfriend. You sit at the table, and I'll get us some sweet tea to go with the salads. You can tell me everything over lunch."

Carley Love complied and sat staring at the table. The next instant, she retrieved a polishing cloth and buffed the surface.

Tall heels clicking on the tile, Ronni came with the drinks, forks, and napkins. She took the polishing cloth out of her friend's hand. "You are gonna wear a hole. This place is polished enough to put your eyes out."

"I TOLD you he'd had an affair," said Ronni.

And Carley Love said, "Thank you, oh great fount of wisdom. That helps."

"Oh, hon, I am sorry. I know this has broke your heart... but really, it shouldn't be so much of a surprise."

"Don't start with the shoulds. I'm seein' all my shoulds. The fact is that I didn't pay enough attention. And Jackson was never...he was just always..." Her chin quivered and tears welled up. "He was always so ste-a-dy." She left off and pushed away her salad.

Ronni said in a tone both soothing and factual, "Well, I'm not certain it technically qualifies as an affair. As I understand it, you two were broke up at the time. That's not really an affair since you weren't living together at the time."

"We were still married!"

Ronni cast her a patently patient look and took up her cold glass.

Carley Love rose from the table, snatched the dust rag and sprayed and polished the counter top. "It just hurts so badly. I feel like such an idiot…a woman lacking so much that her husband left her and preferred another woman."

She put her face close to the wall mirror, as if to find answers in her eyes. Then she polished the already gleaming mirror.

Ronni said, "First off, none of that is true. He said it wasn't your fault and that it was a mistake."

Carley Love moved to polish the stainless refrigerator.

"And Jackson is just a *man*," said Ronni. "I think you had him up on some pedestal. You have seen your marriage as like one of those old romance movies you like to watch. That's a lot of pressure. Jackson's just a man with faults, and you are just a woman with faults. And no marriage is easy. Every marriage has ups and downs and rounds and rounds. It is a wonder you two have stayed married this long.

"And you know, I think he's right that you sure wouldn't want to find this out down the road, after you had gotten back with him. It is admirable that he wanted to be honest about it all. It's open and honest."

"Really…huh. So now you are defendin' him?" Carley Love faced her friend, with her hand on her hip.

"I'm not defendin' him or against him," Ronni said. "I

just said what I saw. Give it time, Carley. Just give it time. Truly, this is not the end of the world. I know it seems like it is...but affairs are not uncommon. This will work out one way or another, but for right now, I recommend a hot bath and a facial cream treatment. Here." She dug into her purse and brought out a small jar. "This just came in our new products. It smells like roses. You'll love it."

"What did I do, Ronni? He left me and took comfort in another woman. You know, I thought that happened to other people, not to me and Jackson. We argued a lot at times...but we were always there for each other. I just always felt we were supposed to be together. What happened to us? I feel like such a failure. At least I can understand Jackson on that score right now," she added in a sad tone.

"I'm the first to admit that I'm no expert on marriage," Ronni said. "Heaven knows the one I had was no great shakes. But it did give me experience, so I feel a bit qualified to say that Jackson is right. It wasn't anything you did or didn't do. It was a choice he made. He chose to run off instead of standing to fight it out.

"And probably that woman laid a good trap, and the poor man fell right in it," Ronni added, lifting a finger for emphasis. "That's how many a happy home is broken up. You see it all the time.

"Now you do have choices, and the best choice right now is to bathe and get some sleep. Remember that scripture—sleep that knits up the raveled edge of care. Something like that."

"That's Shakespeare."

"Oh, well, it is true. I have to get back. I'm workin' the evenin' for one of the girls." She hoisted her purse onto her shoulder. "Just rest. And I left another bottle of wine for you in the refrigerator."

Carley Love gazed at her.

Ronni ignored the look, hugged her, and placed the jar of cream into her hand, then hurried out the door on her heeled sandals.

Twenty minutes later, Carley Love emerged from the bathroom wrapped in a warm robe. She paused, seeing the golden rays of late afternoon sunshine falling through the window. They cut across the room and lit the bookshelf of photograph albums. She crossed and pulled an album off the shelf. She ran her hand in a caress over the white satin cover that had grown faintly yellowed. Lowering herself to the edge of the bed, she opened it on her lap.

The first page contained the wedding announcement.

CROCKER-WELLS NUPTIALS

Miss Carolina Love Crocker became the bride of Jackson Paul Wells, Jr. in a double ring ceremony at Elm Avenue Methodist Church on Saturday morning. The Reverend G. A. Fox officiated.

The bride is the daughter of Mr. and Mrs. Sullivan J. Crocker of Bell City, and the bridegroom the son of Mr. and Mrs. Jack P. Wells, Sr. of Raleigh.

The bride was given in marriage by her father and wore a semi-formal tea-length gown of white peau de soie overlaid with Chantilly lace, with scoop neckline and lace sleeves ending in wedding peaks at her hands. Her shoulder length veil of silk illusion was accented with a satin bow. She carried a cascade bouquet of white carnations.

Miss Margaret Clements, of the city, cousin to the bride, was maid of honor.

Jack Wells, father of the groom, was best man.

A pre-nuptial party had been held the previous night for family and close friends at the home of Mrs. Reba Love Murray, grandmother to the bride. A three-tier vanilla cake with apricot glaze and royal icing, Florentine chocolate cookies, ambrosia, and raspberry-lime punch was served.

SATURDAY, October 21

1:15 p.m.

I just looked at our wedding album. The wedding announcement is yellowed and crumbling at the edges—just like what happened to our marriage.

It all comes back to me, how we started. How young we were, nuts and in love.

It was a June wedding—Creedence singing on the radio about seeing the rain, boys revving up Mustang convertibles, and girls spraying Wind Song on their hair.

I was seventeen, graduating high-school, with long blond hair like corn silk to the middle of my back, short dresses above my knees, and set to marry a boy who had just turned nineteen, was yet bare faced and his mother still wrote out his car payment checks.

For years, when someone would learn of my young age at marrying, they would eye me as if wondering why I'm not barefoot and dragging a truckload of kids behind me. Very often the question has been: "What did your parents have to say about you getting married at that young age?"

My standard reply is: "Can you ever tell a teenager anything?"

The fact of my case was that I had mostly ran my own life since the age of five, when my mother taught me to read. I was the surprise baby of my parents' middle-age. My brother Sully was eighteen when I was born, and he left home when I was yet a baby, so mostly it was Mama and me.

When I was sixteen, my father, who had rarely taken any part in my life, suddenly felt it was his duty to teach me to drive. He was surprised to find out that I already knew, that I had been driving the car to and from the grocery store and other such places since the age of thirteen.

My father, Sullivan Crocker, bless his heart, had viewed the world through a cloud of Jack Daniels. He was a disappointed dreamer, following in his own father's footsteps. He had, in a fit of passion about the earth and the great promise of creating a new soybean variety, taken early retirement from his secure job as a county agent. He spent his days with experimental organic soybean farming and drinking.

My mother was such a contrast of extremes. Her father had taken off and left her mother, and she had always longed for a man to take care of her. She had married my father with this idea and been bitterly disappointed. She escaped from this disappointment by losing herself in fiction stories easily had from the library or paperback racks at the local A&P grocery. She read such varied authors as C.S. Lewis and Harold Robbins. My mother had no idea of her high level of knowledge after all her years of voracious reading. Whenever I pointed out her vast vocabulary and spelling aptitude and that she had a wealth of information stored in her brain, she would deny it. She clung to the conviction that she knew nothing and had no abilities at anything. I suspect to do otherwise meant she would have had to take responsibility for her life.

Jackson and I met at a high-school football game in my junior year. He had come with some cousins, his mother and her family being natives of Bell City. Jackson had beautiful grey-blue eyes and a charming smile and was far different from the local rural boys. He dressed in the fashionable flare-legged slacks and ankle boots, and his hair brushed his collar.

We corresponded by letter and rare, short telephone calls. We dated whenever Jackson came to town with his mother on weekends and whole weeks during that first summer sandwiched between my senior year and Jackson's first year in college. That summer he was required to drive his mother over to Bell City a number of times, because his grandmother was slowly dying in a big old mansion on Main Street, and his mother took her turn as caregiver to the old woman.

I wondered then, and a few times afterward, why his mother did not put a stop to our relationship. His mother's family were the top society of the town, and mine were jumbled between middle and lower. One of Jackson's cousins, a girl in my same grade, seemed to take great delight in telling me, "When Gram heard about you and Jackson, she came up out her death bed for a twenty-minute rant. I wouldn't get too attached to him."

I was bold enough to ask Jackson about this, and he admitted it was true, and then he laughed, saying his mother had told his Gram that if she had so much energy to throw a fit, she could get herself to the bathroom.

Oh, I adored Iris Wells instantly in the curious way that can happen, and to my amazement, the woman liked me. Over the years, we grew close.

Of course, the reason I put off introducing Jackson to my parents was that I was certain that meeting my parents and seeing the rundown state of my home would send him running. However, the day came when I had to be brave. I chose a time that I knew my father would be out, yet still, there was the falling down house and the sagging couch, and my mother sitting there in her customary over-sized flannel shirt and rolled up dungarees that she had worn ever since seeing a photograph of the author of that bestseller, "Peyton Place."

My mother looked up from the current novel in hand and settled an eye upon Jackson. "Hello. Pleased to meet you, young man," she said, gracefully extending her hand and drawing Jackson down beside her in a warm and genteel manner that would have made her own mother and grandmother proud, and astonished me. It came to me clearly: blood tells. My mother was from good stock, and she had not forgotten a thing. She grilled Jackson without appearing to do so.

When my mother learned that Jackson's daddy owned three IGA grocery stores over in Wake County and was a deacon in his Baptist Church, I could practically read her thoughts across her forehead: "Hallelujah, my daughter's prince is here!"

When told of the marriage plans, my mother said without blinking an eye, "Your grandmother and I will handle the wedding."

I've often tried to remember if I ever had any plans of my own beyond being Jackson's wife. To say that I could

easily have gone to any university of my choice is not brag-
ging. My grades were such that had anyone guided me, I
likely could have gotten a full scholarship. However, no
woman in my family had ever gone on to college.

Jackson arrived three days before the wedding, in order
to attend my graduation ceremonies. He came driving over
in his late-model Galaxie 500 convertible. I looked at him
and thought: I don't even know him.

How ludicrous it all seems now. Jackson and I had
not even fully had sex. I was what was known as a
'good girl'. Really it was youth and fear and little
opportunity, not to mention Jackson being of a high
level of common sense, that had constrained us. Now I
was facing leaving all I had ever known and going off
and not only having sex but living with a boy I barely
knew.

My panic at the prospects ahead grew to such propor-
tions as to propel me to run to my mother for help, which
clearly showed the depth of my desperation.

I found my mother in the laundry room. She held an
open book in one hand and pulled wet jeans from the
washer with the other, dropping them into a large bucket.
She flicked me a glance, but neither quit reading nor
handling laundry.

I blurted out, "Mama, I don't think I want to get
married."

Her reply was a chuckle and something about nerves
being natural before a wedding.

I see us still in front of that battered washing machine. I
stood there, while she pulled more wet items from the
washer. I remember her face turning to me, her eyebrows
rising. She then shut the book, dropped the laundry, and

braced a hand on the washer. "You don't want to get married?"

I shook my head and my words came with sobs, the gist of it being, "I'm terrified, and I didn't know what I was doing, and this is all a big mistake."

She gazed at me, pulled a packet of Virginia Slims from her shirt pocket, and said, "You don't have to get married."

My response to this was to wail about how the arrangements were made, the party set, the presents received, and Granny Reba having gone to so much trouble and would be terribly displeased.

I knew by all the years of observing my mother and my grandmother and listening to their comments what a disappointment my mother had been to my grandmother, who had poked and prodded my mother to be more lady-like and mannerly and interested in all the 'right' people and so forth. I also knew my grandmother had thrown herself into great lengths to see that my wedding came up to standard and was a credit to the family. The wedding was set to take place at Granny Reba Love's church, and all the aunts and cousins had been engaged to decorate to the correct amount. The cake was ordered, flowers and photographer arranged, and that very night my grandmother and great aunts were hosting a wedding party, where delicate platinum-rimmed Noritake china and genuine Gorham silverware would gleam against the hundred-year-old family table, with everyone crowded around it. I lost breath at the prospect of dissatisfying my grandmother. The idea of shaming my family brought me near to fainting dead away.

I still remember watching the stream of blue smoke my mother blew out and her flat tone of voice, saying, "We'll cancel. The church, the cake, it can all be cancelled."

"But we have all those presents." Registered china, ruby-red goblets, which I adored, white Corningware, and the very latest in stainless steel tableware from a distant uncle I had not known existed, all displayed on a table in the living room.

"We'll send them back," my mother said, with a dismissing shrug.

"But Jackson is in there...and his parents are comin' today." I was becoming hysterical.

"We'll send him back. We'll send them all back."

Before my eyes my mother came up straight and strong, a majestic hen in faded flannel, ready to protect her chick. "Just say the word, and we will send 'em all back," and she gave a sweeping wave of her arm.

Of course I did not say the word. Thinking of it over the years, I have had to face that I got married as much to avoid embarrassment as for being in love. To this end, I endured the humiliation of Jackson's family seeing my rather dismal home that my mother and I worked like crazy to present as gently worn, as well as my father walking unsteadily around the house in his shirt, tie, and boxer shorts. Despite my mother pouring every whiskey bottle she could find down the drain, my father stayed drunk for those two important days, beginning with the wedding party, where only fruit punch was served because Great-Aunt Sarah was a strong tea-totaling member of the Woman's Temperance Union. At one point she smacked my father upside the head with a tea towel, sending him bouncing into the door jam and then back into Great-Aunt Sarah. My mother stopped a brawl between them by quickly guiding my father out on the porch for air, and finding the flask he had in his suit coat.

Through it all, my soon-to-be in-laws, Iris and Big Jack Wells, smiled and never blinked an eye. And on the appointed morning, I walked resolutely down the aisle on my father's quite unsteady arm. My mother, minus a book, looked like an uncomfortable but amazingly lovely stranger in a pink dress, with a string of genuine pearls at her neck and her hair and face fixed up. I see her still in memory, sitting on the very edge of the front pew, ready at any point to jump up and call a halt and send everyone home, should I give the least sign.

I did not give any sign. I said, "I do," so faintly that the pastor leaned forward and squinted, as if trying to read my lips.

Afterward, when people were hugging and congratulating us, a number of them teased that I had not actually said any vows. They teased Jackson that he was free to back out, and I searched his face for signs that he might.

But my dear mother-in-law hugged me, saying, "Welcome, daughter." I closed my eyes, drinking in her grace and White Shoulders scent.

When I opened my eyes, I saw my mother looking on, saw the tiredness on her face. I went to embrace her, and she was startled. My mother's people were not demonstrative. I can still hear her faint voice in my ear, saying, "I love you." I responded the same. I'm not certain we ever said those words to each other before, and it was not until she lay dying that we said them again.

As we drove away, I took a last look out the window and saw my mother and Granny Reba Love together, holding each other up, each waving a handkerchief after me. In that moment, I realized two things: I had for all my life been taking care of them somehow, and now I was abandoning them. The question of what might happen to them without me swept my chest with near terror.

I stuck my head out the open window, with the urge to fling myself out of the car and run back to them. Instead, I hollered, "Thank you!" Meaning: Thank you for releasing me to a new life!

Not until we turned a corner and they went out of sight did I pull myself back in the window and place myself beside Jackson, turning resolutely from my childhood and family to gaze at the hope-filled road ahead.

SHE LAID DOWN HER PEN, closed the journal, and said in a whisper, "And now you are gone, Mama, and I'm alone."

Doing New Things

SUNDAY, October 22

5:15 a.m.

I just tore out a page on which I ranted and raved like a lunatic. I was going to burn it, but instead I put it in the little secret pocket in the back, because maybe someday I would want to read it.

A bit of wallowing around in hurt is to be expected and even necessary. But at some point a woman needs to pick herself up and go on. As Granny Reba Love so often quoted and has underlined in her Bible—I have been given a spirit of power and love and sound mind. I have been reading Granny's Bible to boost myself.

Jackson called twice yesterday, but I would not answer him. I couldn't speak to him without being some crazy woman that I do not like. Then he texted me: *Please, let's talk about this.*

I am amazed at his texting, as he never did that before our split. Apparently he's learned all sorts of things since he left our marriage. Maybe that woman he slept with taught him. He could have texted that he had had an affair and saved me all the hurt at the restaurant.

∼

CARLEY LOVE DROVE herself and Freckles to the beach. She found a parking space in the blacktopped lot and turned to Freckles, who sat in the rear seat with questioning brown eyes.

"Okay, here we are, two girls doin' a new thing. So let's get to it."

Alighting from the driver's seat, she adjusted her tunic over her denim capris. The sun was warm but the breeze off the Gulf cool. Retrieving her wide-brimmed hat, she slapped it on her head. The breeze pushed the hat askew, so she fastened the fabric tie ends tight beneath her chin. She walked with purpose to the rear of the Escalade to unload her beach chair, small umbrella, beach mat and cooler. She leaned the equipment up against the vehicle and opened the backseat door to attach the dog's leash.

"Okay, girl, come on."

The dog looked at her and remained sitting.

"Come on, girl. We can do this. We're gonna have *fun*."

Carley Love cajoled, tugged, got into the car and pushed. The dog had all four of her paws firmly planted on the leather seats.

"Good heavens, Lord, I could use some help," Carley Love muttered as she scrambled out of the car, righted her hat and straightened her clothes that had gone askew.

She tried again, speaking softly and tugging gently on the lead. In an unexpected move, the dog bounded out the door like a cork, knocking Carley Love inelegantly to her knees. With fifty-five pounds of excited dog jumping all over her, she ended up with her hat pushed fully over her face and sitting on the hard, black-topped pavement, while still holding determinedly to the leash. Freckles gazed at her from beneath the Escalade.

With muttered grumblings, Carley Love got herself to her feet and sorted out. Setting her chin, she loaded herself like a pack mule and trudged with the dog across soft sand. Choosing a spot, she dropped everything, slipped off her sandals, and followed the eager dog to the water's edge, where she padded into the cool salty water washing gently upon the shore. She released Freckles and watched her run and jump. Carley Love laughed out loud. She stopped and looked far out at the expanse of water with wonder on her face.

Sometime later, she sat in her low beach chair, in the shelter of her dark sunglasses, wide-brimmed hat, and umbrella. The wind made a low roaring in her ears. The grey-green Gulf stretched on to eternity before her, and she watched wave after wave roll upon the sand, spend themselves, and edge away. The dog ran and splashed in the surf and tried to bite it. Graceful gulls flew over the water and comical plovers sped across the wet sand, avoiding the creeping waves.

Carley Love sat this way for a long time, her face to the wind and the rolling sea. A number of couples, most holding hands, walked past. Hidden behind those dark glasses, her eyes would follow them, then return to the dog and birds and frothy waves.

When a young couple jogged past, Freckles got excited and ran to follow. Carley Love called to her and gave her a treat for obedience, after which Freckles threw herself down, tossing a great deal of sand in the process. Carley Love brushed sand from the dog and lovingly petted her, laying her cheek against the dog's velvet furry head.

Her cell phone buzzed. It was another text from Jackson. This time she texted in return: *I am okay. Please be okay, too. We will talk soon.*

She sent the message and quickly stowed her phone in the tote, and pulled out the journal.

11:35 a.m.

I am at the beach. It smells so salty good and makes me remember my childhood. The sun is warm and the waves soothing. No wonder Mama used to love coming to the beach. She would sit just as I am and watch me play in the waves.

It is an amazing fact to consider, but this is the first time in my entire life that I have come to the beach alone. Aside from a couple of visits with cousins in my teen years, I have always come with Mama or Jackson. And to so many beaches—Nags Head and Hatteras Island beaches, Corolla, down at Atlantic Beach, Jekyll Island beach, Jacksonville, Florida, countless places here along the Gulf. We used to do things like that. When did we stop? How did we get too busy to go do fun things?

There's a young man who has walked past and now thrown himself down on the sand some yards distant. He's probably from the air base. He is wearing those camo-type cargo shorts and a sweatshirt with the Navy insignia on the back and a military haircut, and those sunglasses military men like to wear. He looks dejected, not that I can see his face, but it is in his shoulders. I remember Jackson saying how lonesome he would get during his time in the Navy, when he was far from home. Maybe that young man is far from home and his loved ones.

I lived with Mama and Daddy Wells all those months that Jackson went through basic training and Navy schooling. Then he was assigned to a ship out of Jacksonville, Florida, and I went down there to join him. I drove the distance across three states by myself, the car packed full. I was terrified the whole way. We stayed in a cheap kitchenette motel room for three days, with an air conditioner roaring in the window and living off bologna and tomato sandwiches, until I found us a small apartment. We had so little back then, but it was some of our happiest times. Jackson would often be gone on the ship during the week and home on weekends, and we went to the beach every chance we got. We were young and in love, our whole lives ahead of us.

When Jackson's ship went on a ten-month cruise to the Mediterranean, I was totally on my own, and it was lonely and awful in that cheap apartment. But staying again with his parents felt like imposing on them, and no way was I going home to Mama and Daddy. I had made my escape from their lunacy and wasn't going back. And I think maybe staying in the apartment somehow made me feel closer to Jackson. I would hug his shirt to me every night.

I remember to this day when Jackson came home on that ship. I remember going to the wide pier and watching the enormous ship as it pushed slowly across the rippling wide grey water. It seemed to take years for it to reach the dock. Sailors in starched white uniforms lined the edge of it, waving and hollering. They all looked alike. As men flowed down the gangway, I pressed forward in the crowd of women, straining to see Jackson in the sea of faces. And then there he was, standing alone in his crisp sailor whites.

"Jackson!" My voice came out only a hoarse whisper, but he heard, and his head came around.

I ran toward him, then stopped, afraid of something, I don't know what.

I think I was afraid that he might have changed his mind in all those months he was away seeing the world and not want me anymore. I remember him opening his arms then, and how I threw myself on him. I remember us holding on to each other so tight I could hardly breathe.

It has always been me and Jackson. Thirty-five years, he has been my best friend. I haven't needed or wanted anyone else.

I made him my world.

~

12:15 p.m.

Well, that young man is still lying over there. It has been well over thirty minutes now. I may have to go check on him. He is going to have sunburn and probably sand flea bites.

I can just hear Jackson telling me that I have too much imagination and that I do not need to butt into the man's business.

~

12:30 p.m.

Okay, it has been fifteen more minutes, and that young

man is still lying there like, well, like a dead body. Too bad I did not bring binoculars and could check to see if he is breathing. I am going over.

※

CARLEY LOVE, bending over the young man, spoke at the same moment that the dog put her nose into his ear. The result was the very much alive man bolted up into sitting position, causing Carley Love and the dog to step backward.

"I'm sorry to have startled you," Carley Love said, as they each stared at the other from behind dark glasses.

"I was asleep."

"Well, you have been lyin' here so very still for quite a long time. I was worried."

The young man removed his dark glasses. He was a fair man of undetermined age, who now resembled a reddish raccoon.

Carley Love removed her own dark glasses and stared wide-eyed at his face.

"Is it bad?" He touched fingertips to his face.

"Well, it's not good—probably gonna hurt tonight. I have some lotion." She stepped toward her chair and beach blanket.

The young man, taller than she had realized, followed. Carley Love adjusted the umbrella to shade him rather than her chair and dug a tube of lotion from her bag. He had difficulty applying the lotion himself, so she helped with the ability of a capable mother who has vast experience.

While they went about this somewhat personal first aid, she said, "I don't suppose you have a hat in your back pocket?"

Of course he did not.

The young man extended his hand to hers for a shake, and they exchanged names. His was Finn MacAuliffe, and he commented on her distinctive middle name of Love, surveying her closely. She offered him a Coke from her cooler and asked what brought him to the Gulf Coast. He accepted the Coke, took hers as well, twisted off the cap and passed it back to her, explaining that he was stationed at the nearby naval air base, and, throwing a piece of driftwood for the dog to chase, said that he raised border collies back home.

He was an easy talker and spoke of his home in the manner of a lonely man. He told her back home was a ranch in Wyoming, and of being a pilot, and how he greatly enjoyed the beach area, although he often missed his favorite dog, Molly, who was looked after by his parents. And sometimes he missed home.

"They say you can't ever go home again, though," he commented, looking out at the Gulf with a pensive air.

Carley Love studied his profile, then shifted her gaze to the water, agreeing quietly, "No, you can't. Things are always changin'."

After a quiet moment, Finn said, "You're easy to talk to, and I've been rambling on. How about you let me buy you lunch and you tell me about yourself."

"Oh..." she looked down at her red-painted toes and brushed the sand away.

"Come on. There's a place just up the beach." He pointed to it.

"Yes, I know—the Tiki Hut. I'm not really hungry, though." Her voice betrayed uncertainty as they gazed at each other from the shelter of their dark glasses.

"You can have a Coke or coffee." Finn stood, reaching his hand down for her.

She peered up at him. "Okay...for just a bit." She took his hand, and he pulled her to her feet.

Together they deposited her beach paraphernalia at her car, and then they walked along the sand toward the café, a brown-roofed shelter, in the distance. Freckles pulled at her leash, and Carley Love almost stumbled in the deep sand. Finn caught her by the elbow. He then kept hold of it the rest of the way to the café, and she did not pull away.

The front of the café was open on three sides, with a plastic barrier in place on the north wall to block winds. To the rear and in the deeper shadows was a bar area, with tables at the front looking out on the bright beach. They took a table at the front rail and Freckles, quite uncertain, settled herself atop Carley Love's feet. There were only a few other tables occupied.

Finn ordered a burger and fries and Carley Love sweet cold tea. When Finn's order came, he pushed his fries toward her, telling her to share. She declined with a polite smile, yet as time and conversation wore on, she absently began to relax and to nibble on the fries. She told of being raised near the coast of North Carolina and having moved to the Alabama coast over twenty years ago. As conversations do, theirs wound to books on local history and on to old classic movies.

It was at that point that she tilted her head, gazing at him with a puzzled smile, and remarked on him being young and liking old movies. She knew few people who enjoyed the old black and white's as she did.

His answer to this was to tell how he and his sister used to come in from school and watch the movies on television with his mother, and then he said quite pointedly and with a chuckle, "I'm not so young...I'm thirty-four."

She fingered an earring, while he continued to explain that he had not enlisted in the Navy until the age of twenty-eight. His gaze dropped to his glass, and he stirred the ice with the straw as he spoke of disappointing his parents by choosing to travel far away. From this he then spoke of having just lost his long-time girlfriend, because she didn't want a life tied to a serviceman.

"She didn't want to leave back home, her family and all," he said. "I got a letter yesterday. She's going to marry one of my old friends." There was pain in his husky voice.

"I'm sorry." Carley Love gazed at him for long seconds and then offered, "It's hard to think of it now, but there will be someone else. She simply wasn't the one."

He gave a chuckle that was tinged with sadness, saying the one female he really missed was his dog, Molly. "That says something," he said, his chuckle more real.

"Yes, it does," Carley Love agreed, with a smile.

Just then three men entered the Tiki, called to Finn and came toward their table. They were the virile Navy sort, boisterously enjoying their time off. Carley Love instantly sat back in her chair, while smiling politely as Finn introduced her. In a bold move, one of the young men plunked himself in the chair next to her, leaned close and draped his arm across the back of her chair.

She stared at him in a pointed manner, while he continued to grin at her.

Just then Freckles made herself known beneath the table, with a low growl.

The young man looked down with a startled expression.

"My dog is remindin' me it is time to leave," said Carley Love, rising gracefully.

She thanked Finn and made polite goodbyes, jammed her sunglasses back onto her face, and headed away so quickly that Finn had to hustle to catch up with her.

He apologized for his friend's forward behavior. "He's really a pretty good guy, just likes to come on to the ladies like he thinks he's...well, he's just a jerk."

She smiled at him but did not slow her pace through the thick sand. He took her elbow again, and she allowed it.

At the car, she got the dog inside and threw her tote bag on the seat.

"Look," Finn said, standing too close for her to open the driver door. "I really enjoyed talking with you. Do you think you would let me take you to dinner tomorrow night? Or if you're busy, just name a night."

Carley Love slowly removed her dark glasses and looked up at him. She opened her mouth, closed it, looked to the side for a moment, and then a gentle smile curved her lips.

"Thank you, Finn," she told him. "So very much. I have enjoyed chattin' with you. I...well, I can't explain how you've given me a priceless gift today. But I am old enough to be your mother."

His brows went up, he tilted his head and searched her face. Then he said, "But you sure *aren't* my mother."

Carley Love's response to that was to laugh aloud. "And I do *not* view you as a son, either." A blush came over her cheeks. Then, her tone firm—"But this is enough—for both of us."

She put her hand on his arm and went up on tiptoe to kiss his cheek. He took hold of her, but she eased from his grasp, opened the door of the Escalade and slipped onto the seat.

"Hey, take my phone number," he said quickly.

She shook her head and slammed the door. She hesitated long enough to lift her hand and press it to the window, then shifted into gear and drove away.

"Well," she said aloud, looked in the rear view mirror and saw him there, gazing after her. "Well."

~

SUNDAY NIGHT

9:30 p.m.

I want to record this. Today I went to the beach alone. I laughed and splashed my feet in the water. I met a young man, who was attracted to me. I really think he did not realize my age. We had conversation, good conversation. And yes, I flirted. That sure felt strange. Here I can say I am gratified to discover I can still flirt. Rusty as a nail on a hundred year old barn, but the ability is not totally dead.

It strikes me that I haven't flirted with Jackson in a long time.

What happened today makes me realize quite sharply how I have not taken time to relax and have fun, nor have I felt a woman, an attractive, desirable woman for a long time.

I have been immersed in being a caregiving daughter, a mother, a wife and a capable homemaker, and somehow lost the me who is first of all a woman.

Well, whatever happened with me at the beach this afternoon emboldened me to stop at Winn-Dixie and buy a thick t-bone steak and come home to grill it. The first time in my life that I have ever grilled anything.

It wasn't nearly as difficult as I had imagined. I turned on the propane tank just like I've seen Jackson do. The electric ignite button would not work, so I got matches, but using them about gave me a heart attack. I threw the matches into the grill from three feet away. Good thing I stood back. When that gas finally caught, it was with a loud whoosh and flames shooting almost up to the tree limbs.

But I have now done another new thing to take care of myself and didn't catch my hair or anything else on fire. The steak was delicious! I lit a candle on the table, although that just made me more lonely, eating by myself.

CARLEY LOVE ARRIVED at the office, stepped through the door and turned the sign to Open. "It's me, Miss Lila. Good Monday mornin'."

"Coffee, please," the older woman called from her office down the short hall.

"Yes, Ma'am." She quickly cleaned the pot that had been left dirty over the weekend, set coffee to brew, and tidied up.

When she took her boss a mug of coffee, the woman cast her a quick glance from the computer screen and said a perfunctory, "Thank you."

Rather than leave, Carley Love hesitated, then moved to check the dampness of the fern near the window. Glancing again at the older woman, she swept her hair behind one ear and lingered near the corner of the desk.

"Do you need something, Carley?"

"Well...I was wonderin' if you might tell me how old you think I am...I mean if you didn't know me." The woman looked straight at her, and she added, "You are the most honest person I know who doesn't mind tellin' the truth."

The woman removed her reading glasses and surveyed Carley Love in the manner of assessing one of her real estate properties.

"You do look younger than your years, Carley. I would say ten years younger, early forties. You're attractive, but mostly what it is that makes you appear attractive is your youthful attitude. And likely your graceful movements," the woman added, reaching for her coffee mug. She stuck her glasses back on her face and returned her attention to her computer screen, signally the end to further conversation.

Carley Love left the room and returned to the reception desk. Minutes later the phone rang. "Lila Ackerman and Company."

"Hello," said Jackson.

Her eyes widened. "Hello."

"Not answerin' your phone?"

"I've been busy. I haven't checked my phone."

"So I heard about you yesterday with a bunch of sailors at the Tiki Hut."

"What?"

"Carryin' on with a bunch of sailors. You were seen."

"I was not *carryin' on* with anyone. And who is this tellin' tales?" Her voice rose.

"Gordon saw you."

"Who's Gordon?"

"I work with him. You met him a couple of years ago at the office New Year's party."

She frowned. "Well, I must be more memorable to him than he is to me."

"Were you there? With a bunch of sailors?"

"I was there, but I was not *carrying-on*, as you put it. I had lunch with a kind young man and some of his friends stopped by the table. And I'll tell you somethin' else—you do not need to take this tone with me, considerin' you are the one that left our home and had an affair with that Angie bimbo!"

Jackson responded instantly, "It wasn't an affair, Carle'Love. And she isn't a bimbo, and her name is Anita, not Angie. It was a *mistake*. A *one-time-big-fat-mis-take!*"

And he hung up.

She stared at the receiver and stated aloud, "You do not help your case by refutin' the term bimbo."

She looked up to see Lila on the far side of the counter, gazing at her.

"I...it was Jackson, not a client."

"I gathered that."

Carley Love said, "People can make stuff up out of whole cloth."

"Yes, then can." Lila passed a file across the counter, saying, "Please have Doreen enter this info in the computer, if she possibly can get it straight. I have an appointment with a client." She turned and left through the front door.

Carley Love watched the older woman leave. Next she grabbed her journal from her purse, opened it and noted furiously.

9:30 IN THE MORNING, and I have something to say—

God knows I have nothing to be ashamed of. I have done nothing wrong. I should have gone out with that Finn, that's what I should have done, if I'm going to be accused. I have a sense of Granny Reba Love and Mama just laughing at me. They both led much more wild and free lives than I have.

Maybe I have lived my life trying too much to be what I thought they *should* be.

Mirrors

~∽~

CARLEY LOVE DROVE the Escalade through bright sunshine and back roads of the county, until she arrived at the congested area of the shopping mall. She parked near Dillard's department store, went inside and perused the shoe department and purses on her way to the Cosmetics department, where she found Ronni at the Chanel counter arranging the display case.

"Well, girlfriend," Ronni said, "I am glad you made it, and I didn't have to drive down to your place and drag you out. You have been shut in that house all week. Did you get to work today?"

"Yes." Carley Love said. "And you were the one who told me to rest. That's what I've been doin'."

Ronni eyed her. "That's good news. Now amuse yourself for another thirty minutes. I agreed to work through the lunch hour today in exchange for the rest of the day off, and I have two big spending regulars comin' any minute."

Carley Love, holding her purse close, wandered the glimmering cosmetics counters, looked at various items, raised her eyebrow at prices, and shot a perfume sample on her wrist. There were mirrors everywhere she turned, and she kept taking peeks at her reflection.

"Would you like a free make-over session?"

The voice brought Carley Love's gaze up from the brightly lit counter to see a young clerk whose eyes were dramatically outlined in black.

"Oh, I'm just looking."

The young woman had close cropped hair and large dangling earrings and bright crimson lipstick.

"Come on and have a seat. It's free, and you might like somethin' new." The young woman patted the tall stool.

"Okay." Carley Love edged herself onto the high seat.

With swift motions, the woman snapped a cape in the air and fastened it around Carley Love's shoulders and proceeded to wipe away her makeup and apply new, while Carley Love sat still as a statue.

Fifteen minutes later, and her credit card dented, Carley Love carried away a fancy bag of makeup promising dewy skin. She wandered back through the cosmetic department, again snatching glimpses of her reflection in the many mirrors. Several times she stopped to stare at herself with a curious frown.

When Ronni saw her, she said, "Oh, good grief, you look like one of those Kabuki dancers."

She took Carley Love's hand and dragged her to a chair that she turned out of the makeup department lights, and shoved a mirror into her hand.

"Well, I guess it is pretty pale. But down at her counter, it looked rather good," Carley Love responded in a mystified tone.

Ronni said, "I know. She had you in the magic lighted mirrors. Those young girls…"

She went to work, wiped the makeup all off once again and reapplied, and the whole time she gave her opinion of what Carley Love needed to do in her life.

"With your Mama finally gone, you have empty-nest syndrome. That on top of gettin' married so young that you didn't even know who you were, and then you made Jackson and Royce your whole life. When you didn't have Royce full-time, you took on your mother. You have always based your entire life on someone else's needs and expectations. Now you have to start over and base your life on you."

"Thank you, Dr. Joyce Brothers," said Carley Love.

"Who's that?"

"Oh, good mercy," said Carly Love, her voice quivering. "You are not even old enough to know who Dr. Joyce Brothers is. I am over the hill."

"Stop that. You are only as old as you feel."

"Keep tellin' yourself that."

Ronni gave her a sharp eye.

Carley Love said, "If age doesn't count, why are you usin' that stuff that is supposed to be *anti-aging* and *hides wrinkles?*"

"Well…" Ronni's eyebrows knotted as she sought words. Finding them, she said with certainty, "The point is to bring out natural beauty. Makeup is to enhance, not shout. Ideally it shouldn't be noticed. And less is more. Now look."

She swiveled Carley Love to face the mirror.

Carley Love looked, and her expression softened with wonder. She looked from the mirror to Ronni, who was putting bottles into a bag, and then back at the mirror.

Ronni said, "I have far more experience than those young women."

Carley Love, still studying her image, said, "You know, when Jackson and I married, I wore black-rimmed glasses and had crooked front teeth."

"Really? See, there's nothin' wrong with improving oneself. Here, take these samples and work with them awhile."

Carley took the bag and looked again in the mirror. "He loved me then, just like I was."

Ronni put her cheek next to Carley Love's. They smiled at each other in the mirror.

"I love you, girlfriend," said Ronni.

"I love you, too, darlin' woman," Carley Love responded.

Ronni, squeezing Carley Love's shoulders, said, "You and Jackson really have loved each other, girl. No matter what happens, that's somethin'."

She turned from the mirror and put her makeup supplies away, "I never got to have that. Andy wasn't around enough in any sense of the word. When he died in the car wreck, had they not told me, it would have been a week before I missed him.

"And, well, my life, even with my daughter and all my huge family can be pretty tiresome alone."

Then she turned back to Carley Love and said brightly, "Come on, girlfriend, let's go have lunch...and I want to hear again about that young Navy guy. Every last detail. He sounds just right for me."

~

CARLEY LOVE DROVE them a short distance down the busy highway to a deli at a small strip mall. As the two women approached the door, chatting about their meal choices, someone shouted, "Carley!"

The women turned in unison.

"Trey!"

Carley Love smiled as Trey Cummings, collar of his dress shirt open and sleeves rolled, strode across the parking lot on his long legs, while a shorter man followed more slowly.

"Hey." Trey flashed both women his bright smile when he stepped up onto the shaded walkway. His gaze lingered a moment on Carley Love, then he turned to introduce the man who had joined them.

"This is Eric Wright. We were just headin' in, too. Can I invite you two beautiful women to lunch?"

He was already opening the door. He fell in step beside Carley Love, leaving his friend to walk beside Ronni.

FORTY-FIVE MINUTES LATER, the group came out the doors of the restaurant, bidding their good-byes.

"Hey, I almost forgot," Trey said, pivoting back toward the women. "We're havin' an open house next Friday to announce Eric's joinin' the firm, and I'd love for you to come. You'll both get an invitation in the mail, but please consider this my personal plea."

As he spoke, he gave Ronni a brief glance to include her, then returned his eyes to Carley Love. "I could sure use your help in hosting, if you would, Carley. We don't know how many people are goin' to come through the offices, but we have at least six major clients that we want to feel especially attended to, and you're good at that." His eyes looked straight down into hers.

"Well...I...I'd love to. Thank you for askin' us." Carley Love's cheeks grew pink. She cast a glance at Ronni, who was grinning sweetly and put in, "I'd love to come, too, Trey."

"Great! Thanks! And now we'd best be gettin' back to a wonderful afternoon of endless meetings," Trey said with a wry expression.

He and Eric headed away with waves, and Ronni put her arm through Carley Love's as they walked to the Escalade.

"And there you go," she said.

"Stop grinnin' like that."

"Like what? I'm just happy for you to have a second date."

Carley Love pressed her lips together. She got behind the wheel and looked over at Ronni settling herself into the passenger seat.

"You did a fast maneuver to get me sittin' beside Trey."

"That's what a friend is for," Ronni answered. "And I think he would have shoved me out of the way, if I hadn't moved," she added, pulling her lipstick from her purse and flipping down the visor to look in the mirror.

Carley Love thoughtfully watched her friend, then lowered her own visor. "You did seem to enjoy Mr. Wright," she commented.

"Hmmm."

Carley Love replaced the visor and her lipstick, then started the car. She stated, "It's not a date. Not like we are going to be alone. It is attending an open house to celebrate with a friend and to help out."

Ronni inclined her head. "Okay. That's true. But now you have got to have a new dress." She motioned for Carley Love to hurry up and get the car in gear.

The two women shopped for clothes as do two good friends on a mission. Carley Love had an eye for classic style and Ronni one for flamboyance.

"I will not wear *that*," Carley Love said more than once. "I'm not thirty anymore."

"Oh, honey, you aren't dead yet, either. Show some skin. It goes like this." Ronni pulled the shoulders down on the dress Carley Love modeled.

Carley Love's expression turned serious as she studied her reflection. She came out with, "I am sort of hot."

"Girlfriend, you are sizzlin'."

They fell together laughing.

"Okay. I'll take it," Carley Love said the words quickly, then added with her customary practicalness, "I can always return it if I can't get myself to wear it."

Friday, October 27

9:30 p.m.

Ronni and I ran into Trey at lunch. He and a friend came in right behind us. What are the chances of that?

Well, actually, not so unusual, as we went to Charlie's Deli, which serves a lot of organic food and is a popular spot for the professional business crowd.

At least Trey is of acceptable age. I found out he's forty-six. But he seems like someone who has always been mature. And he knew who Dr. Joyce Brothers was! He remembered seeing her on television and on magazine and book covers. We talked about it for half the lunch.

It is amazing how much fun it is to share a knowledge in common. I hadn't realized how much I missed having such discussions. Jackson and I used to talk like that, remember things passed or compare current to past.

And I flirted.

I started to get really embarrassed about it, but I decided that there is nothing to be embarrassed about. I am watching myself is all. It's like getting a fresh look at myself in a mirror.

I'm so excited that Trey has asked me to help him hostess his office open house. Ronni and I had a bang-up time shopping for dresses for the occasion. We haven't done that in ever so long, just gone out and had girl-time together. It was lovely.

Ronni said something today that made me realize she harbors a deep loneliness inside. How have I missed this? She's always so assured and seems to have no leanings toward men other than having a good time. As long as I've known her, she's only had one not-so-serious boyfriend— and I know she has had offers.

I guess we are all alone in our lives to a certain extent. This is because we can never really know someone, nor ourselves. The reason we can't is that we are all the time, every single day and with every single situation, learning and growing and changing.

Maybe we just have to get used to not knowing in this world. God knows, and that's the thing to remember. Keep my focus on God and trusting Him with my life.

That is truth, but harder to live for an imperfect human. Reminds me of the old hymn...can't think of the whole of it, but part of it says, "prone to wander, Lord, I feel it...prone to leave the Lord I love." And that is so true for me.

Could I live with Jackson not knowing if he might up and leave me again? Could I love him that way?

Isn't that the point of love? To love without strings? Trust God, love people.

This is me here, God, not Mother Teresa.

And now that hymn is stuck in my head, but I cannot for the life of me remember the title.

Mistakes

~~~

THE MORNING SUN shone brightly through the window, and Carley Love, still in robe and slippers, sat peering at the computer screen through her reading glasses. Finally, she sat back, removed her glasses and rubbed her eyes.

"I can't do it, Freckles. I cannot get things to balance."

At the mention of her name, the dog came up off the floor and wiggled over to press against her mistress for a petting.

"Well, there's nothing to do but keep on keepin' on," she said to the dog.

She fed Freckles and made herself toast. The front doorbell rang, sending Freckles barking through the house. Carley Love followed more slowly, glanced through the side window lights of the door and saw the figure on the other side—a red-haired woman in a blue duster carrying a plastic tote.

"Hi, Miz Wells."

"Hi, Nan...I clean forgot it was your Saturday. Please

come in." Carley Love stepped aside for the woman to enter.

Nan said, "If you want, I can come back another day. But I'm not sure when that can be. I'm booked tight."

"Of course you are. I did quite a bit of cleaning the other day...but I guess the living room could use going over, and the floors. Just go ahead and do whatever you see to do." Carley Love waved a hand. "I'm going to get showered and dressed."

She was dressed and brushing her hair when her cell phone rang. Seeing Royce's name on the phone screen, she smiled broadly and pleasure echoed in her voice as she answered. "Hello, honey. How are you today?"

"Hi, Mom. What are you doin'?"

"Nothing...absolutely nothing. What's up?"

"Well, you know that girl I told you about?"

"Simona? Of course I remember." She pressed the phone tighter to her ear.

"I want to bring her to meet you and Dad tomorrow. If it isn't too short of notice, I'd like to bring her to Sunday supper...and hope you will make your chicken pot pie. I've been braggin' to her about it."

"Oh, you have. That sounds like you are butterin' me up."

His chuckle came across the line. "It's just that Simona got a modeling gig in Atlanta—her work often comes on the spur of the moment—and she's headin' back up there for a week, so I'd like it to be tomorrow. I told her all about you and Dad being broke up. She understands...her parents are divorced, too. But I'd like you and Dad to meet her together, if that's okay."

Carley Love's reaction to all this was a large intake of

breath that she quickly covered by saying smoothly, "Of course, it is perfectly fine. I would love to meet your Simona, and havin' you two to Sunday supper is perfect. I imagine your father will want to be here. I'll call him."

"Thanks, Mom."

"Honey, do you want to ask Simona's parents?"

"No...her mother lives in Atlanta and her father lives up in New Hampshire—he's on a trip to London, anyway."

"Okay. Just us. And chicken pot pie." She grinned into the phone.

"Great. And thanks again, Mom. See you tomorrow!"

"Three. Come at three."

"Got it. Love you."

"Love you, too."

Carley Love stood for five seconds looking at her wiggling toes. Then she started to punch the button on her phone for Jackson, stopped, set the phone down and rubbed her hands together.

She went into the bathroom and applied a bit of makeup and lipstick. Looking into the mirror, she said, "I am callin' Jackson Wells." She cleared her throat and said, "May I please speak to Jackson?" She rolled her eyes, then closed them. "Please let Jackson answer. Don't let it be *that woman*."

She punched the button for Jackson on the speed dial. Rings came across the line. She had about decided he was not going to answer, when suddenly his voice sounded in her ear.

"Hello."

"Jackson?" She gripped the phone and barely breathed.

"Yes, Carle'Love, it's me. Who did you think?"

"Well, I just wondered if someone else might answer."

That sat there between them a long second, before Carley Love said, "First, I want to tell you that I am sorry for speakin' so sharply on Monday, you know, when you called me about hearin' I was with a Navy man. None of that was true. Well, I was with a Navy man and at the Tiki Hut, but it was absolutely innocent as could be, Jackson. I was *not* with a bunch of Navy men. I simply helped a young man with his sunburn and then had a Coke with him. His friends showed up, and I left. That's all—no matter what that gossipin' man told you.

"And I don't think you should believe gossip about me, anyway," she added.

"I'm sorry, too. You're right. I shouldn't have believed gossip."

"No, you shouldn't."

"I said that."

Carley Love stood blinking as the line hummed between them.

Then she explained about the Sunday supper to meet Royce's girlfriend. "He wants you here, and I told him that was only right, and that I thought you would want to come."

"Of course I want to come."

"Good. It's important. This is the first time he has ever pointedly asked me to make supper for one of his girl-friends. It will just be us. Her mother is in Atlanta and her father lives up in the northeast but right now is over in London."

She paused in momentary thought. "I guess that answers a lot about who her people are. It isn't like I can call over to Mobile or Pensacola, or even up to Raleigh and ask friends what they know about her family. These people are *international*." Another pause and she added, "Probably for sure they are not Baptists."

Jackson's chuckle came across the line. "I imagine they aren't. But then, neither were you when I married you."

Carley Love's response was pert, "Then there's hope for Simona. And I already know what to do. Just what your Mama did for me—welcome her and pray."

They both chuckled lightly.

Carley Love raked a hand through her hair and said, "I haven't filed the divorce papers. Have you?"

"No," he said.

That knowledge sat there for several seconds.

"We are goin' to have to talk finances, Jackson."

"We're okay for now."

"Well, I just bought three new outfits that my salary won't quite cover."

"Take it out of savings."

"You aren't pullin' anything out of the account. How are you livin'?"

"I had some cash saved. I'm okay."

"*Where* are you livin'?"

"I'm stayin' with a friend."

"And who would that be?" Her voice rose and the toes of her left foot tapped.

"Gordon."

"Oh." Pause. "Are we talkin' Gordon the Tiki hut gossip?"

"Yes."

She opened her mouth, closed it, then said, "I plan to serve supper around four. Royce and Simona will be here at three."

Jackson said he would be there at the same time.

They bid each other goodbye, and Carley Love hurried to find Nan in the dining room and tell her very important guests were coming for Sunday supper. She explained this as she opened the drawer of the sideboard and pulled out the antique lace tablecloth and chest containing the good silverware. Her expression was that of a woman making mental lists.

Nan said, "I think you want to check out the hall bath toilet, Miz Wells. The handle appears to be broken."

"Really?" Carley Love came back from her mental list making. "I guess I'd best call a plumber."

"Good luck with that," said Nan.

~

SATURDAY, October 28

9:30 p.m.

Whew! I am exhausted. And I keep thinking of one more thing to do for tomorrow's Sunday supper. I just now got up and tucked the two bottles of wine that Ronni brought out of sight at the rear of the refrigerator. This is not hiding, but choosing what I wish to deal with. I've got enough on my plate right now.

I have the pecan pie made and half the chicken pot pie. I'm waiting until the last minute to put it all together with the biscuit topping. I even remembered the red-checked table linens, and to dress it all up a bit, I had Nan put my grandmother's lace tablecloth over it, letting the red checks show through. It is really pretty. I am using my grandmother's fine china and Mother Iris's crystal, too. Nan said it all looks like something out of Southern Living Magazine.

I am made aware how much I learned from Granny

Reba, Mama, and Mother Iris. I keep having a sense of them being close and looking on. I have even caught myself glancing upward a couple of times. It is as if they hover, as if I could reach out and touch them.

I was so nervous to call Jackson to invite him. It is silly, but I got the idea that woman—Anita or whatever her name is—might answer. He had not called me since our argument on Monday. For all I knew, he had given up wanting to get back together and was with her now.

But Jackson answered, and I went right into my apology. My rudeness the last time we had spoken had been weighing on me like a wet wool blanket. I am grateful that he apologized, too, and he told me that he is staying with that Gordon guy. I asked. And I sure hope he didn't make that up. Of course, I don't favor Gordon much, either.

So you see, I have now become suspicious. That's what happens when trust is broken.

Well, I won't think of that now. Let me keep my eyes on God. And on all good, such as the ability to entertain at a day's notice. And to fix a toilet, too!

Nan was right—there was no getting a plumber so quickly and on a weekend. She suggested an 'Out of Order' sign on the door. I was not having that, and I refused to call Jackson.

I have seen him work a toilet over many times, and I'm handy. I went to Home Depot and came back with the new handle. Who knew there were different types? I did not figure that out until I tried to make the first one fit. I had it on, but mostly by accident, because the thingy slid on and would not unscrew, no matter how much I tried. It is a shame there wasn't a video of me, all these tools around me, hair on end, but wearing silver heart dangling earrings and working with Grand-Canyon Red fingernails, all the while praying aloud for God to help me. I get points for not taking a hammer to it. I remembered how Jackson would use pliers to hold one side and a wrench to turn the bolt, and I managed to do that! Went back to Home Depot, and this time I knew just what I wanted.

Experience really is the only teacher. Mistakes teach you, no doubt about it. You learn where you don't want to go.

I think how Jackson says his affair with that woman wasn't an affair but a mistake.

All in all, learning by mistakes is a frustrating and heart-breaking system, but there is no doubt that it results in thorough and complete knowledge. I could replace anyone's toilet handle now.

~

SUNDAY, October 29

2:10 a.m.

Well, I couldn't sleep for thinking about the mistakes Jackson and I have made. I just ended up scribbling all my jumbled emotions on two tear-smudged pages, which I instantly tore out and tucked in the secret pocket of this book. Really, that pocket is no longer secret. It now bulges.

What the writing helped me to see is that while I am hurt at Jackson's having an affair, I can accept that. What has most thrown me is that *he left me*.

I realize now that this has been the biggest fear of my life. The fear is mostly of myself. I feared being like my mother and grandmother and great-grandmother—a woman men leave.

You know what? The only one who will be with you on this earth all of your life is God.

If Jackson and I get back together, I might keep expecting to wake up and find him gone. How would I ever sleep? Or when I go off to the store and then come home, I'll probably be holding my breath, wondering if he has taken off again.

Family Treasures

SHE WAS at the kitchen sink and saw Jackson arrive. Taking a deep breath, she smoothed her hair and went to the door.

"These are for you." Jackson thrust forward a colorful bouquet of flowers.

"Thank you." Timid delight washed over her face. "They'll be lovely on the table."

She cast him a smile without looking him in the face and turned to open a cabinet door. She stretched upward on tiptoe.

He stepped behind her and reached easily to retrieve the vase. He stood close and looked down at her. She cast him a quick glance and moved away to the sink.

He stood several more seconds gazing pointedly at her. Then—"What smells so good?"

"Oh!" She set flowers and vase beside the sink and bent to the oven. "I found a Romanian recipe for sweet rolls."

She peered through the oven window. Jackson's head came beside hers. "They are like crescent rolls filled with jam. I think another five minutes."

She straightened and stepped away from him. With a raised eyebrow, he pointed to the pitcher of cold tea. She nodded. He set about making himself a glass, while she arranged the flowers into a vase.

With furtive glances she saw him walk to the dining room doorway. He complemented the table and Carley Love thanked him. She asked him to light a fire in the fireplace on the veranda. He instantly complied.

She returned to arranging the flowers, closed her eyes, and bowed her head, murmuring.

"Is the lighter still in the junk drawer?"

His voice brought her looking around over her shoulder. "Yes, yes, it should be." She wiped water droplets from the outside of the vase.

He retrieved the lighter and headed away through the dining room and out to the veranda.

She carried the vase of flowers to the dining table, rearranged items and set the vase in the middle. Studying the table, she adjusted the placement of items that didn't need adjusting and surreptitiously observed Jackson through the opened French doors, her gaze following him as he mounted the steps with an armload of wood and crossed to the fireplace.

She stood there for long seconds contemplating his shoulders and back, until the oven buzzer sent her scurrying back to the kitchen.

Minutes later when Jackson came in to the sink to wash his hands, she passed him one of the sweet rolls on a napkin.

"It's great," he said with the first bite.

He held the roll toward her mouth. She took a bite and said with delight, "It *is* delicious!"

His eyes rested on hers as he popped the last bit of roll into his mouth and licked his tongue across his lips.

She turned away from him, took a deep breath, and inventoried her preparations on the counter.

The next instant, Jackson was close beside her. She looked up at him. His gaze drifted downward to her lips, which parted.

The next instant, she planted her hands on his arms and pushed from him. "No. There's no time for us to deal with us. Today is about Royce."

He said, "O-kay, I'll go tend the fire."

He moved a step, paused, and looked back at her. She turned to the counter.

Minutes later music floated through the house, Alan Jackson singing, "Remember When."

Carley Love stilled, turning her ear toward the music.

Jackson, glass of tea in hand, came to the dining room doorway and leaned against the frame, watching her until she looked at him. He ventured a grin. She rolled her eyes, while her lips spread into a slow grin in return.

Freckles barked, and Carley Love stepped to the window. "They're here!"

Jackson came behind her.

Carley Love said, "They're in a car. It must be Simona's."

He gave a low whistle. "A Beamer Sport. The girl has high-class taste."

"Of course she does. She is with our son. My goodness... she's a tall drink o' water."

"Your country 's showin', Care'lina Love."

She smacked his arm even as she moved to the kitchen door, to open it and let the dog run out ahead.

"Welcome, you two!" She watched her son and his girlfriend bend to pet Freckles and then come toward her waiting on the porch.

"Hi, Mama." He had a bouquet of flowers for her, too. "And this is Simona," He beamed with adoration at the woman, glanced at his father, but looked mainly at his mother.

"Welcome, sweetheart. I'm so glad to meet you." Carley Love's voice was warm, and she enveloped the younger woman in a hug, despite having to reach up.

Jackson stood there smiling at the three, and then he hugged his son and nodded to Simona, welcoming her.

Royce's next words were, "Mama, we're sure starvin'. Can we eat now?"

Carley Love laughed and went straight to finishing up the pot pie and setting the meal on the table, moving smoothly and gracefully as a woman does when she feels fully in her element.

Jackson sat in his customary place at the far end of the dining table, and Carley Love took her place on the end nearest the kitchen. Royce bowed his head and Simona followed suit. Jackson looked expectantly at Carley Love before bowing his head.

Carley Love cleared her throat and closed her eyes. "Thank you, Father, for this abundance of food, and for bringin' us together to share it. Bless us and keep us in your care. Amen."

"Amen!" echoed Royce, as he dug his fork into his salad.

Carley Love and Jackson shared a smile.

Over the meal, they learned of one another, and, while Simona was a quiet woman, she responded to Carley Love's gently drawing her out, mostly about family. The women spoke of their respective grandmothers and recipes and family traditions, while the men watched and put in pithy comments.

After the meal, they moved to the veranda in front of the warming fire. Jackson stayed standing to poke the logs and add one from time to time, keeping it blazing. The other three sat on the loveseat and went through the photograph albums Carley Love had placed there for this purpose. The photographs were of a young Royce, which delighted Simona.

It was during this time of sitting close together that Royce took the opportunity to say, "We have somethin' to tell you, Mama...Dad."

His hesitant smile again rested mainly on his mother.

"Simona and I are married."

Carley Love stared at the young couple, her son with his arm around the young woman's shoulders. "You're married?"

Royce nodded. "We got married Friday." Nervousness flickered over his features, and Simona's gaze went to his profile.

"You did? Without...us?" Carley's voice turned faint.

"Well...we..." He glanced at Simona. "Simona's parents are far away, and it would have just been a whole lot of mess tryin' to get everyone together. And we wanted to go ahead and get married."

Another moment of shocked silence, in which everyone gazed at Carley Love.

"Of course you did," she said with suddenness, a smile blooming on her face. "Oh—congratulations! Come here, you two. Oh, my goodness!"

~

THE SUN WAS ALMOST GONE in the turquoise western sky and night creatures sang faint and sporadic songs in the pleasant fall evening, when they all stepped from the house to bid goodbye.

Simona easily hugged Carley Love. "Thank you...thank you so very much."

"I'm glad you've come, darlin' girl, So very glad."

Then Royce hugged his mother and said, "Thank you, Mama. I love you."

Carley Love held to him. "God bless and keep you," she whispered in his ear, and he kissed her cheek.

As the young couple headed away down the walk, Royce draped a warming arm around the taller Simona, who leaned into him.

Jackson stepped beside Carley Love and likewise put his arm around her shoulders.

Watching the BMW's red taillights head away down the drive, Carley Love leaned her head into Jackson's shoulder. She squeezed her eyes closed and tears slipped out. Straightening, she brushed them aside and stepped out toward the kitchen.

"I'll help you clean up," Jackson said, following.

"There's not much. Simona already filled the dishwasher. That girl's a jewel."

"You still have a sink full."

"Granny Reba Love's china and your mama's crystal. I always hand wash these."

She washed and he dried.

"The supper was really good," Jackson said. "You need to make those little rolls again."

"Thank you. I intend to."

A long minute of silence ensued, until Jackson said, "We've become my parents."

Carley Love chuckled. "We have."

Again silence.

Then Carley Love added, "But I don't recall ever seein' your dad dry dishes...nor walk out on your mother."

Instantly she bit her bottom lip, looking down as she soaped a crystal goblet.

Jackson said, "Well, he did, actually."

Her head came up, and she looked over at him with wide eyes.

"Leave, I mean. I doubt he ever dried a dish." He dried a plate as if polishing it. "Dad told me about it one time. One of those early times that you and me were havin' a fight. Dad and I went fishin', and I let it out about you and me not gettin' along."

He set the plate aside and took up another. "Dad told me how one time he had packed a suitcase and driven all the way to Wrightsville Beach, intendin' to never come back. Said he was sick of everythin', was leavin' Mama with the stores and everything else. He'd even taken half the money from the checking account. But after sittin' for some hours on the beach, he ended up comin' back home. He had left Mama a note in an envelope on the mantle, sayin' he wanted a divorce. Mama had found the envelope but said she hadn't opened it. He told her to burn it. He never knew if she read it or not.

"Dad said marriage was a perplexity but that every day he chose to stay married to Mama. He said love was like putting things in a basket. You just kept choosing to put things in, and that was how love grew.

"I guess I should have remembered that before gettin'

the wild hair to leave," he added in a wry tone as he set the plate aside and picked up a goblet.

Carley Love ran a soapy cloth over a dessert plate. After a full minute, she said, "I'm glad he came back. I loved your Mama and Daddy. I still miss them." Her speech was hoarse.

"Me, too," Jackson whispered. He leaned over and hugged her shoulders and rested his chin on the top of her head.

"I...well, I'm not ready to talk about us," said Carley Love, her voice shaky. "I'm too tired and too much has happened, with Mama and now Royce. It's all just too much right now."

He made no reply to this.

Carley Love breathed deeply and cleared her throat, then said, "I have not signed the divorce papers, and I won't before we talk. I do think the same as you have said—that we have had some wonderful years together."

Her voice dropped to a ragged whisper. "Jackson, I have loved you since I was sixteen. It's just that I just don't know if I can..." She broke off.

To that, Jackson said, "I'm not up to talkin' about it, either. At least not tonight."

Carley Love looked at him, at his profile as he gathered fine crystal goblets into his thick hands. Her gaze softened.

He carried the glasses in to the dining room table and returned.

Carley Love said, "I think Simona is pregnant, that's what I think. I think that's why they went ahead and got married. When Royce found out she was pregnant, he wasn't going to wait."

She gave him a sideways look, and he nodded, saying,

"You're probably right. And those two are well grown. They are entitled to make mistakes and learn from their own path just like the rest of us."

He looked pointedly at Carley Love, but she was gazing at his hands rolling down his sleeves over his forearms.

She came back to herself and turned to dry the counter, saying, "I'm awfully glad they have decided to have a wedding party to celebrate. I have looked forward to Royce's wedding forever, so I'm grateful. Simona was such a kind heart to ask my help in bringin' it together."

She breathed deeply and came out with, "We will be grandparents, Jackson."

"Let's not get ahead of ourselves," he drawled, and then—"but how do you feel about that, Granny Carle'Love?"

She replied instantly, "Ready or not, here it comes...just like everything else."

They shared a grin and each looked away with thoughtful expressions.

Jackson went to the door. "Guess I'd better get back. Early meeting tomorrow."

Carley Love followed him out to the porch. "Oh, my! The sweet olive is strong today. Simona asked for a vase of sprigs for the wedding party." She leaned to sniff the tiny, close growing blossoms. "You bought and planted it for me," she said with suddenness of thought.

He nodded, memories in his eyes for a moment, before bending to pet Freckles.

Gazing at his dark head, she said, "Thanks for comin'. It meant so much to Royce...and to me, too."

He slowly straightened. "I *wanted* to come "Care'lina. Royce is my son, too." He swallowed and wrapped an arm around her shoulders, saying softly into her hair, "We'll get through this."

They bid each other goodnight. Carley Love turned quickly into the house, closed the door, and moved to the window to watch him reach his pickup truck, get inside and drive away down the lane.

~

SUNDAY

9:45 p.m.

Writing in this journal is similar to organizing a closet. I pull out everything that happens in my life and look it over, deciding what to keep and what to throw away. Just like with my real closets, though, I find it extremely difficult to throw things away.

This day is the day my son told me thank you for something I did, something that meant a lot, and told me he loved me. I press the precious look on his face into my heart—because the fact is now my son has found a mate and is truly gone from me. When a boy grows to a man and takes a woman, he's pretty much gone from his mother. And a part of me is grateful. Jackson and I have done our jobs. We've raised a good man.

I expected to be told they planned to get married—not that they are already married and now planned a wedding party! My word, young people today certainly get things scrambled around.

Royce kept stressing they wanted it kept simple and not to spend a lot of money. I said that was sensible. It is important to start out on the right foot as a supportive mother and mother-in-law—and mind my own business. Certainly not to ask the questions in my mind, which are: Does Simona really want a small, plain affair, and where are her parents in all this? I did not need Jackson's warning looks to keep my mouth shut about any of that. Besides, eventually I'll find out about it all. I've learned that much. Eventually everything comes to light and at the right time.

Thank you, God, for bringing my son a good woman! Simona is beautiful inside and out. She is a model, mostly for catalogs. While she does clothing, what she models most are shoes. She says because of that she has to be very careful about her feet and legs. I believe someone who has good feet is stable and grounded in soul. She is a head taller than Royce, who took after my side of shorter people, and which does not bother either of them. Royce just beams up at her and treats her like a precious jewel. They are so in love. This is it for my son. I know it as surely as Mother Wells must have known it for me and Jackson.

I was afraid I would not know what to say, her being international and all, but she was quite easy to talk to. She has only a hint of odd accent on certain words and phrases. Simona said it is Romanian Southern Style. Too cute. And it turns out her mother is American and originally from Charleston. Funny how small the world is. She said she was raised by her father's mother in Romania until she was twelve, when she elected to live with her mother in Atlanta.

Imagine a mother who would turn over the care of her daughter to a mother-in-law in a foreign land, and a father who allowed this. I don't know what to say to that.

Simona said my Sunday table looked a lot like her grandmother's had looked. Her warm tone of voice spoke volumes. And with a few comments, I learned that her grandmother raised her in church—Catholic.

I said, "Well, I go to the First Baptist. Maybe you and Royce would like to go there with me sometime." She just smiled at that. That girl's grandmother raised her polite and smart. I don't know if she is still going to the Catholics, but if she does and takes Royce, that will be answered prayer. I never did specify Baptist when I prayed, so thank you, God. I can pray for Baptist later.

Another thing I learned was that she is, of all things, a vegetarian. I apologized for the chicken and scolded Royce for not telling me so that I could have made something different. But Simona said she had told him not to tell me, because she wanted to taste my chicken pot pie, said her grandmother used to make a similar dish.

It comes to me that none of us are just plopped down in this world. We come with stuff from other people—me with all kinds of stuff from Mama, and Mama with stuff from Granny Reba. Stuff came from my Daddy, too, and Royce has stuff from both me and Jackson, and Simona has stuff from her grandmother and her mama and daddy and so on. I bet Jackson got bringing flowers from his Daddy, now that I think of it. Both Jackson and Royce brought me flowers—like father, like son. They each do know me well. I love bouquets. I laugh and get tearful at the same time, thinking of it.

And thinking about what Jackson told me about his daddy. I cannot fully take in that Big Daddy Wells left Mother Wells. I can believe Mother Wells never said anything to him about it. That woman had starch in her backbone.

I think about what Jackson said when he left this evening—We'll get through this. He thinks we'll get back together. I am not so sure. I'm not sure if I have enough starch for it.

And now I hear Mama just as clear screaming at me: Are you insane? Snatch him up! What about your future? Do you want to end up old and crazy and alone like I was?

Well, Mama, I may make your biscuits, but I am not you.

God, I guess I am no surprise to you. I do seem to be a daily surprise to myself, though. Please help me find my honest way through this mess.

⁓

MONDAY, October 30

12:15 a.m.

Can't sleep, so here I am with a glass of wine, again. And with the photo album of Royce as a baby—and with all my dreams and regrets and prayers, too.

To this day, I give thanks for getting to have a child and be a mother. I prayed when I did not immediately get pregnant when I wanted to, which is pretty funny when you think how everyone thought I got married because I was pregnant. The day the doctor's office called to say I was pregnant is etched in my mind. I stood at the kitchen wall phone and repeatedly quizzed the nurse: Could a mistake have been made? What were the error rates on these tests?

There never was a baby more eagerly desired, anticipated, and planned for. I spent hours buying and sewing and reading on how to do everything perfectly. Mother Iris about bought out Belks' baby department for him. Big Daddy even bought stock in North Carolina National Bank, which proved a wise investment and sent Royce to college the one year he chose to go, and he still has some left over.

Of course, the delivery was not so sweet. Royce decided to come almost three weeks early, causing Jackson to have to drive like a madman to the hospital in the midst of a rare March snowstorm. His parents came slipping and sliding in their Cadillac right along behind our chugging Ford Galaxie.

But my body did not cooperate with Royce's entry into the world. I think somewhere inside of me, I decided to hold on to him. My labor went thirty-six hours, until finally the doctor did a caesarean.

When it was all over, Jackson told me that he had been afraid I was going to die. That was the first time I ever saw him cry. It is safe to say that he was also equally as wrung out as I was, because all those hours until the surgery he remained at my bedside holding my hand. When I awoke after surgery, there was Jackson gazing at me with the silliest grin, and then our dear Royce was brought and laid in my arms, where I kept him for weeks and weeks, barely laying him down.

There is a photo of Mama holding him and her face so tender as she gazes at him. And a still-lovely totally white-haired Granny Reba Love with him in the pedal car she bought him. A beautiful Mother Iris and Big Daddy, so proud of their grandson of two years. And then his eighth birthday and Mother Iris with the distinctive white streak of hair that she finally quit dying, and Big Daddy with his shock of iron-grey hair.

They are all gone now. All those people who were once with us, people who lived and loved before us, and now are gone. Makes me think of that quote by Robert Frost—"In three words I can sum up everything I know about life: It goes on."

Writing it all like this is like looking at family treasures. And now this journal falls in the treasure category. It is a treasury of my memories and tangled emotions.

And for my eyes only! When Jackson and the kids were here, I actually locked it in the top drawer of Granny Reba's mahogany desk.

Offerings

SHE LOOKED into the expanse of her bathroom mirror and spoke to herself a stream of encouragement. "I can do this," and "Ask and you shall receive," and "I have a lot to offer."

She called Ronni to consult on her choice of outfit. "I decided on my black and cream slacks outfit. You know that one with the long cardigan."

"I've always liked that sweater. Are you wearing the windowpane pants with it or the black?"

"The windowpane."

"Go with the black. That's more power. You notice Lila is always wearing black."

"Huh. Okay. Seems like I'm going to a funeral, though."

Ronni laughed. "That's just us Southern gals. Although, do you happen to have a pair of cream color slacks? Those would be dramatic with that sweater, too."

Carley Love said no, she didn't, and frowned at herself in the mirror.

"Then go with the black. You do look stunning in black. And if Lila says no, you come on over here and put in an application at the cosmetics department like I said. You got this, girlfriend. Just remember that you are an asset to Lila and Company."

Carley Love hung up the phone, changed her slacks and talked to herself in the mirror twice more.

When she arrived at the office, she went directly to Lila's office. Her petite boss was bent over her desk scattered with papers and files.

Hearing Carley Love at the door, Lila cast a quick glance, saying, "Good morning, Carley. Please make fresh coffee."

"Yes, ma'am."

Ten minutes later, she returned with a full, steaming mug and set it firmly on the desk in an expert manner calculated to get attention.

"Thank you," Lila said without looking up.

Carley Love moved closer, craning her neck to see what the older woman read. It was a printout of a listing.

Just then Lila closed the file folder over the papers and handed the file up to Carley Love. "Ready for Darlene to update on the computer. Then bring the file back to me."

"The Castleberry beach house?" Carley asked, opening the file. "I didn't know the Castleberrys were selling."

"They aren't. That info is from ten years ago when I sold it. I've had an inquiry for a beach house in that area." She turned to her computer screen and slipped on her glasses.

Carley Love held the file and looked from it to her boss. She opened her mouth to speak when a voice spoke from behind her.

"Lila, I need to speak to you about the shoppin' mall project." Norma Fay, tall and lanky, dressed in flowing wide-legged slacks, strode passed and slipped into the chair in front of the desk.

Lila looked above her reading glasses at the woman, who launched into conversation without a word or glance at Carley Love.

It neared noon when she was able to catch Lila alone and getting ready to leave.

"I'm going to lunch," Lila said, gathering her purse and sweater. "Please stay until Doreen gets here. She's been held up showing a property."

"Can I speak to you before you go?"

"Go ahead." Lila spared her a glance.

Carley Love forced the words out in a rush. "I've been part-time now far longer than had been anticipated. I believe I've done a very good job. I'm always willing to work extra when needed, and I believe I'm an asset to the company. I would like to be put on full-time."

Lila had pulled out a mirror and was checking her image. Seconds passed before she looked up and snapped the mirror closed.

"Carley, I agree totally that you are an excellent employee. I have nothing but praise for you. But right now I'm not in a position to bring you on full time. I'm not even going to the Bahamas this winter," she added with a rueful tone.

"I see," Carley Love said.

"I can keep you on three mornings a week as we are, with the possibility of full time in the future. That's the best I can do."

Carley Love nodded.

The older woman looked as if she might say more, but instead she took up her purse.

There came the sound of the front door chimes and Doreen calling gaily, "Yoo-hoo! I'm back!"

~

CARLEY LOVE SAT behind the wheel of her Escalade in the Wal-mart parking lot, talking to Ronni on her cell phone.

"At least I asked," she said.

Ronni came back with, "That's right. That is a step in the right direction. Now, you can just come up here and put in an application for the cosmetic department. My manager is all the time wanting good-lookin' mature women to sell to the older clientele.

"They don't want them too old," she hastened to add. "Just enough of an age to make the older women feel comfortable and hopeful. You'll be perfect at that."

"Oh, Ronni...I don't know." Her eyes followed a young woman in glowing purple spandex who was power-walking through the bright sunshine to the front entry of the store. "I'm no expert at makeup. You're all the time pointin' out ways I can improve my own."

"Honey, I can teach you the basics in no time. And all you really have to do is look nice and smile a lot and be sweet and flattering. You're a master at that. People just love you."

"How much would it pay?" Her gaze followed an immensely tall man with a multitude of piercings and a mural tattooed on his neck moving slowly, while a small boy, a toddler, trailed behind him.

"Well, they start people with no experience out at minimum wage. But you do get employee discount on purchases throughout the store. In any case, it would be more than you are gettin' now."

Carley Love frowned at a woman dressed in printed flannel pajama pants and fuzzy slippers.

"Well, I'll think about it. But I just can't do it today. I'm exhausted." She paused. "I'm picking up some Halloween candy—I forgot all about it being Halloween."

"Do you even get trick-or-treaters out where you live?"

"We usually get a few...local children. I just want to have it in case." She added, "I used to always get Reese's Cups and Snickers and hide them around the house for Jackson and Royce."

～

TUESDAY, October 31

10:10 p.m.

I ate half a bag of bite-size Snickers bars, so I took the rest of the bag out to the garage and put it in the freezer. Not one trick-or-treater came. It was depressing to my already depressed state, evidenced by another episode of pouring my emotions out on the page that I tore out and put in the back hidden pocket of this journal. It is definitely bulging too much now to be called hidden.

Lila turned me down for working full-time. The fact is that it is the slow time for real estate. Home insurance is still a mess after last year's hurricane, and people are busy with holidays and don't want to think of moving.

I appreciate Ronni's encouragement to put in an application to work at her cosmetic department, but the idea makes me want to throw up. Working around all that chrome and glass would get on my last nerve. The idea just seems non-productive for me. If I have chosen real estate, then that's where I need to focus.

Although maybe I had best face the fact that I can't be all that choosey. Obviously things are not going along in my life as I had planned.

SHE CLOSED the journal and gazed at the photograph of her mother and grandmother. Touching her fingertips to the photograph, she whispered, "I know—this, too, shall pass. No more whinin'. Tomorrow, Scarlett, right Granny? I'm a Love woman."

In the kitchen, she poured a glass of wine. She sipped it while standing at the counter and thinking. The next moment, she retrieved a pair of scissors, flipped on the back porch lights and stepped out the door. At the sound of rain, she paused and watched the water stream from the roof, before walking quickly around the corner of the porch to the rosebush. She snipped the three ragged blossoms.

A short time later, she snuggled in bed, falling asleep with the scent of roses coming to her from the blossoms nearby on the night chest.

Surprises

FRIDAY, November 3

5:30 a.m.

I am wrapped in a blanket on the porch this morning. The tea olive is blooming like crazy and smells divine.

Jackson has not called all week. I considered calling him. A couple of times I so wanted to talk to him. I think about him going ahead and filing the divorce papers and can hardly breathe.

But I am doing my best to not let my emotions run me, to be practical. I'm needing my space. I am giving myself time to find out what is right for me. I cannot base my life on what he decides. I have to decide for myself.

Trey has called me twice this week, making certain I am attending his firm's open house tonight. I was surprised at his eagerness to have me come and help host. I guess it is okay. This is something a friend does for another. But I can't recall ever going to a party without Jackson since we got married—I mean a social event with both men and women. So, I guess this is another new thing.

Yesterday I determined to start cleaning out Mama's things. I tried to start with the closet but got overwhelmed. That closet is full, if profoundly neat—Mama was committed to keeping everything in plastic bags and containers.

But I couldn't bear to face the enormous job, so I shut the closet doors and went to the old marble-topped chest in the hallway. Again, everything neatly placed in plastic bins. My goodness, it is amazing what Mama kept. There was every pad of paper she had ever gotten from a charity solicitation mailing. And there was one check-copy pad. Just one. An old yellow plastic medicine vial, with Granny Reba's name on it, holding safety pins.

People die, and all their stuff is left just as it was. It is pretty eerie. And a good lesson in how little material things matter in this world.

I simply couldn't begin to deal with any of it. The most I did was remove the stack of notepads and the vial of safety pins, because at this point the vial is a family heirloom. Guess what—now those things are cluttering my correspondence desk. I won't need any notepads or safety pins for as long as I live.

WHEN CARLEY LOVE pulled into the parking lot of the Cummings Law Firm, the sun was low in the western sky and cast a golden glow over the white-painted brick building. She approached the double oak doors with a massive tote bag in her right hand and a bunch of white and silver balloons floating from the left. The weight of the bag and the tug of the balloons caused her to walk erratically in her heeled sandals. A young man exiting the heavy door held it open for her to enter and helped guide the balloons in behind her.

Trey stood at the far end of the spacious room, speaking with his tall secretary. His head came round at the sound of Carley Love's entry.

"Carley!" Delight registered on his features. "Thanks for comin'! You remember my secretary, Evangeline?"

"Yes, I do. Hello, Evangeline." She gave the woman a wide smile.

"Hello, Mrs. Wells." The taller woman gracefully inclined her head in greeting. A forty-ish woman, she was beautiful in an exotic way, close-cropped dark hair and eyes carefully made-up.

Trey said, "Ladies, I'm runnin' late. Please excuse me... I'm goin' t' duck into my office to freshen up. I leave the rest of the arrangements for the evening's event in your capable hands."

He strode away down the hallway. Carley Love smiled up at the statuesque Evangeline, who gazed down, then cast an arched eyebrow at the balloons, which floated at her eye level.

"Well, I brought lighted goblets..." Carley Love said, glancing around the room with its darkly colored walls and heavy leather furniture, "...to brighten the rooms a bit. It is a party, after all."

"It is an open-house t' display our offices and introduce a new member of our firm. We are attorneys-at-law," the elegant woman added.

Carley Love's response to this statement was to blink,

look downward in the manner of a naughty child, then glance around the room with a skeptical eye, while her toes wiggled in her sandals.

The next moment, she straightened to full height. "Right, such a good point. Although, you know in real estate, we set the scene. And since this is a celebratory scene, and Trey said he wanted to welcome his clients and provide an opportunity for everyone to get to know the firm better, we could reflect more of a casual, welcoming atmosphere."

"Maybe these silver and white balloons here in this corner..." She moved to the area behind two heavy leather chairs and attached the balloons' ribbons to the wall with push pins. "...and these two over here." She fastened the floating balloons at the opposite corner.

"There. I think silver and white make a rather chic statement, don't you?"

Evangeline gave a faint, indulgent smile.

Carley Love looked in the open doorway of an adjacent room. It proved to be a conference room, with a long table and chairs. A credenza stretched along one wall. She anchored two balloons at the back of it, where they floated at the edge of a darkly-framed wall mirror, lifting the heavy atmosphere.

At the end of the room were double glass doors leading outside to an ivy-covered brick walled patio, with a table and benches. A wall switch illuminated the space with lights from a post and wall sconces. She tied the strings of the last balloons on the back of a wrought-iron chair and, leaving the doors wide, returned to the lobby. Out of her tote bag came goblets filled with strings of fairy lights, which she scattered throughout the rooms.

In the lobby, the caterer had arrived, and Evangeline directed him to set up a long cloth-covered table in the middle of the room.

Carley Love said, "Might I suggest...if we did away with the table and used this desk here and other small surfaces throughout these rooms, we'd create more space."

Evangeline gazed down at her without expression.

"That way people would not bunch up, but could sort of graze," Carley Love explained in a sweet fashion. "That long credenza in the conference room is perfect to hold food trays and the punch and drinks." She paused, waiting.

Fifteen minutes later when Trey, in casual shirt and with hair still damp, appeared from his office down the hall, he found doors opened, chairs moved, overhead lighting dimmed, and festive goblets of fairy lights in sparkling display. Carley Love was in Evangeline's office, standing behind her at the computer.

Just as Trey stepped into the doorway, the swinging jazz of Count Basie flowed out of the ceiling speakers.

Evangeline jolted at the sound and quickly turned down the volume.

Frowning at the computer, she shifted the frown to Carley Love, then saw Trey in the doorway.

"Good choice of music," he said, giving the woman a wink.

She gave an accepting small smile in return.

Trey took Carley Love by the hand and drew her with him into the lobby and over to a tray of food, saying, "Man, I'm hungry. Missed lunch today."

"Grab a bite, but come on," she told him. "Your guests are arriving, and you're up."

She gestured to the headlights showing through the

window. He crammed cheese and a cracker into his mouth and hurried with her to open front doors. She shifted to place herself second and him first, saying, "You are the master host." She brushed cracker crumbs off his sport shirt.

Glancing upward, she saw him gazing at her. She ducked her head, red flushing her cheeks.

"I really am grateful for you comin'." He slipped his arm around her shoulders and gave her a squeeze. "Social things are not my forte."

She looked up at him again, her eyes for a moment on his face and jaw that tightened as he watched a second car stopping beside the first at the far end of the lot. Men and women alighted from the vehicles, calling familiar greetings. Trey quickly explained to Carley Love that two of the men were members of the firm from the offices in Pensacola. The couples came toward them hand in hand, and Trey introduced Carley Love.

A sporty white Mercedes roared into the lot. Eric Wright, the firm's new attorney, alighted from behind the wheel, rounded the rear of the car and opened the passenger door. A woman got out, and as the couple came toward the door, Carley Love's mouth formed an astonished O.

"Ronni?"

A faintly sheepish expression passed over Ronni's face, and she said smartly, "I told you that dress was the one. Trey, isn't her dress fabulous? I picked it."

The two women embraced, then Carley Love pulled back and looked at her friend with a confused expression. "Why didn't you tell me you were comin' with..." She broke off.

"I really didn't know until this afternoon. I didn't know if I could get off work and then..." Seeing another couple approaching, she trailed off, "Oh, we'll talk later."

Carley Love watched her friend, who wore a slim-fitting, sexy dress, be led into the offices by her escort.

A stream of people arrived, and a flurry of greetings ensued. When they were alone again, Trey said in a low voice, "Ronni's right...your dress is great."

His eyes were intent on her.

"Thank you." Her gaze slipped to the side. "Oh, look, that's Lila. I didn't know she was comin'."

The older woman came forward across the pavement in the manner of Queen Elizabeth, in a pale grey suit and patent pumps, with a black patent purse dangling from her arm.

Both Trey and Carley Love greeted her at once.

She responded with, "Good evenin', Trey...Carley." Her gaze lingered on Carley Love.

As the sun set and stars appeared faintly in the sky above, they continued to greet a multitude of guests. Trey stood it, moving from one foot to the other, until a certain pretty young woman clerk arrived.

"Melody! You take greeting duty. I promise you a bonus."

He pulled Carley Love by the hand, and led her inside, moving from one snack tray to another, speaking to people as they went. Trey kept her close and at every opportunity fell silent to let Carley Love carry the conversations.

She smiled and made small talk, prodded Trey to mingle, cleaned spilled drinks, found chairs for elder guests, brought a young, awkward paralegal together with a group of people the same age, and found baking soda in water and a sofa in a large office for a young pregnant guest, who needed to rest. People—Trey said far more than he had expected—seemed to come and go in waves and only the few who actually worked in the offices stayed long.

When Carley Love saw things settling down, she headed for the ladies room and ran into Ronni coming out. Carley Love pushed her friend back into the room and shut the door.

"Now, tell me—so you and Eric are..." Her arched eyebrow demanded an answer.

With a trembling grin, Ronni gave a roll of her eyes. "Okay. I fell for him that day we went to lunch. I know it's crazy. I have to be nuts." She turned to look at her image in the mirror over the sink, as if to find an answer there.

"Eric came to the store the next day after our lunch—he looked me up and pestered me for my phone number, and then he called me just thirty minutes later!" She put her head back with a laugh. "He has called me every night this week and practically begged me to come here with him and is takin' me to dinner after."

She turned to face Carley Love, her eyes shimmering with tears. "We just seemed to click. It's like we've known each other forever. And he sure doesn't seem like anyone I would ever in my life be interested in—he's from up north in Wisconsin, for cryin' out loud, and he's short and balding —and he's such a nerd! It's just crazy!"

"Why didn't you tell me?" Carley Love asked.

"I couldn't. Well, at first I didn't think there was anything to it, and then when I started to realize that I was gettin' nutty over him, I felt embarrassed. It was only today, this evenin', when he wanted me to come, that I realized this is really something between us. Actually, I was scheduled to work, but then the boss changed the schedule...it was like it was meant to be.

"This becomin' a partner in the firm means so much to Eric. He wanted me to share it. He's a *good* man. He's kind... and he is a believer. I mean in a quiet way. He's...he's steady, Carley, you know? And he wants me, and I want him." An expression of wonder passed over her face. "And I'm scared to death!"

Carley Love put her arms around her friend and hugged her. "I'm glad for you, darlin' woman. This is a blessin'."

"But what if it doesn't work out? What if I'm wrong about him? What if I'm imaginin' all this?"

"Oh, honey, don't sink it before it's barely begun."

A knock sounded on the door, and a woman's voice called, "Hey, you ever comin' out?"

The two women came out arm in arm, and the woman waiting stepped back and stared, then dashed through the door.

Eric Wright came to claim Ronni and to take her out to dinner. "Thanks so much for helping with tonight, Carley."

She smiled at him. "Glad to. Take care of my girlfriend."

As she watched the couple leave hand in hand, she felt her ring finger with her thumb in an absent manner. The next instant, she swiftly lifted her hand and contemplated the empty space on her finger.

Dropping her hand, she strode across the lobby and into the conference room, picking up discarded cups and plates as she went. She tossed the refuse in the large bin on the patio, where she saw Trey chatting with a group of men. Returning inside, she went to the credenza and picked at what fruit was left and poured herself a glass of punch.

"Carley."

She turned to see Trey coming toward her, with a distinguished silver-haired man following close behind. "I want to introduce my father."

"Just call me E.H.," the man interjected with a smile, taking her offered hand into both of his. "The Third here tells me you contributed greatly t' the success of tonight's event...and to choosin' the music. May I have this dance?"

"Oh, I—"

"I saw you swayin' to the music. "In the Mood" happens to be a favorite of mine. Turn it up, won't you, boy?" He tossed the instruction over his shoulder at Trey, as he swept Carley Love into his arms and danced her around the conference table and into the lobby.

He was smooth and she was stiff. She looked doubtful. He grinned. The few guests remaining moved back.

The song ended, and Rod Stewart's sultry voice floated in the air. E.H. kept hold of her and continued dancing. She began to find her footing. Her eyes widened when he placed his cheek to hers and pulled her close.

As the music ended, he danced her to the side and stopped. She breathed deeply and declared, "It's been a long time since I've danced."

"I thank you, darlin'. And now I believe The Third wants a dance." He still had hold of her hand and passed it to Trey, who took her into his arms to the old Bunny Berigan tune, "I Can't Get Started With You."

She grinned up at him, and he grinned down at her. When the song ended, he did not let her go, but kept dancing into the following tune.

Just after eight o'clock, Trey closed the doors behind the last departing guests. Carley Love and Evangeline were cleaning up, but Trey told them to leave it for a special crew coming in the morning. He helped Carley Love gather her sparkling goblets and carried the heavy tote bag to her Escalade.

"Would you like to go out to dinner?" he asked, his eyes intense.

She shook her head. "I'm full. I finished off that last tray of smokies."

"I'm offerin' steak."

She chucked and shook her head again, although saying warmly, "Thank you for includin' me tonight. I had a really good time. But I'm ready to go home."

A hint of disappointment touched his eyes, but he smiled as he nodded in understanding.

She slipped up into the seat behind the wheel, and he stood in the opened door. They gazed at each other.

He said, "Text me to let me know you got home safe, okay?"

"Okay."

Again they gazed at each other, then he swiftly bent to brush her cheek with a kiss, closed the door, and stepped back.

She started the engine and waved as she backed away.

As she pulled the Escalade out onto the boulevard, she turned off the radio and silence descended. Two miles and she left the brightly lit boulevard, driving through the velvet night, eyes on the two-lane blacktopped road lit only by the vehicle headlights. Twenty minutes and she pulled through the entry of her own driveway. Halfway along, she saw bright light pouring from the opened garage door.

Jackson's truck sat parked off to the side.

She eased the Escalade into the garage and shut off the engine. Through the windshield, she saw Jackson in the adjacent workshop, the fluorescent fixture hanging from the ceiling shining like a spotlight on his dark head and shoulders.

She got out of the Escalade, and he came to the doorway of the workshop, screwdriver in hand.

"Hello," she said.

"Hi." His gaze moved down her body and back up to her eyes. "I needed a part for a carburetor. I'm helpin' Royce with an old truck."

"Ahh."

"Friday night on the town?"

"No." She shook her head and gave a faint smile. "Trey's —the Cummings' Law Firm—had an open house. I helped with it."

"Uh-huh. Well, y' look great." His eyes bore into hers.

"Thanks." She averted her eyes and raked a hand through her hair. "I'm mostly exhausted now."

Again their eyes met. They each waited as if for the other to speak.

"Well, goodnight," she said.

"Yeah...g'night." He abruptly turned back to the workbench.

She headed through the door to the house. "I'll lock up when I leave," he called after her.

"Thank you."

She stepped into the kitchen and stood blinking, even as the dog wiggled around her.

Ten minutes later, barefoot and tying her robe, she heard Jackson's truck engine. She went to the living room window and peered out through the shelter of the blinds. She watched his truck back from its place and head down the driveway, watching the truck's taillights until they disappeared.

She turned and looked around the dimly lit living room. Bending, she pet the dog. "I sure am glad for you, Freckles girl."

~

FRIDAY, November 3

10:00 p.m.

I heard a night bird through the open window, a lonesome sound. Even the air is sweetly lonesome. My tattered robe and fuzzy slippers and the quiet solitude is sure a far cry from earlier this evening when I wore a femme-fatale dress in the midst of a crowd and ended up being danced around by two handsome men.

I certainly surprised myself. Men looked at me. I enjoyed it. I enjoyed feeling my full, ripe womanhood that all the years of living and learning have managed to grow. I very much enjoyed assisting people to enjoy themselves, and I'm sort of amazed at it, whatever that says about me.

I braved Trey's intimidating secretary, Evangeline. I had forgotten all about her and how I feel inept and small around her. I truly am small compared to her. She is an Amazon woman and stunningly beautiful. What Mama would say is: She thinks she's the Queen of Sheba.

When I was melting away in front of her, I reminded myself that Trey had asked me to come. I was not an intruder. And frankly, they did need help. While Evangeline may be excellent at ordering an office (or an army, I'm sure) her talents fall short for a friendly social event. My few ideas added just a bit of sparkle and openness and made the atmosphere more inviting. I think I may have even charmed Evangeline just a bit.

It sure did come as a surprise to find out that Trey, who always seems so confident and urbane, was uncomfortable with a social event. He more or less let me carry the conversations.

Of course I knew quite a number of the guests, some from church, others who have business with Lila. And Lila herself. Her expression at seeing me with Trey did tickle me. Not that Lila ever displays much emotion, but I saw her eyebrows rise.

The really big surprise—Ronni and Eric Wright are a couple. Good heavens! Ronni never said one word to me about him. Not one word. I'm hurt, or maybe more like I've lost one more person. Which of course is silly—and bears testimony to how wrong feelings can be and lead us astray.

But I am wondering what sort of friendship Ronni and I have that she didn't confide in me. Is it that I am no good at relationships? Maybe no wonder Jackson and I are all messed up. Maybe I haven't let Ronni get a word in, talking all about myself as I have been. Maybe it is true what Jackson says—I don't listen.

Well, I am truly happy for Ronni. Even if it means our friendship has changed. Ronni doesn't need to tell me anything. She has a partner now, someone with whom she can share all the secrets of her heart.

Just like I am writing all of mine now in this journal, because I don't have that special person.

I used to tell everything to Jackson. I told him things I couldn't tell anyone else. He was my other half.

It comes to me suddenly that I am telling things to God now. I do that on these pages. Here I am honest. God knows me better than I know myself, and maybe here on these pages He helps me to see me.

Valley Of Confusion

SHE STOPPED JUST inside the doors of the church sanctuary, letting her eyes adjust after the bright sunlight outside. As she moved further inside, she greeted people, hugged a few, kind people who spoke condolences about her mother, while making her way down the aisle and looking for a place to sit.

"Carley Love!"

She turned and smiled. "Hello, Trey."

"Care to sit here?" He gestured to the pew.

"Uh...thanks."

She slipped into the pew, leaving room for him on the end. A man stopped to greet him and chat. Others around them exchanged comments and greetings or simply nods and smiles.

Evangeline passed in the aisle on her way to a woman one pew up on the other side, who motioned ardently. Evangeline paused to exchange greetings with Trey and Carley Love, then moved on to sit with the woman. The music director stepped forward in front of the choir, the lights above dimmed, and the music began.

At the cue, Carley Love stood with Trey and sang a modern rendition of "Blessed Assurance."

She and Trey glanced at each other and smiled.

Carley Love's gaze drifted toward the stage, and stopped at Evangeline, who was turned, looking her way. Seeing Carley Love look at her, Evangeline faced forward.

AFTER THE SERVICE ENDED, while everyone around them rose and began to stream out of the sanctuary, Trey asked Carley Love, "Would you join me for lunch?"

She hesitated, and then—"Yes, that would be nice."

His grin flashed, and he moved aside to let her go ahead of him, guiding her with his hand pressed to the small of her back, slipping past the line to greet the pastor, out the doors and down the steps.

"The Mariner okay?" Trey asked.

"Lovely."

Carley Love agreed to meet him there. Driving in the slow-moving heavy Sunday traffic of people heading to the beach, eyes hidden behind large dark glasses, she kept glancing at her image in the rear-view mirror. At one stoplight, she retrieved lipstick from her purse and applied it. At another stop light, Trey eased his black Lexus up beside her in the right lane. He waved at her, and she waved back.

"Lord, help me not to be foolish," she murmured.

He went ahead to the restaurant and leaned waiting against the fender of his Lexus when she pulled to a stop beside it. He opened her truck door and again walked with his hand at the small of her back.

The hostess greeted him by name and asked, "Your usual table okay?"

"Your usual table?" Carley Love questioned, when they had gotten seated.

He grinned. "The owner and I are buddies—we handle his legal work."

As they perused the menu, they made banal conversation about the weather and economy and real estate, past weather, and coming weather, until the waitress brought cold sweet tea for each of them and took their order.

The topic turned to Pastor Conroy's sermon on Ephesians and grace and the importance of living by grace.

"I like how he teaches on specific scriptures," said Carley Love, stirring the slice of lemon around in her glass, "and relates it to daily living. He makes me think about my life."

Trey agreed and said, "Pastor Conroy is who got me back in church. Our firm did some work for his family. He started with encouraging me to read the Bible, and eventually I did, and one day just found myself going to church. I hadn't even realized how I had been seeking, and finally began to realize that fact." His voice and eyes reflected humor.

The waitress brought their meals, and as they ate, they related their childhoods, both having the experience of a mother taking them to church and a father who stayed home. This sharing brought them leaning forward on the table toward each other.

Carley Love said, "From as far back as I can recall, Mama read the Bible to me and helped me memorize scripture at bedtime." She chuckled as she said, "I remember her stamping out her cigarette and comin' to sit on the side of the bed. My granny and great-granny and Mama all went to church together, and I have never as long as I can remember doubted the existence of God. I've always prayed." She gave a rueful grin. "Although, now, lest I give a wrong impression, I struggle daily with truly relyin' and followin'. I'm a work in progress."

He nodded in agreement. "My mother taught me, but she died when I was a thirteen, so that shook my faith." He sat back in his chair and spoke slowly. "I guess I've been looking ever since, and I think now I'm findin' something true to hold on to."

Carley Love said softly, "Jesus, the author and finisher of our faith."

He nodded.

She sat back and her tone grew lighter as she said, "Your father calls you The Third."

"Yeah. I am Ernest Havelock Cummings III. That was a mouthful for a baby, so Dad called me The Third, and Mom called me Trey. I continued with Trey. It's easier, and I don't get confused with Dad."

She studied his face, and he looked back at her.

"How are you doin' now—I mean about your mother," he asked.

"Better. I'm tryin' to get myself to start the hard job of sorting out her things.

"Mama will always be with me. Jackson always said I was Mama made over. It's true, and sometimes I don't like it." Her lips curved into a wry grin. "Me and Mama and my Granny Reba Love. Sometimes I don't know where they stop and I begin." She paused a moment, then added, "It was complicated with us."

He nodded, sipped from his glass, then spoke as if it were hard to bring out the words. "I remember my mother's voice more than anything."

He shifted to lean his arms on the table, and his voice was warm. "I can hear her singin' sometimes. She was a professional singer...small clubs in New Orleans, Tallahassee, and churches, too. Sometimes I hear her singin' *'Georgia...Georgia'*." Her name was Georgia, and "Georgia On My Mind" her signature song. And she could sing "Ain't No Grave" in a real gospel style."

He turned his cold glass with his fingertips. "Dad never recovered from losin' her. It's all pretty complicated between us, too..."

Once started talking of his private life, the words flowed from him, about the loss of love in college and struggling with growing up with only his inattentive father for guidance.

Carley Love listened with her gaze fixed on his face. Every now and again, she would prod him with a gentle question or comment that brought more from him.

Later, when he walked her to her Escalade in the parking lot, he walked close, his hand on her back, his hip brushing against her.

She remotely unlocked the door, and he opened it for her in a courtly manner. They politely thanked each other for the lunch. His eyes drifted downward to her lips.

He cleared his throat. "How 'bout dinner Wednesday night?"

"I...I think that would be lovely," she replied and smiled up at him.

Eyes shielded by dark glasses, she drove the crowded boulevard carefully, until she turned onto the empty county road, where she picked up speed. She fished her cell phone from her purse and punched the number for Ronni.

Rings came across the line, two, four, five, and then Ronni's voice: "Hi. Sorry, maybe, to miss your call. Leave a message, or not. Have a blessed day."

"Ronni, it's me. I just had lunch with Trey. I agreed to a date Wednesday night. And now I am in somethin' of a state...well, talk to you later."

She punched the button ending the call. Her lips trembled.

Then she jutted her chin. "Girl, it was just lunch and now it is just a date. Not an affair. There is no reason to get all in a tizzy about it."

She breathed deeply, then murmured, "As a man thinketh in his heart."

Then loudly, "I am *not* thinkin' of an affair, just because imaginings cross my mind."

And then, whispered, "Help me, Lord."

SUNDAY, November 5

4:30 p.m.

I went to church today for the first time in weeks. I hadn't known how much I had missed it.

Do I know myself at all? I keep surprising myself.

I had not planned to sit with Trey, but I did anticipate he might be there. You know, in trusting that no one will ever read this, let me say that Trey's warm man hand on the small of my back felt amazingly good.

Trey and I went to lunch together. We really talked, and that was nice. And I'll say something else—I do listen.

I've a better picture of Trey now. He was close to his mother but lost her when he was barely in his teens. His father had a lot of live-ins. There was a lonesome tone in his voice when he said this. He said he almost married in college, but his girlfriend died in a boating accident. Thus, he has lost the two women in his life to mean the most— not that he put it that way, but my observation as a woman. He is a kind, good man. And I'm attracted to him.

There I've said it.

It is true that I might simply be attracted to him because he is attracted to me. I am flattered and at a terribly lonely and vulnerable time in my life. For a moment, when we said goodbye, I thought he was going kiss me. I got terrified and looked away. Then he asked me to dinner on Wednesday night, and I said yes.

Maybe I more understand what Jackson was trying to tell me about how he had felt frustrated and confused with his life and himself.

I don't think where I find myself is totally Jackson's fault. All of my heartache, anger, blame, is from within me. I'm reacting to confusion within myself. It is like a great big valley of confusion that I have to get through, in order to find myself again.

SHE FELL ASLEEP WRAPPED in a blanket on the kitchen porch chaise, near the fragrant sweet olive shrub. When her phone rang, she jolted awake, sending the journal and her pen flying from her lap. Feeling for the phone on the nearby table, she knocked it to the floor. Spying the phone in the pool of light falling from the kitchen window, she stretched to reach it, and tumbled onto the porch floor.

"Oh, shimmy." She grasp the phone and scanned the screen, then sat up on the floor and answered with a puzzled frown. "Hello, Lila…How are you?"

"Just fine. Look, Carley, I need you for certain to come in tomorrow, and plan to stay through early afternoon. I need to speak to you about something."

"O-kay. I can do that. What's up?" She pushed to sit on the chaise.

"I'll tell you tomorrow. Goodnight." The line fell silent.

Carley Love said, "Huh," and slipped the phone into her robe pocket. She retrieved the journal and pen and took up her empty tea cup and saucer. She was just inside the kitchen with all of it, holding the door for Freckles, when her phone went off again.

She plopped everything on the table and answered. "Hi, Ronni."

"Hi, sweetie. I couldn't return your call earlier 'cause I was havin' family dinner at my aunt's. I only have a minute—Eric is supposed to call. What I want to say is don't make a big deal out of this date with Trey. It is only dinner, Carley, and a married woman is allowed to have dinner with a man friend."

"I agree…but name one you know who does that."

"Well…okay, I can't right now, but I do believe there is nothin' wrong with it. Especially for *you*, Miss Proper…and Trey, too. Oh, Andrea is callin' in, and I need to talk to her."

"Okay, bye."

Carley Love breathed deeply and again pocketed the phone, frowning and gazing at the floor for long seconds.

The next instant she pulled her phone out again and scanned recent calls. With a sigh, she pocketed it once more. She put the tea cup into the sink, folded the blanket over her arm, and headed through the house, turning out the lamps as she went. Freckles followed.

In the bedroom, she pressed the stereo button, and Faith Hill's voice sang out about fireflies. Humming along, Carley Love positioned herself against a generous pile of pillows in bed. Calling the dog, she patted the bed. Freckles' brown eyes looked upward at her, but the dog did not move from her cushion.

Carley Love gave a disappointed shrug and opened the journal on her knees, put her pen to the paper.

She paused as George Strait's voice filled the air, singing "You'll Be There."

"Mama, I'll see you there," she whispered.

Her cell phone rang. Simona's name showed on the screen. Carley Love smiled, picked up the stereo remote and lowered the volume on the music before answering.

"Hello, darlin' girl."

"Hello. I hope I'm not callin' too late," said Simona.

"No, not at all."

"Oh, good. I wanted to let you know that we booked the venue for the party."

"The venue," Carley Love repeated. "How exciting. Where's it goin' to be?"

"The Gulfside at the beach. Do you know those condominiums?"

"Oh, yes, I do. Very nice."

"And that way my parents and the few friends coming

from Atlanta can stay overnight. The event room opens out onto the beach. We thought maybe we would reenact our vows—well, actually make up our own vows, because at the courthouse we didn't really say vows. We thought on the beach at sunset."

"Ah-huh. That sounds lovely."

"Well, I need your email to send you all the details we have so far."

Carley Love smiled. "Of course...you know, how about I text you the address?"

"Perfect."

Carley Love said, "I've been thinkin' of ideas for the decorations, if you still want my help."

"Oh, I do. We just don't want to spend extravagantly. We don't think that is wise or at all necessary."

"I understand, sweetheart, but it is a special event to celebrate your marriage, and that is important. It really is all of your traditional parties in one and a once in a lifetime opportunity to have all of your friends and family celebrating with you. So you just don't worry about the money for decorating—or for the food and entertainment. Jackson and I will fund all that."

"That's very kind of you, Mrs. Wells. I'll have to make sure it's okay with Royce."

"I understand." A smile traced Carley Love's lips.

Simona continued, "We have the music taken care of. Royce has a friend who is a DJ for parties. And we really do want to keep it simple and conservative. Royce hates what he calls *folderol*." Her laughter came lightly across the line.

"Yes, my son has not liked fancy fussing since baby-hood." Carley Love laughed. "And I think since we are going to be family, you could go ahead and call me Carley, or Mom."

"Okay...Carley. Thank you," came the shy reply.

"Now a place to start with the party is with one particular thing you want in the way of decorating. What would that be?"

"I think...I think I would really like to have gardenias for my hair and for the tables." The young woman spoke with soft hesitancy. "I know they are expensive and right here in winter, too. But just a few, if we could."

"Oh, honey, I know where to get them! I have a friend who can get them wholesale from a greenhouse. Got that covered. Now what about food?"

They spoke a few more minutes, then said goodbye. Carley Love quickly sent her email address in the promised text, set the phone aside, and took up the pen again.

10:10 p.m.

A busy night here. Lila called and says she wants me for sure to come in tomorrow and she wants to talk to me. Wonder what that's all about. It doesn't sound like she is going to fire me.

Ronni called and according to her, I am too proper to have an affair. She is *right*. And I'm not sad about it. I would say it's according to me, too, and I'm relieved to know that much about myself.

And Simona just called to discuss the wedding celebration. She said the venue is booked—at the beach. In late November. A chancy proposition. But I did not speak of it.

The plans are made, no need to throw a damper on her spirits.

It appears that Simona's parents are having no part in helping with the party. Well, why should they? Simona and Royce are fully adults living their own lives. And of course they are simply being kind to include me in the party plans. Royce knows it means a lot to me. I told Simona, though, that I would handle the decorations and food, and promised not to be extravagant. When I think of how lean Jackson and I lived our first fifteen years—I learned how to make something from nothing—which Ronni is always telling me, so maybe I do that in more ways than one.

I have not heard from Jackson. Not one word all weekend.

What did I expect?

As Mama would say, My arm ain't broke. I could call him. But I just can't. Besides, it's too late tonight anyway.

I guess it's "tomorrow, Scarlett."

About Successful Living

MONDAY, November 6

10:30 a.m.

Lila went out as soon as I got here. She said she will talk to me when she returns. I doubt she is going to let me go, but what do I know? I didn't see what was coming with Jackson and myself. How can I trust myself with any insight?

I'm upset at myself and upset at him right now. I called him first thing this morning. He never gets up later than 5:30. I called him at 6:30 and got no answer, which was better than if that woman had answered—a possibility that made me so anxious I felt sick. What would I have said if a woman answered his phone?

Anyway, I left a message telling him I was going to take money out of the savings account for the wedding decorations and to put a deposit on the food.

Rather than call me back, he answered me by text, two letters: OK.

I guess he doesn't want to talk to me. Maybe he has decided to go through with the divorce.

There is a hard truth: I don't want to let him go and I can't imagine getting back with him. What can I say to that?

I was up in the night, and I went poking into Mama's closet. In a box, I found my Granny Reba Love's old wallet, of all things, and it still had her driver's license, with her picture only a year before she died, and voting card and stuff like that.

Think of a person who kept such a thing for over over twenty-five years—as well as two packages of unopened Super Glue, the tubes hard as rocks, more yellowed greeting cards and envelopes, a small New Testament, and a real old photo album with blurry photographs. Oh, recognizing a young Granny Reba in a lot of them both warmed my heart and made me teary. Everyone in those days had nicknames. Granny was 'Susie-Q' for some reason that I never learned. Think how prosperous my grandmother's family had to have been to have a camera and be able to take so many photos.

I tossed it all into the trash, and then I fished it out, except the glue. I just can't throw a Bible in the trash, and Granny's wallet and the cards and photographs could have historical value. I might someday decide to put the photos of Granny in one of those ancestry books. So now I am a person who...

∿

THE BELL over the office door rang out. Carley Love's head came up with a jerk.

Doreen breezed in with a smile. "Hi, girlfriend. I am so happy to have made it on time today."

"Congratulations." Carley Love snapped her journal closed and reached for her purse, tucking the book securely inside.

"Did you hear the news?" Darlene asked.

"What news?"

"Lila didn't tell you?"

"Tell me what?"

"She's bought a new building. She's movin' the office. She's already sold this building." She leaned forward and spoke with a lowered tone. "That attorney E.H. Cummings was in here last week, and I overheard them talkin' about it. I sort of got the idea that she is partnering with someone, maybe him. He took care of some of the details, and it sounded like they are makin' future plans. It sounded to me like she's going to expand."

Carley Love raised an eyebrow. "Lila has always run things herself...and expanding this year?"

"Just relayin' what I heard. And really, now with real estate way down is the time to take advantage. And have you noticed how much Norma Fay has been gone up to Montgomery? I mean, she is like some phantom agent around here now...which is good for me," she said with a grin and a wink. "Miss Lila had me take over one of her clients. The lady is real hard to please, but I bet I can do it."

LILA DROVE her long black Cadillac down the boulevard in a manner that pressed Carley Love back in the passenger seat at takeoffs from traffic lights. She turned onto a street of the old part of town, drove beneath stately trees, and pulled into a small parking lot in front of a white clapboard building, where strong young men swarmed the roof and threw down shingles with abandon. A porch ran the length of the front, a great live oak spread limbs over half of it, and sago palms gone wild sat at the corners.

"Did Doreen tell you about the building?" Lila asked.

"Yes. Just a bit ago."

"Trust Doreen to know all that's going on."

"She said you are expandin'." Carley Love's eyes were curious.

"Not expanding so much as making changes that I've thought about for some time and decided to go with." While she spoke, she reached into her purse and pulled out a packet of gum.

"I had this opportunity and took it." She popped the gum into her mouth and opened the car door. "Come on and I'll show you around."

The older woman quickly alighted from behind the wheel.

"Isn't this the Monroe building?" asked Carley Love, hurrying to catch up with the older woman, who walked in surprisingly quick steps, and in low-heeled pumps, despite her advancing age.

Lila nodded and said without stopping on her way to the weather-beaten wooden and glass double front doors, "It's been vacant since Hurricane Katrina. Two bad hurricanes in two years was enough for them. The elder Monroe retired and moved up to the Carolina mountains. His son went over to Mobile. I got it for a song."

Inside, workmen were tearing up carpeting. Carley Love followed Lila through the rooms, listening as she pointed out features and spoke of her plans in her brief, no-nonsense fashion.

Fifteen minutes later, the women returned to the front entry and then out onto the porch.

Lila turned to Carley Love, "Here's my offer. I want you to help with décor. I offer you half days all week. If business picks up in the spring, I'll be able to put you on full-time as an office manager, if you're still interested at that time." Her expression questioned and she added. "I don't think selling real estate is for you, Carley, but you are good at organizing and handling social things."

Carley Love pressed her lips together and furrowed her brows. When she spoke, it came slowly. "Okay. I think that will work for me."

"Good," said Lila. She opened her mouth to continue, when a batch of shingles came falling down in front of them.

Frowning, Lila stepped off the porch and hollered upward, "Hey, up there! Watch where you throw those shingles! I'm not paying you to destroy these boxwoods."

"Yes, ma'am," came the answer.

Lila motioned to Carley Love, and the two women went to the Cadillac. Lila started the engine, then turned to Carley Love.

"Now, I have another offer. I want you to plan an open house for us. One similar to what the Cummings' offices held. A simple come and go, but I want it to be festive for Christmas. We'll show off our new offices and have a Christmas party for clients and associates at the same time. And I will pay you separate for planning the party."

Carley Love took this in, and asked, "How much?"

"How much will you charge me?"

Breathing deeply, Carley Love looked out the windshield for long seconds, and then turned an assessing eye to the building.

Finally she said to the older woman, "Five hundred, and you pay for the catering, of course, and all disposable supplies and anything extra special that you particularly want."

Lila inclined her head and stuck out her hand. "Done."

The women shook hands, and the older woman put the Cadillac into gear.

"You know, dear," said Lila, as she pulled into the flow of traffic, "I would have paid twice that." She slid her eyes to Carley Love. "Start high. You can always come down."

CARLEY LOVE PUSHED through the heavy glass door of the department store and hurried toward the cosmetic department.

Ronni was busy with a customer. Carley Love waited off to the side, perusing the Clinique counter until the customer left.

"Guess what," she said to Ronni.

Ronni smiled. "You ran into that Navy fella again."

"Oh, no." Carley Love shook her head. "Lila's bought new offices and given me more hours through the winter. And she's hired me to plan an open house to celebrate the new offices. She payin' me to do that!"

"I'm glad for you, darlin' woman. That is good news." Ronni moved down the counter, putting away items she had brought out for the customer.

Carley Love followed, saying, "What's really exciting is that I know I can do this. I can. Well, I'm not so certain about drawin' up a plan." She frowned. "Lila wants a written plan. I've never done anything like that. I am tryin' to be grateful, because it is professional and something I need to learn."

"You can do it. They have computer programs for that." Ronni crouched down to unpack a supply box, putting items into the case.

Carley Love leaned over the counter. "I thought maybe I could hang around until you get off work, and we could go to supper and you could help me talk out my ideas."

Ronni shook her head. "I'm sorry, I can't tonight. I'm workin' into the evenin', and then I have to get home and make sure Andrea is doin' her homework. Her civics teacher called me. Andrea's got a whole bunch of zeros where she isn't turnin' in work."

She straightened. "I need to spend more time with her. She's jealous of Eric." Her chin quivered with the last.

"Oh, honey." Carley Love reached out to cover her friend's hand with her own.

Ronni swallowed and breathed deeply. "No one in my family is happy about me and Eric. My aunt Geraldine is havin' a hissy about him not bein' Catholic and bein' from up north...and he and my brother Elvin...well, they don't see eye-to-eye on anythin'. I'm sure you can imagine." She bent and came up with a tissue, picking up a hand mirror to check as she wiped her carefully made-up eyes.

Carley Love said, "I'm sorry."

"I just never thought they'd be so mean about it." Ronni's voice broke.

"You know," Carley Love said gently, "I imagine it is

more that they are used to havin' you to themselves. They just need time to adjust. It's a big change for them."

Ronni sniffed and glanced to the end of the counter, where a customer was looking her way. "I've got to work. I'm happy for you," she added, forcing a smile.

Carley Love watched her friend walk away to the customer. Turning from the counter, she left the store far more slowly than she had entered, and not looking at any of the colorful temptations of the women's department on either side of the isle.

She slipped up into the driver's seat of the Escalade, started the engine and touched the stereo button. Country music floated from the speakers. Navigating the late afternoon traffic, she exited the expressway and drove home along the narrow country road. The sun, low in the western sky, spread golden rays over the fields and through the pecan orchards.

Quite suddenly she cried aloud: "Whoo-hoo! You got a cool job, Carley Love!" Grinning and doing a little hip dance in the seat, she added, "This could be the start of somethin' good, girl."

Then she sighed and relaxed, a smile remaining at the edges of her lips.

George Strait's sultry voice sang out a ballad about hope and love and life, and Carley Love sang along in a low voice, knowing all the lyrics from memory.

"How do you know where you're goin', if you don't know where you are?" she whispered, as the song faded.

Punching the button to silence the stereo, she removed her sunglasses and slid her eyes to the ball that was the golden setting sun.

"Where am I, Lord?"

FRECKLES GREETED HER EAGERLY, and she ended up going down on her knees, while the dog licked her all over the face.

"Thank you, friend," she whispered, burying her face in the dog's neck.

An hour later, in pajamas and robe, with a half-eaten sandwich and cold tea abandoned, she sat at her desk in the alcove, peering into the screen of her notebook computer and making notes.

At last she gave a satisfied, "Well! To use an old expression, Freckles, gettin' info on the Internet is the bomb."

The dog's head came up, dark eyes curious.

Carley Love said to her, "And I can sure spend money fast...so I'm glad you don't criticize."

Her cell phone rang. She checked the screen, smiled, and answered eagerly. "Hi, Trey."

His deep voice came over the line. "Hi. How are you doin' this evenin'."

"Good. Had a really good day."

"You did?"

"Yes. Today Lila told us she has bought a new building for the office—the Monroe building. You may already know about it."

"I think Dad is workin' with her. Didn't know what all it was about, though."

"Well, that's it. And I'll be workin' more for her. We're goin' to be doing an open-house like you did. December first. Mark your calendar—you're invited."

"Well now, thank you. I'll plan to be there."

"Good."

"Um, I was just callin' to make sure we were still on for Wednesday night."

"Yes, sir," she said, her voice turning soft. "I look forward to it."

"Me, too," he said in such a way that she smiled into the phone.

They made a few more comments and then said good-bye.

She sat there a moment pressing her lips together and staring at her toes wiggling in her fuzzy thong slippers.

With a determined expression sweeping her face, she again pulled out her phone and punched the button for Jackson.

The rings came across the line. Three...four...five times. She rolled her eyes upward and started to hang up.

"Hey, Carle'Love," came his drawling voice, startling her.

"Hello."

The line hummed for several seconds, and Carley Love said, "I just wanted to let you know there will be some charges comin' on the card. From online stores. Three of them."

"Okay."

"Well, we should both know and keep track." She read off the names of the vendors and the amounts.

"Got it," he said.

"It's more than for the wedding party. Lila's bought a new buildin' and is holdin' a Christmas open house party the first of December. She's hired me to plan it."

"Really? That's good."

"Yes. And there's a chance I'll take the office manager job in the spring. Lila's talkin' about it, anyway."

There was a beat before he said, "It all sounds good. I mean, it sounds like you want that."

"I do. At least I think I do. I guess I'll find out." She got to her feet and moved to the sink. "But right now, I really do want to plan the party for the office. I can use a lot of what I bought tonight at both the wedding party and the open house. And I'll be paying for it all in the comin' week, when Lila gives me the advance."

She paused, biting her bottom lip.

Jackson said, "I think that's great. You and Mama used to do that sort of thing all the time back home. People looked forward every year to the stores' Christmas breakfast parties, remember?"

"Yes, we did," she said slowly, staring at the night-black window. "Remember the year Mr. Moore was supposed to be Santa but got knocked out by an icicle falling on his head as he came out his back door, so your daddy had to play Santa? He was the only one of Mr. Moore's size to fit the costume."

She chuckled and heard his chuckle come over the line.

"He only did it because you begged him not to let the kids down."

"And he ended up havin' a grand time...was the best Santa ever."

"Yeah."

Silence stretched again.

Jackson said, "You spend what you want, Carle'Love. I've always known I could trust you with money...and I hope you've known you could trust me that way."

"I have, Jackson. I have." After a moment, she added, "I've always been grateful about that, too. You've been a good provider for us." Still gazing at the night-black window, she saw her image reflected there.

"I'm glad you think so," he said quietly.

Silence fell again, until Carley Love said, "Well, I just wanted to tell you about the charges. We have to be careful. I hear there's a lot of fraud with online shopping."

"I do keep watch," Jackson said.

"Oh...okay."

"Hey, Carle'Love...how about dinner at the Barbecue Barn Wednesday night?"

She opened her mouth and then closed it.

Jackson said, "Are you there?"

"Yes. I was just lettin' Freckles out the door." She quickly stepped to the back door and opened it, while saying, "I'm sorry, but I already have plans for Wednesday."

"Oh."

"How about Friday night?"

After a moment, he said, "I've got to work on Friday night. Could you do Thursday?"

"Yes...yes, I can."

"Great. Then I'll pick you up at six-thirty?"

"That'll be fine."

They said goodbye, and she closed her phone and sat blinking. All of a sudden she threw back her head and laughed. "How did I get here?"

A full minute later she said, "And where is here?"

∼

STILL MONDAY

9:15 p.m.

My dance card appears to be getting full. Jackson and I

172

have a date for Thursday.

I called him to tell him about charges coming through on the credit card from my Internet shopping.

Who am I kidding? I called him because I just had to tell him about Lila hiring me to plan a Christmas party for the new offices. I told Ronni and Trey, but who I really wanted to tell was Jackson.

A job, not asked to help or volunteering to help. Lila asked me and is paying me. When she asked how much I wanted to do the job, I had no idea what to say. I did think to send a prayer to God. That shows progress for me. Still, Lila said afterward that she would have paid more.

Never mind about that. I am excited about doing something for the first time in ever so long. Lila has bought the old Monroe building, with that fabulous hundred-year-old live oak stretching over it and giant sago palms at each corner. They've gone wild and Lila wants them trimmed, but I'm going to ask her to wait until spring. I like them overflowing like that.

Jackson reminded me of how I used to do parties all the time years ago. I haven't thought of it in so long. Me and Mother Iris did something in the spring and again at Christmas for each of the stores. Boy, we sometimes pulled all-nighters then. And I remember helping Granny Reba Love with her church ladies parties, and Mother Iris with her neighbor ladies.

How did I stop doing that? How did I quit belonging to women's clubs and gatherings?

Well, I had Royce, and we left the stores when Jackson got his electronic engineer degree, moved down here, and I took on all sorts of other endeavors. Somehow my life just changed.

Maybe that part of my life has circled around again. Now within weeks I have the wedding party and the office open house, and before both of those, there is Thanksgiving, which Royce says he and Simona will be home for, because he is not missing out on my Thanksgiving meal followed by napping in the recliner. He never even thought to ask me if I was going to do Thanksgiving this year. I suspect he put off the wedding party until after the holiday. Boy, Simona is surely seeing the true side of him.

Good grief. So much happening. It's like that quote: Nothing happens and nothing happens, and then all of a sudden, everything happens.

A wonderful thing about today's world is online shopping. Retail therapy available twenty-four hours. I found these wonderful little solar powered lanterns and string lights that will be adorable for the wedding reception and the office party. Great prices.

I also got a deal on a purse with a hidden gun pocket that locks. I'm going to use the hidden pocket to carry this journal. No one will know it is there, and I can keep it with me and locked up.

Although it won't be good if my purse gets stolen.

But I have never in my life had my purse stolen.

HER PHONE RANG, startling her out of sleep. The big blue numbers of her bedside clock read eleven-forty-two. Next, she saw the name on the phone.

"Ronni?" She came straight up in the bed.

"I'm sorry to wake you, but..." Her friend broke into sobs.

"Oh, Lord, what's happened? Did you have a wreck? What's wrong?" She threw her legs off the side of the bed, as if to be ready to race somewhere.

"Eric and I broke up. He...he...and I..." Again came sobs garbling her words.

"Honey, I can't understand you."

The sobs lessened, and there came shaky breathing. "We had a big fight and I broke up with him. He called Andrea a big...a big spoiled brat," she said, and the sobs came again.

"Oh, darlin' girl, I'm sorry." Carley Love pulled her legs back up onto the bed and covered them as her friend explained further through sobs.

"I can't go against my own daughter. I am her mother."

"Uh-huh," Carley Love said.

"He's like all the rest—he doesn't want a woman who has family. He doesn't want to understand."

"Uh-huh."

"Better to find out now."

"Uh-huh."

Carley Love sat with the phone pressed to her ear, her head tilted as if straining to hear, brows knotted together and alternately nodding and shaking her head, opening her mouth to interject a word and then closing it, until she finally said, "Are you okay now? You want me to come up?"

"No. I'm better now," her friend said in an exhausted tone. "I'll be okay."

Carley Love waited, and then, "Well, okay. But you call me again, if you want to talk. I don't mind. I love you, girlfriend."

She clicked off and stared into space for long seconds. Then she yawned and slipped down onto the pillows, whispering as her eyes fell closed, "God bless us all."

Love, After All

TREY PICKED her up at six on Wednesday. He drove them to Pensacola Beach. It was dark when they crossed the long bridge, and Carley Love remarked on the beauty of the lights stretching the coastline. Trey agreed with a smile that caught her attention. She gazed at his profile for long seconds. When he glanced her way, she faced forward, saying the lights looked like strings of stars.

When Trey directed the Lexus into the parking lot of a large water-side restaurant, Carley Love exclaimed, "I love Harpers! Jackson and I..." She faltered. "We came here on occasion."

Trey said smoothly, "I trust it meets with your approval then?"

"Oh, yes."

They smiled at each other.

He parked, got out, and rounded the car to open the door for her. Keeping hold of her hand, he started for the restaurant in long strides, then adjusted himself to her shorter ones.

A hostess greeted him by name and led them to a table at the window looking out onto the sound. A bottle of wine in ice sat waiting on a stand nearby.

He pulled out the chair for Carley Love.

She said, "I feel like a princess."

"Good."

Once settled, she gazed at the table with fascinated delight. "You didn't need to impress me, Trey. I'm already pretty impressed with you."

"I'm glad of that. But none of this was hard. A phone call. The owner and I are old friends."

"Do you know all the owners of restaurants hereabouts?"

"Just the better ones. And it seemed like a good time to celebrate."

She watched him reach for the bottle of wine, pull it from the ice and remove the cloth covering the mouth. He took up her glass, poured it half full, and set it in front of her.

"Thank you." She gazed at shimmering liquid in the glass. "And what are we celebrating?"

"Another day in paradise," he replied, filling his own glass. "And the success of the firm's open house...and that you agreed to come to dinner with me." He lifted his glass toward her.

She touched her glass lightly to his, took a sip, and smiled at him.

A waitress appeared with an appetizer tray containing various seafoods. She took their order and left.

Carley Love turned her attention to the view out the wide window and remarked on the beauty. This prompted Trey to speak of the efforts of his somewhat eccentric but talented client to establish the restaurant as it now had come to be. When the food was set before them, the conversation moved on to the deliciousness and feast for the eyes, too, and onward to telling of their respective restaurant experiences. They chatted easily, with long but comfortable silences between subjects.

When they had both finished eating, Trey asked, "Is the wine not to your likin'?"

Carley Love gestured at the table, saying, "Every bit of this is to my liking, Trey. The entire meal was fabulous."

And he said, "But?" His eyes, lit warmly by the candle on the table, looked at her with kindness.

"Oh...well, it's just that I don't much drink. I feel a little inexperienced and ignorant about that, especially after you've gone to such trouble and expense. It's just that...I don't care to drink."

He inclined his head, his gaze dropped to his own glass. "I understand. More than you know." Then he gave a rueful and boyish grin. "I guess I was tryin' to impress you.

"And you are not at all ignorant," he added. "You had everyone at the open-house enthralled. I got calls, actually."

"You got calls?" Her eyebrows rose.

"Yes, ma'am. Wantin' to know who you were, and if you were available. I said no." He gazed at her in such a manner as to cause her to grip her napkin.

"Would you like a cup of coffee?" He motioned for the waiter.

"Tea, actually. They bring it in a pot here."

The waiter appeared, and Trey requested a pot of tea. He looked at Carley Love, "Is there a preference?"

"Darjeeling, if you have it."

"Enough for two," Trey told the man. Relaxing in his

chair, he returned his attention to Carley Love. "You know, Carley, I find bein' with you relaxing. I don't feel as if I have to carry conversation, or put on about anything."

"That is a high compliment." A shy expression swept her face. "And I feel the same," she added, as if just then realizing.

The tea arrived, and they fell again to chatting. The restaurant, which had not been crowded, became virtually empty. At the same time, both noted a waiter standing to the side, yawning.

"We'd better let the staff finish up," Trey said, "And I'd best get you home."

As they were leaving, a man and woman called and waved to Trey from the bar area.

Trey took Carley Love by the hand, weaving between tables. He introduced her to his friends. The man gave a friendly greeting, the woman spoke politely, while she covertly surveyed Carley Love, and Trey's hand holding hers.

Carley Love stood with a fixed smile. In an absent manner, her thumb felt her ring finger. Instantly she relaxed her thumb. Another few minutes, and she looked down to her right hand held in Trey's, his hand alternately squeezing and relaxing, as he had done at the open house. Her gaze slid downward to the woman's knee that shifted forward, causing her tight skirt to edge upward, while the woman directed her comments and total attention to Trey.

As the conversation wore on, Carley Love's smile began to fade. At last she pulled her hand from Trey's, getting his attention, and excused herself to go to the ladies' room.

Trey was waiting when she came out. He apologized for not being able to get away from his friends earlier.

"Lucky for me, Lauren had some information that will help me with a case I'm handling, and since she was excited about being an attorney for NOW, it was only polite payback to listen to her about it."

"Now?" Carley Love said, with a puzzled expression.

"Nation Organization for Women."

"Oh, yes."

A smiling hostess opened the interior door for them to exit into the entryway. They both stopped abruptly, seeing pouring rain.

"You wait here. I'll get the car." Trey sprinted the short distance to the Lexus. Carley Love stepped out under the portico and watched the car approach. The door swung open and she slid inside.

Trey drove easily, and they listened to music and made sparse conversation. Carley Love yawned and sat back in the luxurious seat. He smiled at her and again took her hand.

A moment later there came a bump. The car veered slightly; Trey let go her hand and grabbed the wheel with both hands.

"What is it?" Carley Love came up in the seat.

"A flat tire."

"Oh, dear."

Trey guided the Lexus smoothly to the side of the road. Rain beat on the roof of the vehicle.

"Do you have an umbrella?" Carley Love asked.

He cast her a curious look. "No, but I don't think that would be much help with a flat tire."

"I just thought that I could hold it for you, and..."

Just then a feminine voice sounded. "How can I help you, Mr. Cummings?"

Carley Love jumped, startled.

Trey spoke the details of the situation and the female voice confirmed the location. Carley Love's gaze moved from Trey to the ceiling, where the voice appeared to come from.

The female voice said, "A repair service will be to your location in approximately twenty-five minutes, Mr. Cummings."

"Thanks," he answered.

"You're welcome, sir."

Carley Love saw the rain flowing over the windshield, saw lightning split the sky in the distance.

Trey said, "The rain might cause a delay with the road-side repair truck, but I don't think it should be long. Meanwhile, we can still have music." He raised the volume.

Carley Love shifted to lean her head back against the seat, saying, "I should see about gettin' that service for my Escalade. We had it at first, but I let it lapse. We never used it. I was usually with Jackson, or always could call him, or Royce."

To this Trey said, "Jackson would change the tire, wouldn't he?"

She shrugged. "Probably or like you did, call someone," she added quickly. After a moment, she said, "Jackson has instructed me, but I never have had to do it. We could do a Google search as to how to do it."

Trey laughed to the point of throwing his head back. "I don't think we need do that."

It was thirty minutes and several updates from the disembodied voice before the road service technician arrived. By then the rain had slowed to a drizzle. Trey got out to join the young man. Carley Love relaxed against the headrest and closed her eyes. When Trey returned to the car, she jerked herself out of half-sleep.

"All set, and only mildly wet," he told her.

When they arrived at Carley Love's driveway, the headlights played across the ditches, showing water rising. Trey stopped the car and lowered the stereo volume. Light rain could be heard pattering on the car roof.

"I've had a lovely time," Carley Love said warmly.

"Me, too."

Their gazes lowered to each other's lips.

Carley Love shifted her eyes forward out the windshield. She noted the water standing on the walkway in the headlights.

"I'd best take my shoes off. Bare feet don't mind water."

"Sit tight, and I'll come around and get you."

"Oh, no need..."

He was already exiting the car. He slammed the door, rounded the hood, opened the passenger door, and with smooth motion scooped Carley Love into his arms, carrying her like a knight in shining armor, his shoes splashing water as he went.

He set her onto the porch and she got her balance.

"Thank you, Sir Galahad," she said with feeling, then, looking at his shoes, "I hope they aren't ruined."

"What?"

"Your shoes."

He shook his head. The next instant, he put his hand to her chin and tilted it upward, saying, "I'm grateful you came to dinner with me."

"I am, too, Trey. I really am."

In the low glow of the porch light, they gazed into each other's eyes, intent, measuring. Then his lips came down on hers. Her eyes closed as she wrapped her arms around his neck. He held her against him, and their kiss turned hard and searching.

They parted in slow motion. Carley Love stared at Trey's chin. He cleared his throat and his breath teased her temple. Her arms fell from around his neck. His arms loosened, but continued to encircle her.

After a moment, Carley Love eased back a step. His arms fell from around her.

He gave a crooked smile

She said, "I...I thank you, Trey. Now we won't ever have to wonder."

"No, we won't," he replied in a frank and serious tone.

They exchanged a smile of humor that turned to shared understanding.

He raked a hand through his hair. "I do love you, you know. I hope we can..."

She put a hand on his arm. "We have a special friendship. I love you, too."

He nodded.

She fished a key from her purse. He waited for her to unlock the door and step inside. Then he softly said goodnight, gently kissed her forehead, and headed away. She stood in the doorway watching him hurry in his long-legged stride back to his car, each step sending up splashes of water in the faint light from the porch.

~

THURSDAY, November 9
12:45 a.m.
The date with Trey was fabulous, and we finally kissed.

And it was pretty much nothing. For either of us. We are friends. Not lovers.

Dear God, I am grateful as all get-out that the whole foolishness of my fantasy crush is over. It was exhausting.

Tonight showed me myself. I love getting dressed up fancy, but after an hour, I start to itch where it is not polite to scratch. I cannot tell the difference between costly wine and the cheap stuff Ronni brought me. In truth, the most exotic I want to drink is a good cup of Darjeeling tea.

So here I am in my ancient chenille robe and fuzzy slippers, every bit the grandmother that I likely will soon be, and having just looked up what the National Organization for Women is. In my defense, I have heard of it, just couldn't remember what it was when Trey mentioned it tonight. My first thought when Trey told me what NOW stood for was, Women for what? The name would have been better to have said *of* women. Or maybe National Organization for the Advancement of Women, like the NAACP. Or maybe National Organization for Women's Education—or National Organization for Women's Better Attire. Lord knows that would be helpful, given what I witnessed tonight—namely a woman, who is definitely old enough to know better, no matter how svelte she is, wearing a skin-tight skirt that appears nothing less than wearing Spanx as a dress item.

Well, I am laughing at myself. It all could have been a big mess with my foolishness over Trey.

But then, only by trying things, even foolish things, do we learn. Which is a lesson to me on my judgement of the woman's attire.

Maybe it is foolishness that opens our hearts and teaches us the most. All of which is to say tonight was a watershed moment for me—quite apt with the deluge of rain.

The truth of it that I know surely in this moment is that I am still in love with Jackson Paul Wells, after all.

~

SHE STARED at what she had written.

Slowly, she lifted her head and turned, gazing for long minutes at the French doors.

As if coming to herself, she drew a deep breath, exhaled, and set the pen aside. She removed her heavy robe and crawled into bed, fluffed the pillows against the headboard and retrieved her reading glasses and Granny Reba Love's Bible, propping it on her knees. Reading lasted less than ten minutes, for slowly her legs straightened and her hands let go of the Bible as she fell over asleep.

Had anyone been watching with eyes that could see, they would have observed four ghostly women in flowing gowns of various pale hues hovering over Carley Love.

"I wish she didn't have to make every little thing so dramatic," said the closest woman.

"Look whose talkin'. You were just like that," said the one hovering further upward. "We got through and she will, too."

"I wish she would find my Bible under my bed." The first woman frowned and pushed back her short hair. "It is more right for her to use her mother's Bible."

"I was as much her mother as her grandmother. She's got mine, and I actually used it."

"Oh, Mama, I used mine."

"Hmm."

"Carley Love's goin' t' be all right," said the third woman, more distant. Her voice was cultured, her white hair sweeping back from her face like a halo. "She has starch, and my son does, too. There's always rough patches in a marriage, and a couple just has to stick it out."

Two women looked at the third and frowned.

The fourth woman called from the far distance, "Leave my great-granddaughter to her own life. The Father does not need your help."

The three women floated upward, but the one closest to Carley Love bent low over her and whispered, "Darlin' girl, my Bible fell under the bed. I love you...love you...love."

And then the women were gone.

Getting Comfortable With Not Knowing

CARLEY LOVE WAS UP EARLY and working at her computer while having her first cup of coffee. Finally, with a sigh, she rose to pour a second cup. She gazed out the window and saw sunlight making patterns on the nearest pecan tree trunk. Glancing at the clock, she retrieved her cell phone and called Jackson.

His voice mail answered. She left a message.

Five minutes later a text came: *In a meeting. Will call when I get out.*

She considered the text, then set her phone aside and went to dress. She chose an easy draping sweater, slim denim jeans, and tall leather boots. Out the door, the scent of the sweet olive tree came to her. She paused, sniffed the blossoms, and picked a small sprig that she carried to the Escalade and tucked into the air vent.

At the office, she made fresh coffee, began packing items to be moved to the new offices, and handled the reception desk, which was, as she said to Ronni on the phone, "Dead as a doornail."

"What does that mean?" Ronni asked.

Carley Love replied, "I guess just dead as it'll ever be. I'll see you for lunch."

The next minute, Doreen came from the break room, reading from her phone, "It is an expression dating back to Shakespeare's time. And Charles Dickens used it in *A Christmas Carol*. It may come from doors nailed back then. That seems unclear. I looked it up on the internet on my new phone!"

Carley Love said, "O-kay. Thanks," with a faintly stunned expression.

Nearing noon, Lila called and instructed Carley Love to leave the reception desk to Doreen and come to the new building to help with measuring rooms and to decide on furniture.

Carley Love arrived at the new office, parked, and went rapidly up the few steps. The door was wide open, Lila stretching a measuring tape its width. As the two women worked on measuring and sketching and discussing various décor, Lila asked about plans for the Christmas open-house. "Do you have the written plan ready?"

"Almost. I'm still working on a few more items. Mr. Clarence sent the catering proposal this mornin'. I've just glanced at it, and the charge looks reasonable, but I need to go over it to make sure the menu is right."

Lila headed down the hallway to the entrance, but stopped so quickly that Carley Love almost bumped into her.

"Oh, good heavens, look at this." The older woman gestured into the restroom. "The counter top has not been replaced. And it looks like a ten year old painted the walls."

"I'll call them," Carley Love made a note on the pad she

was using for the measurements.

"We shouldn't have to call them," Lila rubbed her forehead. "I'll call. I have a few things to say to him."

Carley Love watched Lila stalk ahead down the hall to the reception room and to the lone desk sitting in the entry. She watched the woman dig into her purse, pull out a small bottle of antacid tablets, shake out two, and pop them into her mouth.

"Well, we've done all we can do here," Lila said. "Forward that catering info later."

"I can handle the caterer," Carley Love said. "If I find he's changed anything you asked for, I can let you know."

"I want to see it," Lila responded in a clipped voice. "You can be done for the day. I'll see you in the morning."

With Lila in the lead, the two women parted beneath the massive old live oak and went to their respective vehicles.

Carley Love emitted a large sigh as she flung herself behind the wheel of the Escalade. In the rearview mirror, she saw Lila's black Cadillac back swiftly and head at a rapid rate of speed out onto the road. Carley Love's gaze followed the vehicle until it disappeared into traffic.

She noted sprinkles on her windshield and took note of dark clouds building in the distance. Just as she turned the key, her phone rang. Seeing Jackson's name, she answered quickly.

"Carle'Love, this is the first..." The line crackled with static.

"Jackson...you're breakin' up."

She checked the cell phone screen. The call had dropped.

She punched the button. The line rang and rang. She

ended the call and sat there. The phone rang again.

"Jackson?"

"Yeah. I could hear you but I guess you couldn't hear me."

"Well, I can now. I just wanted to suggest that you come to the house for supper tonight, rather than goin' out. I'll make us somethin'."

There was silence. She looked at her phone screen, then put the phone back to her ear, saying, "Jackson, I can't hear you. Are you still there."

Still no answer. She looked at the screen and saw the connection had ended.

Rubbing her forehead, she gazed out the windshield at the heavy dark clouds, then put the Escalade into gear, halting when a text alert came from her phone.

I'll call again this afternoon.

She texted in return: *Do you want to come to the house for supper tonight instead of B.Barn?*

She waited. When no text came immediately, she headed the Escalade out onto the street.

Ten minutes later, she parked and hurried across the parking lot to the restaurant with an umbrella against a light drizzle.

Inside, Ronni motioned from a booth. She had her cell phone at her ear.

"I'm sorry to be late," Carley Love said, as she slipped into the opposite seat. Seeing Ronni on her phone, she stopped.

Ronni said, "I love you, too, honey." Her lips formed a big smile. "Talk to you later...yes, I will," and she smooched into the phone before ending the call.

Carley Love said with a raised eyebrow, "Eric?"

Ronni gave a tentative smile. "Yes."

"Ah. So you two are back together then?"

"Uh-huh." Ronni nodded in a happy fashion and her voice lowered. "But we're keepin' it a secret for a while. There's no need to get everyone riled up. We've got to go slower, give people time to get used to the idea."

"How will they get used to it, if they don't know?"

"What I mean is I want time for Eric and me to get to know each other before we involve my family. I want to make certain where this is headed. When we become serious, then I can start bringin' him around, slow like."

"Uh-huh. Well, tellin' someone you love them sounds serious."

Ronni smiled sheepishly. "Yes, it really is."

The waitress appeared with two icy glasses of cold tea. She took their order, and when she left, Ronni continued.

"Eric just isn't used to big families—certainly not a big passel of passionate Cajuns like mine. He only has a brother, and they are not close. He's never been married. I thought if we just didn't involve my family right now, maybe I could find a way to slowly let them in, and he would get used to me havin' the family I have, and they could all get used to each other."

"Uh-huh." Carley Love squeezed a slice of lemon into her cold tea.

"Besides, I'm so nervous about it all. I keep waitin' for Eric to disappear," Ronnie said. "And really, is my seein' him any of their business at this point? Oh, I know it will be Andrea's business if Eric and I get more serious, and yes, even my aunts and all of them, but right now, it doesn't seem so. What do you think?"

Carley Love's eyes, which had been focused on stirring

the straw in her drink, came up with surprise.

"Well..." She looked into Ronni's questioning face. "We never have to tell everything we know."

Ronni broke into a bright smile. "That's what I think, too." She went on happily chatting about Eric and upcoming plans for a date with him, detailing what she was going to wear and small things she found adorable about him, pausing only when the waitress brought their meals.

Carley Love watched her friend's face closely and smiled softly.

"So, let's hear about the date with Trey," Ronni said all of a sudden.

"It was very nice."

"Nice? That's how you describe it? I need a little more here, girl."

"Trey and I discovered that we are simply friends—*good* friends, but no spark. Or not one big enough for a fire." Carley Love stuck a fork of salad into her mouth.

"Really?"

Carley Love swallowed. "Really. He's a very good *friend*."

"I guess that's somethin'. So now what goes on with Jackson?"

"We are havin' dinner tonight."

Ronni's eyebrows went up.

Carley Love continued, "We're supposed to go out to the Barbecue Barn, but I've suggested we eat at home. I think more privacy is prudent. That way we can both say stuff without worryin' about people watchin' and listenin'."

She paused and took a deep breath, then said, "I'm ready to talk with him now. I think what the date with Trey showed me is that I am still...attached to Jackson."

"Or is it simply that change is frightening?" Ronni

suggested, pushing her plate away from her.

"Perhaps. Or habit...or simply longing for what was. Or just being so darn tired. Whatever it is, I have to find out what it is, and I'm ready to talk with him," she said, her tone certain, her eyes steady. "I owe him that...I owe us both the chance to speak the truth and listen to each other."

Ronni reached across the table and laid her hand atop Carley Love's, giving it a squeeze.

Ten minutes later the two women stepped outside the restaurant to find rain had stopped, but water puddled across the parking lot and grey clouds hung heavy above.

Ronni said, "Smells like the Gulf. They're sayin' a tropical storm."

"I haven't kept track. Seems late in the year."

"My uncle Leon's hobby is weather. He says there's been a number of big storms in November. The last one dumped a lot of rain. He thinks this one may do the same."

Ronni turned to hug Carley Love. Calling, "Be careful" to each other, they each picked their way around puddles on tiptoe to their vehicles.

Just as Carley Love slammed the door closed, her phone rang. It was Jackson.

He said quickly on her hello, "Dinner at home sounds great. No need for you to get out. I'll stop and bring barbecue home. That way you don't have to cook."

Her smile came quickly, "I'm not cookin'. Just heating up. Your country-boy son wants Gigi's barbecue for his wedding, so I went there and got two sample dinners."

"Okay, that sounds good. And you might want to get some staples in the house. I've been watchin' the radar. This storm could bring a lot of rain. I'll check the generator when I come tonight, make sure it's ready in case the power goes out."

"I have plenty of everything."

"Look, I'm sorry but I have to run again. We've had a system go down at the airport. See you tonight."

"I understand," she said quickly. "See you." She opened her mouth to say more, but he was gone.

AT HOME, she let Freckles out to roam the yard while she brought in three armloads of firewood from the covered bin. The wind came in gusts and snatched at her hair. She gathered chair cushions from the porches and stacked them in the dining room. After playing with a knotted pull rope with Freckles, they returned to the kitchen. She put the kettle on the stovetop and flipped on the small television on the counter. She watched the smartly made-up weather woman report on the storm in the Gulf and show graphs of past storms and their tracks.

She switched off the set and carried her tea, with the dog at her heels, through the house to her bedroom.

On passing the opened door to her mother's room, she stopped, then turned into it, switched on the overhead light and stood a moment looking around. She set her cup on the dresser and crouched to look at the low bookshelves beneath the window. She selected two antiquated books— one on table and buffet settings and another on creating centerpieces. She gave each a brief glance, and then her gaze slid sideways, toward the bed.

The next minute she was on her knees reaching beneath the bed. She pulled out a book—a black Bible.

"Mama," she whispered, as she opened the book and scanned the names recorded on the genealogy page, written in her mother's hand.

She dived back underneath the bed and came out with dusty slippers and a wad of tissues that had been pushed up against the wall. "Well, Nan, we need to clean here."

She dropped the tissues in the waste bin and slippers in the closet and retreated to her own bedroom. First exchanging her heeled boots for socks and slippers, she moved to her desk with the books and tea.

After a moment of looking at the books, she set them aside and pulled her journal from the desk and took up a pen.

~

THURSDAY, November 9

3:45 p.m.

The oddest thing. I suddenly remembered these old books about entertaining that I had from years ago with Mother Iris. I'd put them on Mama's bookshelves because I had run out of room on mine. While I was getting them, I happened to look at the floor by Mama's bed and then without even thinking about it, I got down and looked under it. I found Mama's Bible shoved under there! I'm so happy to find it. And golly, it sure needs dusting under there. Found a wad of her used tissues. She used to stuff them everywhere. They plain brought tears to my eyes.

Had lunch with Ronni today. Boy, how fast things can change. She is back with Eric. Those two have a good old-fashioned torrid romance going. They have decided to date secretly for awhile and not involve Ronni's family.

When she talked of him, I could see it all: Eric has found the woman for him, and he wants her all to himself. He is going to have a tough row to hoe coming to understand that when he gets Ronni, he gets her abundant and raucous family and friends.

Seeing Ronni's face bright with happiness did my heart good. I kind of think hiding this relationship from her family is not going to work, because Ronni is so dang happy again. They are bound to guess. Although, most people are generally taken up with themselves and not given to noticing what goes on with others.

Maybe that is part of what happened to me with Jackson. I was so taken up with the stress and strain of taking care of Mama and trying to carve out some sort of life of my own that I didn't notice what was going on with him. He was focused on his career and earning a living.

It is a hard truth to see. How could I *not* pay attention to Jackson?

Maybe that is just one of those life lessons. I don't think it has anything to do with how much one loves another. It has to do with life pulling and tugging people off course. Distracting, like when one is driving along and looks away to something on the side, and wham! A wreck happens when you weren't looking.

I only just now realize how I have been running from my life, trying to distract myself.

Yes, I have been running from every daunting decision, all the confusion of feelings that I couldn't deal with. I have been running from connecting with Jackson for fear of what I would have to face. Running from all the overwhelming things that I don't know but feel I should know.

Life—and we humans—sure are some big mystery.

Maybe the best we can do is work on getting comfortable with not knowing, and meeting whatever comes knowing that God has equipped us to deal with anything, and with grace.

Although, having grace and using it are two vastly different things, I suppose.

Lord, let me get better at using grace.

～

CARLEY LOVE WAS MAKING cold sweet tea when her mobile phone rang. As she reached for the phone, she glanced at the red enamel kitchen clock; it read five-fifty. Her phone screen said *Jackson*.

"Hey, I hope you aren't gonna get mad," he said, "but I have to cancel on dinner. We've got an emergency with equipment at the airport."

Her mouth made a line, and then she breathed deeply and replied, "I understand." She paused and added, "I'm not mad. These things happen."

"We've got to have this equipment for the storm planes."

"I know, Jackson. I do. We'll try for this weekend, when hopefully this storm gets out of here."

"I'll try to get someone to sub for me tomorrow."

"Okay. Call me when you can, to let me know you're all right."

There was a pause and then, "I love you, Care'lina."

The line turned to static. "Jackson?" But the connection had broken.

Untold Stories

"Don't come in today," Lila said. "I'm not planning to open the office the entire weekend. This storm's unpredictable. I heard it's stalled out there."

"Yes, Jackson called earlier and said the radar indicated it's milling around about twenty miles out. Gatherin' more rain to dump on us. How are things where you are?" As Carley spoke, she moved to the window to look out at the growing pool of water that was the backyard.

"Just fine," Lila replied in a clipped tone. "I have never lost electricity here. I'm doing some work on the computer...if I can just get rid of this headache."

"Do you have everything you need? I'd be glad to go to the store in the Escalade for you."

"I'm fine. I'll see you Monday morning, unless I call you and say otherwise. Goodbye."

Carley Love pocketed her phone, fed Freckles, and poured a second cup of coffee. Carrying the steaming cup back through the house, she paused at her mother's bedroom door and gazed into it for some seconds. Stepping into the room, she flipped on the light. Setting her coffee cup aside, she went to the closet and opened wide the double doors. She stared into the depths and raked her hand through her hair. Then, still in her bathrobe, she began pulling clothes from the hangers and shelves, making piles on the bed and the floor. Certain items she held to her nose and inhaled. She cried into a crimson robe. She pulled shoes from the racks and threw them out of the closet into piles. After the shoes, she went deeper into the closet, hauling out plastic tubs, an ironing board, sewing machine, stack of pillows. Finally out she came tugging an old trunk.

After pausing to stretch her back and catch her breath, she opened the trunk. Wrinkling her nose, she waved a hand, as if to clear the air of the smell of mothballs.

A gentle expression came over her face as she reverently lifted out a pink crocheted baby jacket. Next came a matching baby blanket that she caressed with her fingertips and eyes. Carefully laying the items aside, she knelt on the floor in front of the trunk and continued to delve, pulling out each item to examine in the manner of someone who is enthralled with finding treasure—a bundle of Valentines tied with faded ribbon, a Benny Goodman LP, a worn, colorful wool granny square afghan that she hugged to her.

Tears came with photographs of her mother and father in childhood and her brother Sully's newborn book. A beautiful blue vintage nightgown with robe got her to her feet. She held it up to her to model in the mirror.

Back on her knees, she continued to delve down and down through unrecognized clothing and memorabilia, until she discovered a scrapbook at the bottom. She sat cross-legged to examine it. The cover crackled when opened. Neatly posted clippings and letters filled the pages.

She ran her hands over the papers and read, with her dark-rimmed reading glasses perched on her nose, while sporadic storms and the morning hours came and went.

By the end of the scrapbook, she was sobbing so hard she bent her knees and rested her head on them.

Freckles' cold nose nudged her arm and then found her neck. The animal had braved coming into the room. Laughing and drying her eyes with her sleeve, Carley Love hugged the dog.

"You sweet thing."

Her gaze came up to see sunlight glimmering on the raindrops splattering the window pane. "Oh, come on, Freckles! Let's get you and me outside before rain starts again."

She went to her room and dressed in sweats and a rain-coat, and pulled on rain boots. She and the dog exited the room through the French doors, crossed the porch and splashed down into the yard. With the dog running and jumping beside her, she sloshed through grassy puddles and out into the openness of the small meadow. Picking up a stick, she threw it for the dog, who went bounding over the ground, splashing water, to retrieve it and run with it clamped in her mouth.

Carley Love stood in the meadow with legs splayed, laughed at the dog. She put her smiling face into the buffeting wind and tingle of misty air, inhaled deeply and smiled.

"Oh, my, Mama. I smell the salty ocean, just like you always said."

～

FRIDAY, November 10

2:15 p.m.

With the storm, I am rather stuck here, so I have commenced going through Mama's things. I have this odd feeling that I must clean out these things in order to move forward in my life. It is remembering, and in the remembering, a letting go.

Although we Love women are apparently not good at letting go. Mama still had the old family trunk. Soon as I lifted the lid, the scent of moth balls came wafting up, the scent still there from generations past.

I found letters from Daddy to Mama. Oh, how young they were! The letters reminded me of how much older my parents were than all the other girls' parents when I was in school. I remembered Mama got her hair dyed because she didn't want to be called my grandmother.

Daddy was barely out of his teens when he wrote the letters from away on Roosevelt's CCC program. Of all things, on a crew that was building a factory to make starch out of sweet potatoes. This sort of thing would have been right up my daddy's alley. Indeed, in one of the letters, he mentioned constructing a still and brewing moonshine out of sweet potatoes. He was clearly proud of himself. The letters were postmarked Columbia, South Carolina, but the way he talked, it was a rural area, where they were required to live in tent barracks, and it was a bitter winter. He was trying to earn money to go to Aggie college.

Daddy had surprisingly good handwriting. He wrote "Dearest June Marie Love," an amazement. The man who wrote these letters is a pure stranger to me. The letters are those of a young man with feelings of love and missing his girlfriend and hometown. A young man with tender hopes and dreams of an education and a family and a career. He spoke, too, of Mama's letters to him, thanking her for writing two in one day, and for sending him a sweater to keep warm, and a box of sweet breads. He asked about her mother and grandmother and friends, and cautioned her to remember that he loved her.

I heard their voices, my mother and father, in these letters in a way I never remember hearing them. They were gentle and funny and tender, oh, so tender.

And Mama had kept these letters all these years. Had she taken them out and read them over the years when Daddy let her down by his drunkenness and ridicule and bitter anger? Over the times she wondered how they would pay bills and the days her husband spent obsessed with soy beans and the nights he went missing? I think of my parents, two young eager people once so terribly in love, and how they changed.

Other people parade through my mind—Granny Reba Love, and Mother and Daddy Wells, and Ronni, and then me and Jackson. What does life do to us? How do we lose our loves and dreams, and ourselves?

Those are questions that are too big for me. Only God knows any of us as we really are. Which is a comforting thought. "Him that cometh to me I will in no wise cast out." Just as I am, I come.

3:40 p.m.

A few minutes ago lightning struck nearby, maybe one of the pecan trees. The sound caused me to let out a scream and sent Freckles under my feet, poor baby. It's grown quite dark outside now and has been raining heavily for an hour. Water is edging up the yard toward the patio. It is a river across the backyard. I have never seen it do that, not in all the years we have lived here. Our house is two feet up on a solid foundation, though, and we should be safe. Royce called to say roads are flooding that have not in the past. I have started a fire in the fireplace and have a flashlight ready, just in case.

I went all the way to the bottom of the trunk and found another box of old photographs, really old, Mama as a toddler—the cutest one of her in a line of little dancing girls, big bows in their hair. Mama on a tree swing, Mama so small with both of her parents. Then her as a teen at the beach, so pretty.

And then, last thing, a scrapbook Mama had started way back in her elementary years. It began with clippings from graduating elementary school, report cards, birthday cards, and on to the junior and senior classes. They put all those students' pictures in the newspaper back then. Lots of handwriting beside each blurry student photo. Small clippings of social events—they had write-ups that reported who was visiting who, who went where, parties held at so-and-so's. A small clipping about Daddy down in South Carolina for the CCC, and according to this piece, he also worked over in Florida, excavating a cavern. I've been to that cavern! The newspaper announcement of Sully's birth, and one of Mama being elected the Methodist Ladies' Circle president. I never knew that. Then a big newspaper front page: "War Declared!" And a ticket stub from the movie "Bambi" and two ticket stubs from the movie "Casablanca," both from the Carolina Theatre. There was a half of a 78 rpm record stuck on a page—Bing Crosby's

"White Christmas." Then there were whole sections of newspapers tucked in the scrapbook, from VE Day and VJ Day, and President Roosevelt coming to town, and then the news of the new Israel as an independent state. After these the pages sort of dwindled. There were small things—letters, and I read each one, from Mama's friends of the time, and pieces about parties and Granny Reba taking over the Ladies' Circle.

I found my own birth announcement, and one of Sully going away to the Navy, then the newspaper clipping of mine and Jackson's marriage. Then I found a little article of the baby shower for Royce Jackson Wells by the Sweet Springs Baptist Church Ladies, which was Mama Wells' group. Oh, what precious memories that brought!

Then, abruptly, the final page held a newspaper clipping, a small one-column article glued right in the middle of its own black paper page so it stood out as if to shout.

"Halford Jones Dead from Fall."

I had to get up and walk around a bit before I could settle to read it, and then I had to sort of squint at it. And what I think now is how we all should have talked about it more back then.

Since I plan to save this scrapbook for Royce, I think I may tell him what really happened.

SHE WAS ADDING a log to the fire when her cell phone rang. It was Jackson.

"Hi."

"Hey. You doin' okay? Electricity still on?"

"Yes. A few blinks is all."

"Well, if it goes out, hopefully the generator will kick in. I wish I'd been able to check it."

"We'll be okay. I've got flashlights and candles and the fireplace. You had a lot of wood in the bin. Me and Freckles are enjoyin' a cozy fire." Lowering herself cross-legged in front of the fireplace, she stroked the dog, who lay sprawled in the warmth.

She said, "Water has come up to the edge of the patio steps, but it hasn't come further in the last few hours."

"Well, some areas have received ten inches of rain, and the storm's not done yet."

She shifted position and said, "I finally began goin' through Mama's things."

"Oh, yeah?"

She looked at her socked feet and wiggled her toes. "I'm findin' things I haven't ever seen...or at least not in a long time. I found a newspaper clipping on Halford Jones. Mama kept that."

There was a space of silence before he responded. "Huh. Well, that was a long time ago."

"I know. I just thought of it and want you to know I have always thought you did right, and I appreciate you handlin' it. And you did so much for Mama. I guess that got tiresome. I can understand how it would."

"Carle'Love, that's not why I left, if that's what you're thinkin'. I didn't get tired of doin' for your mama, and it had nothin' to do with getting' tired of you or our marriage. Well, at least not lasting tired.

"What happened was that I got tired of dealin' with myself." His words were forceful. "Anyway, I can't get into it now. I've got to get back to work."

"Just know I appreciate you, Jackson. All you've done for us. That's what I'm sayin'."

Another pause. "Well, I'm glad you feel that way," came his hoarse reply.

The line crackled. Carley Love said, "You are breakin' up."

Jackson said he would call again soon, and the connection broke. She slowly set aside the phone.

Reaching again for the scrapbook, she opened it across her lap. Turning to the page with the newspaper clipping, she re-read it, then sat staring into the flickering flames in the fireplace. Her eyes darkened, becoming glazed with memories as her mind sped back in time, and her inner voice said, "So long ago...and another thing I wish I would have talked to Mama about, which, of course, she likely would have waved away."

5:00 P.M. and dark as night outside, with heavy rain, but wind not so bad.

I am going to write it all out, and see what I see. Mama never spoke of it, and her face wouldn't let me talk to her about it. I tried with Jackson. It would just come out of me, how I couldn't believe it, and did he think we did the right thing.

One time Jackson said to me, "Right or not, it's over and done. We can't go back and change it, and I don't think Jones gave us any choice anyway. Let's not talk of it anymore."

I knew he was right. I would let it go, until I'd start thinking of what happened, and I'd have to talk about it some more. Jackson always responded with the same words and would hug me tight, which was what I needed.

The article says that Jones, 52 years old—oh, my, same as I am now, and I had always thought of him as an old man! —was found at the bottom of the back stairs of his hardware store by Jackson Wells. It reports that apparently Jones had hit his head on the concrete step. The county coroner ruled it accidental death, stating that it appeared Jones had fallen while heavily intoxicated.

Well, that last part was true. Jones had been drunk as a skunk and taken a bad fall.

The rest of the article, though, about where it took place and his grieving family illustrates how easy it is for people to make up things out of whole cloth. I wonder how many people knew the truth. Quite a few, I imagine. In small towns, people know.

Once Halford Jones' daughter—can't recall her name, if I ever knew it—stopped me on the sidewalk and told me in so many words: I've always thanked you, Miss Carley, and your mama and Jackson for saving us. She walked right on before I could get out a word of reply. She was a strange bird, skinny as a rail, in her twenties at that time, with an ethereal sort of white wall face and dressed like an old woman.

That day I felt relief, and guilt, not from what had happened, but from being one who had suspected all along that Halford Jones did unspeakable things to his family and being like the rest of the town and turning away from doing anything about it.

We were living in Sweet Springs, east of Raleigh, because Jackson had taken over management of the store there when he came home from the Navy. His daddy had it all planned out. Papa Wells had even put the down payment on our little brick ranch. I was so proud to have our first place. Our hard time then was I wanted a baby, and Jackson focused his attention on getting by at the stores and going to college on the Navy's dime because he wanted out of there. While we were in the midst of our first home and all our precious plans, my daddy died. Not too long afterward, we moved Mama to Sweet's Springs to be near us. I didn't think of it at the time, but she pretty much abandoned Granny Reba Love, although I guess everyone figured Granny Reba had always taken care of herself.

Mama was pretty puny at the first, laying around all day. I finally got in a snit one day and told her that she had to get up and make her own life. And Mama did take hold, started to eat right and fix herself up. She was nearing sixty but still a lovely woman. She made friends and started driving around those who didn't drive, and even took to doing crafts and swing dancing at the community center.

Then came that evening I stopped in at her house and found Halford Jones attacking her.

The Jones hardware store was around the block and directly behind Mama's backyard, with an alley separating them. It was one of those two-story brick buildings that had been there since the 1800s. Mama said later that Jones had been eyeing her and making comments for some time, and she had kept her distance.

Halford Jones was a mean drunk. He had been arrested more than once for battery of his wife. But she never pressed charges. She was just too scared and beat down. Everyone knew the woman and her children suffered. The comment was often that he would kill her someday and that something should be done, but no one did anything.

According to Mama, her apartment had blown a fuse—how funny to think of it, me and Mama lived passed fuses. Anyway, Mama had gone over to the hardware store to get one. It was so hot, she just had to have her fan. She said walking through the back gate and getting the fuse just before closing time was better than driving out to the Ace Hardware store on the highway. She said Jones made some of his rude remarks when he sold it to her, but she ignored him and got herself home. Later she was all comfortable in a seersucker robe and making a pitcher of sweet tea, getting ready to watch *The Carol Burnett Show*, when she heard the back screen door squeak behind her. She turned and there was Jones. She thought she could scare him off, and when she couldn't, she tried to get to the phone on the kitchen wall, but he reached it first and tore off the receiver.

I had just reached the front steps, when I heard Mama scream. I went flying in, hollering like a banshee, "Mama? Mama?" and there Jones had her down in the dining room, was on top of her and with his pants pulled down. Mama was gasping for air. He was choking her with his arm and weight. What screamed through my mind was, *"He is killing my mama!"* I vaguely remember trying to kick him, but all I had on were flip-flops.

Like a bear, he came up off of Mama and went for me. I raced for the kitchen. I remember that I got hold of the heavy glass tea pitcher that had belonged to Granny Myrtle Love, which I have it to this day in my own cabinet. I swung it at him, and it bounced off his shoulder. He grabbed me and pressed himself on me. His breath—I can't write of it.

The next instant, the man went down, pulling me with him. I think I hit the cabinet with my ear. It was like I had lost my hearing, because sound seemed to have ceased. Jones' dead weight pinned my legs.

Dead weight it was, because Mama had hit him on the back of the head with her small cast-iron skillet. Her egg-frying pan. Lord help you if you happened to grab that pan to grill a cheese sandwich. Mama would go on like you had committed a mortal sin.

There she stood with her egg-pan and calling my name. I can, after all these years, still hear her panicked voice calling my name as if from a distance.

The coroner said it wasn't Mama's pan but Jones hitting his temple on the corner of the counter when he went down the last time.

Sometimes I think the coroner made that up to spare us. I asked Jackson once, and he said what had become his refrain, "It's done. Doesn't matter."

I didn't call the sheriff that night. I called Jackson from the phone in Mama's bedroom. I watched him from the door get out of his car, but he did not race. He walked without hurrying up the walkway and mounted the duplex steps. After he looked at the scene and I told him what happened in one sentence, he went straight to call Sheriff Sykes. He started to call the ambulance but replaced the receiver and asked us if we needed to go to the hospital. I did not, but I wanted Mama to go. She had all but fainted onto the sofa. She refused, though. She grasped more what Jackson was doing before I did.

I never did know how far Jones got with her, and I didn't ask. She was a mess and shaking so hard, she couldn't light a cigarette. I wrapped her in the wool granny square blanket from the back of the sofa, despite it being eighty degrees at night. Dear heaven—it is the same old afghan I've just found in the trunk.

Sheriff Sykes came up quietly, too. He and Jackson talked it over in the kitchen. Jackson had known him all his life. I eventually went to stand in the doorway and listen. I would not go in there because of Jones' body laying there. The upshot was that they decided to keep it all quiet. Sheriff Sykes did not know if Jones had life insurance, but said that if he did, his family should get it without question. The sheriff called one of his deputies and the coroner himself and they all handled everything quietly, sparing all of us who lived on.

Just as the sheriff had thought, the Jones family did get a small bit of money, and people rallied around to hold a funeral and pay respects, which may not have happened if the truth of Jones' attack had come out. Maybe everyone was just so glad he was gone and not being an unpleasant concern anymore.

Me and Mama got to go on without some horrible trial and lurid talk, and the widowed Miz Jones got to stand up straight and seemed to bloom. It was rumored that she found money Jones had stashed here and there, that he had been involved with moonshine. Anyway, in the following year, she sold the hardware store building, paid off debts, and moved herself and her children to a lovely big house and acreage where they grew a truck garden and raised chickens. The Jones boy grew up and married and had a passel of children. They all became pillars of the community.

I remember now that Granny Reba Love came over the following week. Granny was nearing eighty by then, but still driving her big Plymouth with the tail fins. She came and stayed a month with Mama, until they were about to kill each other with annoyance.

~

STILL FRIDAY

7:45 p.m.

Well, I just remembered all that happened, and maybe I am ready to put it to rest. I wrote a few things to God and burned the pages in the fireplace. Facing it all has just been such a help, remembering the people and place that I came from. I see my mother, and through her my father, and all of them—my people—as if they were a passing parade.

My heart has just welled up with tenderness and love for all these people. We are humans set on earth, and we go on and on, each of us doing the best we can at any given moment. I think it is awfully heroic simply to keep on living.

Life just flows on like a river, with failures and triumphs. Really, lots of triumphs. The demands of the day-to-day world tend to make us forget the triumphs, but we need to remember them.

We need to remember these stories of triumphs, because they are stories of love.

Fallen Trees And Heroes

A THUNDERING EXPLOSION and the dog's fierce barking brought Carley Love bolt upright from where she had fallen asleep in front of the fireplace. In the glow of the table lamp, she saw Freckles disappear into the hallway, heard the animal's toenails slipping and sliding on the oak flooring.

Freeing herself from the tangle of blanket, she scrambled to her feet and followed, hand flipping on light switches as she went. The dog was at the doorway to her mother's room, ears perked and body tense.

The door, partially open, seemed to sway. Carley Love tilted her head, listening. Then—"Oh, for heavensake." She pushed the door and felt for the light switch on the wall.

Blinking in the sudden brightness of the room's overhead light, she stood staring at the startling sight of a tree limb protruding into the room.

"Well, good Lord a'mercy!"

Just then buzzing and the light above blinking brought her attention upward, where she saw sparks arc. She gave a cry of alarm and cut the light switch off, and stood staring in the darkness. A small damp breeze tickled strands of hair on her forehead.

~

10:20 p.m. This is one long day.

A tree has fallen smack-dab into Mama's room. It was that old pecan tree that Jackson and I had talked of having removed but never got around to it. You just can't cover every base, and heaven knows I try.

It sure is a startling sight. Like an invading monster fell dead in the room. It is a mercy that something didn't catch fire. The overhead light was blinking and I heard hissing, saw sparks. I turned off the light and thankfully thought to also turn off the breakers. Jackson has them all labelled, clear and bold.

Granny Reba Love's rose lamp escaped harm, praise God! I suddenly have become nuts over that lamp. I moved it into the dining room, along with the trunk and containers of pictures and papers, and that framed picture of a Victorian girl that Mama had loved and that had belonged to Granny Myrtle.

So obviously, I'm going to take on all the saving of this stuff. Saving family stuff is in my blood. There is no escaping.

I am not calling Jackson or Royce. There is nothing to be done until this storm passes. I closed the door against the whole disaster. I am safe and sound and have mostly stopped shaking.

It strikes me that this is the first time a tree has ever

fallen into my house. I guess it can count as another new thing for me on my own.

~

IN THE KITCHEN, while waiting for the kettle to heat, she brought her phone out twice, and put it away twice. She opened the back door and looked out to see the steadily falling rain in the glow of the pole light. The breeze was brisk, with occasional gusts.

The kettle whistled. She shut the door and returned to the counter to make a hot cup of black tea thick with sugar.

She switched on the television on the counter, cradled the steaming cup of tea in both hands and blew upon it, as she watched the local news detailing the storm situation. Scenes from around the area flickered on the small screen. There was video of the hard pounding surf and wind damage on the coast, streets running like rivers with water, cars with floodwaters up to their doors.

And then Carley Love's mouth formed an O. She bent close to the television screen.

"Royce?"

But the camera had moved on from the familiar tall pickup truck and now panned into the flooded front yard of an old house. Her gaze fastened on the back of a man caught in the bright camera lights. A man in tall waders making his way across the the sea of yard.

She quickly turned up the television volume and even moved as if to peer around the corner of the screen for a better view, listening as the reporter gave a blow by blow of what could be plainly seen—Jackson slogging through the knee-high water to help a wiry old man trying to get a dog off the top of a dog house and up to the porch of a shotgun house on block foundation above the floodwaters. But the man, bent with age, was no match for the big hound that refused to be moved.

Jackson fairly picked up the dog in one arm and the man in the other. The dog's feet touched the water and paddled instinctively. Jackson deposited them both on the porch and fell over on the porch himself.

"Oh!" Carley Love put her hand toward the television screen.

The old man hugged his dog and smiled and pumped Jackson's arm in an enthusiastic manner. Then he waved at the camera, shouting something that sounded like, "We all right."

Jackson pushed from the porch and waded back across the yard to the driveway and then the street, where the reporter shoved a microphone in his face and asked, "Shouldn't he be evacuated?"

Jackson shrugged and drawled, "He said he wants t' stay. He's okay there. He's been through this before."

As he turned away and the camera cut back to the reporter, Carley Love strained her neck, as if she could see around the reporter.

SHE WAS in the bedroom wreckage, laying towels and blankets by lantern light on the wet floor, when she heard Freckles bark. She hurried to the living room and saw head-lights in the drive. She went to the back door, and Freckles darted out onto the porch.

Royce's big truck rumbled in the driveway, the head-lights shining through misty rain.

"Hey, Mama!" Royce called as he walked in front of the headlights.

A figure alighted from the passenger side and came toward the house—Jackson walking more slowly behind his son.

Royce reached the porch, and she threw herself into his arms. He hugged her hard. She reached a hand out to Jackson, and then the three of them were entering the kitchen.

"I saw you on the news. Well, your big truck and your father."

"Oh, man," said Royce, rubbing his short wet hair. "It was that guy with his dog, right?"

"Yes," she chuckled at his expression.

He launched in to telling how he had rescued a number of stranded cars that afternoon, until his father had phoned him. He told what roads were under water and how he and his dad had pulled one car out of a driveway on the way home that evening. He was alight with adventure and pride.

Jackson hung back, leaning on the counter, letting Royce do all the talking. Carley Love shot him a glance, and he smiled at her and at his son.

Then, suddenly remembering, Carley Love said, "Well, we have a tree in the house. In Memaw's room."

The men instantly headed to the bedroom, both still wearing their waders. Carley Love followed behind them, explaining how she had turned off the electric breaker. Royce took up the lantern and played it over the room. The next instant, he hopped onto the tree limb and up it to poke his head into the attic and call down a damage report. Carley Love protested for him to be careful.

"This thing's not movin', Mama." Royce stomped a heavy foot on the tree for proof.

Just then the dog again went barking into the kitchen. Carley Love followed the dog to answer knocking at the door. It was Simona, standing in the porch light, barefoot and holding her shoes, with her pants legs rolled up.

"My goodness, darlin' girl, you don't have to knock. Get in here."

The next moment, the room went black.

Simona let out a squeak, and Carley Love reached out to touch her. "It's all right. It's just the power gone out. The generator should come on."

The two women stood waiting.

After a full minute, Carley Love said, "Well, maybe not."

There came the sound of movement and a light coming through the dining room.

"Aw, honey, I'm sorry I forgot you were in the truck when Mama told me about the tree." Royce went to Simona.

"I'll check the generator," Jackson said, holding the lantern for Carley Love to locate a flashlight.

"I'm coming, too," said Carley Love.

Jackson got tools from the workroom and went to the generator at the edge of the garage. Standing behind him, Carley Love directed the flashlight beam to where his hands worked on the engine.

Her gaze drifted downward to his damp hair and then over his denim-clad muscled shoulders.

"Hey! The light."

She adjusted the flashlight beam and her attention back to the generator. Another few minutes and the machine roared to life, dropped to an uneven sputter and then settled into a rhythmic rumble. Jackson observed it, his ear tilted.

"I think that's got it." He wiped his hands on a rag as he gave the generator another long look.

She studied his profile, the shadowy stubble over his jaw. His eyes swung to meet hers.

"Thank you," she said.

His response to this was to gaze at her and then nod, saying, "Well, it's runnin' for now." He placed the rag and tools at the corner of the generator. "But anyway, we came to get you and take you to Royce's apartment. It's high, dry, and warm there."

"Oh, no...there's no need." She shook her head.

"Now, Carle'Love, the rain's not done and the water's likely to rise..."

"Do you think we will flood?" In alarm, she glanced at the doorway.

"No, the house is safe. It may come up on the bottom step but not near to reachin' the house. The roads are flooded, though. Little Creek is rushing over the bridge. It may even take it out. So the west is cut off even in the Escalade. Royce's truck can go down Simpson's road, at least it could. Or we can go around to the east and then north."

"If the house is safe, I'm okay here."

"Look, the generator isn't gonna run itself. It's gonna need fillin' with fuel, and it's old. I should have replaced it last year with a more modern setup. It goes out, you won't have any heat."

"I can fill it with fuel, and I have the fireplace."

"And limited firewood."

By now they had entered the kitchen.

"Carle'Love, it's gonna get cold when this thing passes, and there's no tellin' how long the power is gonna be out. And a tree has done fallen on the house." His drawl got deeper with impatience. "Anything could happen, and no emergency crew can get in here. You'd best go to Royce's for a few days. That way no one has to worry about you."

"No one has to worry, Jackson," she said with calm practicality. "I'd rather be sleepin' in my own bed and havin' all my own stuff." She put her hand to her hip. "You thought it was just fine for that old man to stay in his house with water up to his porch."

"That old man is in town, not ten miles out. And he has a boat tied at his back porch if need be to go fifty yards and can walk the rest to dry land." Then he added, "And he isn't my wife. I'm tryin' to look after you, Care'lina."

At this her eyes widened. They stared at each other.

"Well," she said in a level tone. "The house appears to be fine. If the generator dies and the firewood runs out, I've plenty of clothes to layer on. It is highly unlikely to be more than a day or two before the road is passable, at least to the east. I would really rather stay here, Jackson, with all my own things, and Freckles would be more comfortable here. But what I do *need* is some plan about the tree and the hole in the roof. It's rainin' in the house."

He regarded her thoughtfully, nodded and hollered, "Royce!"

The younger man came instantly, Simona right behind his shoulder, as if connected. Without waiting to be told anything, Royce launched in with what work he felt should be done, as he followed his father to the garage to retrieve tools.

Carley Love set about making coffee.

"What can I do?" asked Simona.

"See can you dig out the package of date-nut muffins I put in the freezer. They're labeled."

Forty-five minutes later, Carley Love showed Simona to the guest room, even turned down the covers of the bed, while Simona went directly to the warm shower. In the kitchen, Royce ate a sandwich at the table. She kissed his forehead.

Peeking in the great room, she saw Jackson in his large chair, watching television. She went quickly to the bedroom, changed to pajamas and robe, gathered a pillow and a blanket and returned to the living room.

Jackson had reclined the chair and was fast asleep.

She stood a moment contemplating him.

With a tender smile, she gently slipped the remote from his hand and turned off the television. She spread the blanket over him. As she went to the kitchen to turn off lights, she heard voices from down the hall and a door close. Clutching the pillow, she returned to her own bed and snuggled down.

After a moment, she put out her arm to feel the emptiness beside her.

Storm Clearing

SATURDAY, November 11

6:15 a.m.

What a precious thing—waking to coffee I didn't have to make! When I went to the kitchen, I found that Jackson had made the coffee and gone back to sleep in his recliner!

He spent the night there. I had meant to let him have the bed. I knew he was exhausted from a very long day. But he fell asleep before I could tell him.

Seeing him in the recliner that has been empty for months quite undid me.

The entire eventful night quite undid me. The storm, the tree falling on the house, Jackson and Royce and Simona coming, and then, in the thirty minutes that the guys put tarps over the hole as best they could and Simona and I made coffee and heated muffins, Simona told me some of hers and Royce's plans and confided that she is indeed pregnant. This news came from her quite by accident, and then she worried because she said Royce wanted to be the one to tell me. I promised I would forget that she told me. We are sharing secrets. I think maybe in Simona I'm going to get the daughter I have always wanted.

Thank you, Father God. And I know, Father, that you are in charge of all. You have good plans for Royce and Simona. You love them far more even than I, which is hard to imagine but true.

The catastrophe of the fallen tree is in actuality a blessing. Last night it was like it used to be for the three of us. It has been since Royce's birth, the three of us facing things, having adventures. And now we have Simona and have become four. All four of us were at one time in Mama's room, making order enough to get a tarp over the hole and also moving things out of the room to keep them safe.

I was happy during that time last night. Happy for the first time in months.

Jackson is happiest when fixing a problem, and I am happy when helping him. Like two pieces of a whole. This seems such a funny fact, and one I have always known but paid so little attention to. It comes to me to wonder if one of the difficulties he had, something that caused him to go crazy and leave, was that he could not fix the problem of Mama's decline and me over-extending myself to take care of her. He could not fix his own upheaval and I could not help him. In our confusion and frustration, we turned from helping each other and went in different directions, headlong on our own determined ways.

Well, here we are now, gaining the daughter we have always longed for and are going to have a grandchild. It seems something of a second chance. I see with fresh eyes what I have missed and what will be gone forever if we divorce.

~

JACKSON CAME SILENTLY into the kitchen in his sock feet. "Do I smell cornbread?"

"Yep. And the electricity is back on." Carley Love handed him his mug steaming with coffee. "Thank you for makin' the coffee. It was nice to get up and have coffee made."

He lifted his coffee cup at her in acknowledgement.

Their eyes met and held. He winked.

To this, her mouth opened, then closed and she turned to grab a pot holder and bent to the oven. Just as she removed the hot iron pan of cornbread, Simona came through from the dining room, with a yawning Royce behind her.

"We smelled breakfast. Man, I'm hungry." Royce headed for the table in the breakfast nook that was already laden with covered dishes of scrambled eggs and bacon and early oranges. Jackson ambled over to join him, while Simona shared a smile with Carley Love, who handed her a jar of honey, mouthing, "Royce's favorite."

Carley Love brought the crusty cornbread and sat herself in her usual place. When she settled, she noticed the other three holding hands and their eyes regarding her expectantly.

She sat and took Simona's hand on one side and Royce's on the other, saying, "Well, Jackson, are you goin' to say grace?"

Seemingly startled by her question, he looked at her, then bowed his head, and took a breath. "Bless this food, Father...and thank you that we all came safely through the storm and without any damage that we can't repair. And thank you for Carle'Love makin' us such a good breakfast. Amen."

Royce said a resounding "Amen! Let's eat the grub."

Jackson and Carley Love smiled at each other, and then Jackson told Royce to fill up, that they were cutting the tree trunk out of the house after breakfast.

Yet, despite Jackson saying more than once that they needed to get to work, they all lingered around the breakfast table. Outside the grey sky turned dark and misting rain returned, cleared, and returned several times.

Suddenly Simona jumped up, saying breathlessly, "Excuse me..." and ran from the room.

Royce swallowed and turned to look at his mother, whose apprehensive gaze swung from where Simona had disappeared through the archway to her son.

"Honey, maybe you should go check on her."

Her son's gaze dropped downward. "Yeah, well, she doesn't care for me to do that. Uhm, I guess I need to tell you. Mom...Dad...we're goin' to have a baby. You're gonna be grandparents." He waited, looking from one parent to the other.

Carley Love's eyebrows went up, and she put a hand to her heart. "Well, this keeps getting' better and better."

"Congratulations, son," Jackson smiled widely, while Carley Love rose and went to throw her arms around her son.

When Royce decided to go check on Simona after all, Carley Love began to clear the table. She kept her face averted.

"What is it?" Jackson came beside her.

She set the dishes on the counter and sniffed. "Oh, Jackson...it's...it's wonderful and scary. They're takin' on so much right away."

He reached for her and pulled her against him, holding her, stroking his hand over her back.

"I know. But a lot of couples get started that way...and have since the beginnin' of time."

They stood thus for a long minute. Then Carley Love sniffed, pulled away, and took up the nearby tea towel, saying, "I remember when we had Royce. Remember how we laughed when dressing him at the hospital...at his big feet." She chuckled.

"Oh, yeah. And he's still got 'em." Jackson laughed with her.

"You have always been a good father," she said without looking at him.

"I've tried to be."

She turned to the sink, running the water.

Jackson came behind her, stood close as he slipped plates into the sink. "Well, Granny Carle'Love...you don't look like a granny to me." He pressed against her and nuzzled her neck.

Her breath caught in her throat, and she held herself taut for a moment, before relaxing back against him with a deep, audible sigh.

He pressed more firmly against her, his hand going around her middle while his lips softly kissed her ear and down her neck, which she tilted.

"Mom?"

Royce's voice brought them apart.

"Uh..." He gazed at them. "Simona wanted to know if you have a toothbrush and toothpaste."

"Oh, yes, sweetheart. Middle drawer in the guest bath. And let me make her some lemon ginger tea. It will settle her stomach."

~

STANDING IN THE BACKYARD, Carley Love spoke into her cell phone. "Thank you, Phil. I'll tell Jackson. Thanks again...bye."

She punched the button, dropped her cell phone into the pocket of her jacket and walked toward the porch, her boots splashing in soggy ground.

Jackson came backward through the French doors of her mother's room, bringing a branch that he threw over the rosebush into the yard.

She said, "Phil just returned my call and took our insurance claim."

"Good." Jackson, breathing heavily, removed his work gloves.

"I told him we documented with pictures and that you and Royce were getting the limb out of the way so you could more securely tarp the house. He said our photos would be fine and agreed we need to close the hole. Scattered storms are expected, and it would be impossible to get a crew over here today. He did say you can leave the main limb if you want. Insurance will pay to have that removed. He said the adjustor would be calling you."

"Okay. Good." He wiped his face with his sleeve.

"Hey, Mom, how 'bout some lunch?" Royce dropped out of the ceiling.

"Let's get this hole wrapped first, son."

"We'll have sandwiches ready when you are," Carley Love told the men. She stood watching them a moment. Her gaze moved in the manner of a caress from one to the other, taking note of every movement and expression as they exchanged comments.

Turning, she went along the porch to the veranda and into the kitchen.

Simona held up the tea pitcher, a question on her face.

"I'd love a glass, thank you, dear." Carley Love threw herself down into a chair and removed her rain boots. "They have cleared enough limbs and are about ready to start putting on tarps."

"I think Royce is quite enjoyin' himself through all of this," Simona said.

"Oh, yes. Jackson, too. They love those power tools. And they enjoy workin' together."

Simona set a glass of tea in front of her, and Carley Love smiled. "Such a treat. Thank you!"

"You're welcome. Do you think they might be wanting sandwiches? I saw you have plenty of cold cuts and cheeses."

"Oh, yes. Royce already wants lunch. But come sit down for a bit. Don't overdo."

"I'm fine," the younger woman said, as she came to the table, bringing a glass of water and lemon slices. "I was really sick in the beginnin', but not so much anymore. I think it was the coffee this mornin'. Right from the beginnin' the smell of coffee has made me nauseous. But this mornin' it smelled so delicious, and it tasted good, too. I may have gotten sick, but I sure did enjoy that cup of coffee." She chuckled.

Then, "You know, my sense of smell is so keen since I've been pregnant. Last night in the storm, I smelled the tinge of salt water." She inhaled deeply. "And now the scent of cut wood. I love that smell."

"I do, too." Carley Love nodded. "Everything smells so fresh now after the storm." She swirled the ice cubes in her glass. "Big storms have a way of cleaning the air...sort of cleaning the mind, too," she added, stroking the beads of sweat on her glass.

They each fell into their own thoughts for long seconds.

Simona broke the silence by saying, "I'm awfully glad that you know about the baby. I obviously couldn't hold the news much longer. I'm so excited." Joy beamed from her face.

"I am, too!" Carley Love leaned forward and reached out to lay her hand over that of the younger woman.

After a moment, Simona said, "I told Royce we should have told you right away. I know it was a disappointment for you not to be there when we got married. It was a disappointment for Royce, even though he didn't say. I could tell."

"Darling girl, I'm just so grateful you and Royce are together and welcomin' this precious new life, and lettin' Jackson and me be a part of it all."

Simona smiled softly. "You know, Royce thinks the sun rises and sets with both of you. That's what I liked right off about him. Right when we first met, he started telling me about where he was from. He is like a walkin' advertisement for this area." Her eyes took on a distant glint. "Here is not too very different from where I grew up with my grandmother. She lived in a small village. My grandfather was a carpenter. I don't remember him, but I do remember many things in my grandmother's house that he had made. And my uncle was an accountant, but he cut and sold firewood for a second income, and because he liked doing it. That's why the scent is familiar to me...it brings good memories. I know this is a good place to raise our child, and he will be blessed with y'all as grandparents."

"He?"

"Oh, we don't know yet. Sometimes we say he and sometimes she."

To all this, Carley Love nodded thoughtfully. "So living here with Royce suits you?"

"Oh, yes." Simona's head bobbed. "I'm finishin' up a job —it's my hands bein' photographed for potted meat." She chuckled. "With hands and feet modeling, I can work many months yet. As long as my feet don't swell. It will mean travelin' back and forth to Atlanta, and maybe to Tallahassee. I also work with a photographer there. But the money is good and will help us. After the baby is born, I want to focus on our family for a year or so at least. I'll take some work, but mainly I'll be a full-time mom."

"You seem to have a plan."

Simona opened her mouth to reply, but a buzzing sounded. Both women's gazes went to the source of the sound—Jackson's cell phone lying at his place on the table.

Carley Love stretched to pick up the phone and rose from her chair, saying, "That could be the adjuster."

Phone in hand, she started toward her mother's bedroom. Another ring, and she looked down at the phone, intending to answer.

The name on the screen read: Anita H.

She stopped and stared at the illuminated letters. Red

bloomed on her cheeks. The phone rang again. She put her fingers on the phone to answer.

She stopped, looked ahead and hurried through the hallway into her mother's bedroom, where Jackson stood handing a hammer upward to Royce.

"You have a call," she said.

He responded with raised eyebrows as he caught the phone she all but threw at him.

He looked at the screen and then at Carley Love as he answered.

"Yeah?" He turned and walked out to the porch through the opened French doors.

She stood staring at his back the short minute that he spoke on the phone. When he closed it and turned to her, she pivoted, and stalked to the kitchen.

As the two women made lunch, Carley Love chatted about the wedding celebration and the baby and told Simona stories of Royce's boyhood. Rain came again heavily, and when the men appeared, the four of them laughed about how they had finished covering the hole in the roof just in time.

Again the four sat around the table and chatted pleasantly. Afterward, the men cleaned away the last of pieces of wood and tools, while Simona helped Carley Love with items she intended for the charity box. Simona delighted in a crocheted cotton yarn blanket, and Carley Love gave it to her.

When it was time for them to depart, she pressed a

container of cornbread into her son's hands. He hugged her and she held him tight and thanked him for his help. Then she hugged Simona. She thanked Jackson for his work and kept her gaze in the vicinity of his nose. He put his arm around her and dropped it when her gaze slid upward to him. With the dog standing beside her on the porch, she waved them goodbye.

Not watching until they were out of sight, she came into the house, closed the door, and leaned against it. Freckles looked up at her. "Well," she said to the dog.

Going through to the fireplace, she stirred coals, then laid small kindling and firewood until she had a full blaze.

She went to her bedroom and brought back her mother's Bible and the journal. She opened the Bible to Psalm thirty-four and read and re-read it, until tears fell on the pages. Closing the book, she reached for the journal, but instantly set it aside. "I can't even write about this."

"I can't write, and I can't pray. God, help me."

Curling into a blanket, she closed her eyes and fell asleep with her hands in fists.

"CARLE'LOVE!"

Jackson's voice awakened her. She slowly unfolded her stiff body and sat up on the couch.

Jackson appeared in the arched doorway to the kitchen, in the fading gloomy daylight.

"So the roads are passable," she said.

"Just barely. Don't try it."

They gazed at each other.

"We need to talk, Carle'Love."

She rose to her feet. "As long as you are talkin' with *her*, I don't see that you need to talk with *me*."

Jackson sighed a great sigh of annoyance.

She carefully folded the blanket.

He said, "It isn't anything, Care'lina. She called to find out if everything was okay down here. That's it." He came fully into the room.

"Really?" She looked away, raking a hand through her hair. "And why would she be so concerned?"

His brow furrowed with perplexity. "Well, she works in our department...and anybody would be concerned. Haven't you talked to Ronni, let her know how you are and found out how she is?"

She looked at him and tilted her head. "So now you are sayin' this woman is your best friend?"

He opened his mouth, closed it, and slowly lowered himself to the wide hassock.

She bit her bottom lip, studying him. She said in a soft tone, "You have her name in your contacts...and you walked away to talk to her privately." She turned to the fireplace, took up the poker, and jabbed crumbling embers.

"Of course I did. You were starin' at me like I had horns."

She leveled a look at him over her shoulder. They gazed at each other. His eyes shifted downward.

She took split logs from the bin, placed them with deliberation on the fire, and poked them earnestly to get a blaze.

He rubbed his hands together and said, "Look, I have her in my contacts because she is one of the secretaries at work. I have to talk to her, Carle'Love. She keeps all our schedules, and she wanted to make sure I would be comin' in tonight."

She focused on the flickering fire.

"Carle'Love, don't be like this." Impatience vibrated in his voice.

Her head came round, her entire body following. "Like what? Don't be upset that you are at our home talkin' on the phone to the woman with whom you had an affair?"

His expression was as if she had struck him.

She again looked away to the fire. After a moment, she said, "You see the problem we have?"

There was a long silence before he replied in a firm tone. "Her phone call wasn't anything. It was about work. I have only seen her at work. There is nothin' between us... nothin' at all."

Her back still turned toward him, Carley Love rolled her eyes toward the ceiling, then squeezed her lids closed. Tears slipped out.

He continued, "And it wasn't an affair. I don't even know if I slept with her...well, I guess I did, because I woke up..." He broke off, stood and took a breath.

"Oh, Care'lina, it was an *accident*. An accident that should never have happened...but it did the night after you said you wanted a divorce. I went out and got wasted. It was a stupid move on my part and an accident from too much alcohol."

Frowning, she brushed tears from her cheeks before turning toward him. She opened her mouth and then shut it. Slowly she moved to sit on the edge of the couch and gazed down at her bare wiggling toes.

Finally her words came in a hoarse tone. "Let me make the point that I did not simply up and ask you for a divorce one day. It was a decision I came to after you had been gone for four months. Is that correct as you see it?" She raised her gaze to his.

He said in a low voice, "Yes...yes, it is."

His shoulders slumped as he lowered himself back onto the hassock. They both sat in silence, eyes on the floor.

Then Jackson leaned toward her. "Care'lina, I love you, and I want to make it up to you. I want us to be together like we used to be. It seemed like last night and today showed us how it could be again."

She nodded. "Yes, it did. Last night and today, I thought we were happy again. I did...until the phone call." Her voice ended in a catch.

He gazed at her with no reply.

"I don't know what to say to any of this." She rubbed her forehead. "I've been readin' what the Bible says about marriage and divorce...and forgiveness and love. I want more than anything to be the sort of wise and loving woman who can open her heart and arms and welcome you home. That's how it happens in movies. The two make up and get together again and all is right with the world. I thought this mornin' that I could be that woman."

Her voice broke. "And then the phone call came, and I turned into someone I don't even recognize."

She took a deep, heavy breath and put her hand to her heart. "Jackson, you call it an accident. Well, I can see that...I really can. But like any accident, we are now dealin' with the consequences. Consequences for me mean that I'm all tore up. I certainly am not the same person that I was. I've been through too much, and alone."

She considered a long moment before continuing. "Sometimes it's like I'm losin' my mind. I see things so different from you. You say there's nothing goin' on with this Anita-woman, and then you're takin' phone calls from her askin' after your well-being. That right there is relationship, Jackson. It is called an emotional affair." She stopped and swallowed. "Maybe you don't have that with her, but she certainly does with you."

Understanding dawned across his features, and his gaze slipped downward.

"I love you, too, Jackson. I believe that I will always love you. You are a wonderful man with many talents that I admire—a great father, a man with a sense of humor...a man who can fix and build things. You are generous and kind and will be a wonderful grandfather.

"But right now my love for you is painful. And part of that hurt is from not liking *myself* in connection with you." She jabbed her chest with her finger. "I don't like havin' all this turmoil inside me that comes up when that woman calls you. Anger and fear and pure bitchiness. I never in my life had that." She raised her arm and let it fall.

"I'll tell you flat out, Jackson—I don't think it is right for you to still have anything at all to do with her."

He said slowly, brow furred deeply in thought. "Well...I can't fire her. I'm not in charge of that...and it wouldn't be right."

Her eyes widened. "Oh...no, it wouldn't."

Silence ensued.

She gazed at him.

He scratched his head.

After a moment, she said, "Oh, Jackson, I do still love you, But the trust that I had with *us* is gone. I don't trust that you won't walk out that door again. And I don't trust myself, that I won't end up drivin' you away."

Jackson unfolded himself from the hassock and came to

sit beside her, and looked down into her face. "I hear you, Care'lina. I know it isn't goin' to be easy, and I know most of this is on me. I don't expect you to trust me right away. I can live with that and work on it. Do you hear me? You had nothin' to do with me leavin'. You never drove me away. But you have everything to do with me returnin'. You are my home, Care'lina."

She stared into his eyes that shimmered with unshed tears.

"Jackson, let's pray together," she said in a voice just above a whisper.

Uncertainty flickered over his features, but he nodded.

She held out her hand, and he took it, holding tightly. They bowed their heads. Neither spoke aloud but Carley Love's lips moved.

After long minutes, she said an audible, "Amen."

She watched Jackson open his eyes.

He gazed at her, then said in an apologetic tone, "I have t' go to work. It is what keeps this broken roof over our heads."

"I know, Jackson...and I do appreciate it."

He stood, then—"I gotta get somethin'." He said dashed away through the hall toward their bedroom.

Both Carley Love and the dog stared wide-eyed at the hallway.

Jackson reappeared and held up a black book. "Had to get my Bible. Sure glad you didn't get rid of the stuff in my nightstand," he added with a chuckle.

She chuckled, too, blinking tearing eyes.

He kissed her quickly. "I'll call you tomorrow," and sprinted for the back door. The next instant he reappeared, warning firmly, "Don't try to go anywhere tonight."

"Well, don't you get stuck!" she called, hurrying into the kitchen as he went out the door.

"I won't." The door closed.

At the kitchen window, she watched his truck head away down the driveway.

When she turned from the window, she saw the dog looking at her as if for direction.

"Well, Freckles, I don't know what to tell you. Your humans are nuts."

Moving On

THE STORM HAD DAMAGED the roof of the current Lila Ackerman and Company offices, so Lila decided to immediately move out of it and into the new building, even though the renovations were not fully finished. Everything fell into place when it turned out the movers were available.

"We have your computer," Carley Love told Lila, entering the woman's large office at the new place. A man followed in her wake, bearing a cardboard moving box that he set on the desk.

Lila, who was talking on her cell phone, nodded that she had heard, rose from an overstuffed chair and went out through the glass-paned oak double doors onto the rear patio.

Carley Love set about unpacking the box and assembling the computer. She had it all arranged when Lila re-entered the office, retrieved her purse from the corner of the desk, dug into it and pulled out an antacid bottle, shaking two tablets into her palm.

"You're set up again," Carley Love said, plugging the

electronics into the receptacles on the side of the elegant desk.

Lila's expression registered pleasure as she ran her gaze over the new desk. "Did you check about the delivery of the credenza?"

"Mr. Busby said it's arrived from Mobile and will be delivered tomorrow mornin'."

"They should have just sent it here."

"Yes...probably too sensible a decision for them to handle."

Just then a man appeared in the doorway with a dolly bearing a short cherrywood file cabinet. Carley Love directed him for the placement, while Lila looked on, saying, "What about the files that got wet? Did they get dried?"

"Yes, ma'am, dried but still in boxes—those and the ones Doreen is currently enterin' into the computer are stacked in her office."

"How's she doin' with that?"

"Very well. She has evolved into quite the wiz with the computer."

"Huh...who would've imagined?" Lila pulled a pack of cigarettes from her purse. Her gaze came up to Carley Love, then shifted beyond her. "Hello, E.H."

Carley Love turned to see E.H. Cummings saunter into the room.

"Hello, ladies," the man drawled. "Old Fred would rise up from the grave and demand the place back if he saw what you're managin' to do with it."

He smiled at both of them, and then his gaze shifted to rest on Carley Love, as Lila explained, "We're not done by any means. We've only done the rooms in this half of the building so we can operate, while we work on those on the other side."

Just then a moving man appeared in the doorway with a bookcase on a dolly.

"Oh! That goes over here," Carley Love said and gestured.

Behind her, she heard Lila say, "Come on outside with me, E.H." The older woman led the way through the double doors.

Two boxes were delivered, and Carley Love set about emptying them and placing the contents on the shelves. Through the window, she saw Lila and Mr. Cummings on the brick patio. The two were in deep conversation. A faint smile played at Mr. Cummings's lips, while Lila frowned and blew a stream of smoke.

Carley Love finished unpacking and left the room with the empty boxes, which she carried through the center reception room to one of the unfinished rooms, tossed them inside with others and shut the door.

More men and boxes streamed through the front door, and she gave direction.

Doreen appeared, a bit wobbly on her high-heels, juggling a plastic container, a tote bag, and her enormous purse, with one of the moving men following, bearing a large cardboard carton.

"I wasn't about to let them take Miss Betsy. I brought her myself," she said of her computer, then, "Oh!" as her enormous purse slipped from her shoulder and the container tilted, spilling a computer mouse and various papers. Carley Love caught the mouse before it hit the floor and quickly gathered the papers, then followed Doreen and her moving man down the hall to the younger woman's new office.

The burly man set the large box on the desk, gave Doreen a flirty smile, and left.

Doreen thrust a file folder toward Carley Love. "Here. Don't lose your party info. I got the last bit of it entered this mornin'. I'll email you the file and you can print it out for Lila. She always prefers that."

"Thank you, Doreen! Oh, but you shouldn't do it on Lila's time."

"It was all of fifteen minutes. I promise I will make it up somewhere." She gave a dismissive wave of her long silvery fingernails. "You know, we can consider doin' your work simply more education on my computer skills. Here...plug this into the back of the monitor."

Carley Love complied, saying, "I'm learnin' the book-keeping program. It's pretty much like what I've been using for my home accounts."

"Girlfriend, why stress yourself when you have me to do it?" Doreen gave her a saucy grin.

"Well, looks like you ladies are settlin' in."

Both women turned toward the door. The tall, graceful figure of E.H. Cummings smiled as he surveyed the room.

Carley Love said lightly, "We're doing our best to get it over with."

"Miss Lila says that you are plannin' an open house the first of December...somethin' like you did for The Third's office."

Carley Love said, "Yes, we're plannin' somethin' similar... but you know I didn't do the open house for Trey's office. Evangeline did most of it. I just came in and added a bit of sparkle and helped where I could."

"Ah," he nodded, thoughtfully gazing at her. "Lila tells me that you're a party planner on the side. Do you think you'd be available to help me with a small dinner party this Saturday? I know it is short notice, but it's informal and just eight people at my house—ten, with you and me. I'd be delighted for your help to dress it up a bit. You know, give it some style and help me host, too. It would make it special."

"Well, I..."

"You're free." Doreen was suddenly beside her, a planner open in her hand. "The Fredericks cancelled...remember?" she said looking pointedly at Carley Love.

Waving a pencil toward Mr. Cummings, Doreen said, "Party of ten, you said...uhmm...with us providin' the decorations?" Without waiting for an answer, she added, "What time and what's the address?"

CARLEY LOVE STOPPED at the Dollar Tree and was checking out when her cell phone rang.

"Hold on, Ronni, I'm at the checkout. I got a really good sale on glass goblets!" She propped the phone atop her purse, finished the transaction, and rolled the cart containing her bags from the store, while picking up her phone. "There, okay. Oh, Ronni, I have another party job!"

"I got your message...Can you hear me okay? We've been havin' trouble with the phones since the storm."

"I hear you. My cell has been okay, but the landline phones were out at the office until late this mornin'. We had a leak there right over the file cabinets...just soaked files. Lila is fit to be tied, and we've all been runnin' around like fleas on a dirty dog tryin' to get papers dried and things packed and carried to the new office. The movers could fit us in today, so Lila snatched the oppor..."

"Well, honey, I have to interrupt. I'm so glad about your party job. I really am...you are just movin' on, girlfriend. This will be so good for you. And I am movin' on, too! In half an hour I'm leavin' for Jacksonville. Eric and I are goin' on a cruise, and we're gettin' *married!*" Ronni fairly screamed the last.

"You *aren't?*"

"Yes. I am." Ronni's firm statement was followed by delighted laughter. "I can't believe it myself. We're gettin' married on the ship. It was all arranged this mornin'."

Carley Love touched the back of her hand to her forehead. "My goodness..." She looked across the parking lot toward the skyline now coral with the setting sun. "Congratulations, girlfriend."

Ronni's voice dropped low. "What happened was Eric's ex-girlfriend found out about him and me, and she started after him again. She is playin' the oh-I-need-help card. Men can't resist that.

"Well, I tell you, Eric is the best thing to happen to me since I gave birth. My whole family may disown me but I'm snatchin' up this blessin'."

"I'm happy for you, Ronni. I wish I could be there to celebrate with you." Her tone was hoarse.

"I wish you could, too, honey-bunny." Then, softer, "I just know this is the right thing for me, but please pray for me."

"You know I will." Carley Love pushed the shopping basket across the pavement to the Escalade with one hand, not seeing the car that braked hard for her. "God bless you and keep you—both of you."

"How is it goin' with Jackson?" Ronni asked.

"Oh, I don't know. I saw him only a few minutes on Sunday. He came when the insurance adjuster looked at the house. But I didn't have anything else to say to him. I'd said it all on Saturday. And apparently he didn't have anything to say, either."

"Oh, girl...just a minute." Ronni's voice came muffled as she spoke briefly to someone in the background. "Now look, Carley Love, that woman at Jackson's office is like Eric's ex. She sees Jackson has made a firm turnaround and she's reachin' out to grab him."

There came a clattering sound. "Ronni? Are you still there?"

"Yes. I dropped the phone 'cause I was holdin' it between my chin and my shoulder while I pack, which only teenagers should do. Look, darlin' girl, now is not the time to back off just because you feel hurt and are afraid of more hurt."

"It seems your romance with Eric is givin' you a different perspective."

"Yes, it is. I never imagined I would meet a man like Eric. He's...well, he's just so right for me. And he *needs* me. He *really needs* me.

"Men *need* us to help them, that's what it is. They are a mess when it comes to relationships. That's the woman's territory. We have to help them," Ronni stated firmly.

There came a voice in the background. Ronni answered it and then said into the phone, "Oh, honey, I've got to go. Look...well, I just want you to be happy, too, Carley Love. I want the whole world to be happy. And please be happy for me."

"I am happy for you, sweetheart. Have a wonderful time! Call me when you can."

Ronni was already gone.

Carley Love sighed deeply, slowly pocketed her phone, and stowed her purchases into the back of the Escalade. Her expression one of deep thought, she pushed the cart to the front of the store and returned to slip into the driver's seat of her vehicle, started the engine and drove away.

At the exit of the parking lot, the black Escalade stopped with a jerk. It backed up, swung in an arc and, with a squeal of tires, sped back to the front of the Dollar Tree store. Carley Love jumped out of the driver's seat and ran to the cart she had left moments before—and the purse she had left in the cart seat. Snatching it, she hurried back to her vehicle, slammed the door, and drove away.

WEDNESDAY, November 15

8:00 p.m.

I've been carrying my journal around in my purse, thinking that I would write all about what happened on Saturday with Jackson and Royce and Simona—and That Woman who called—and now it is Wednesday night, with Saturday further and further away and more and more happening. It's just that I'm having the hardest time to write here. After the weeks of pouring everything on these pages, now I can't get myself to form words. It's as if my emotions are all in a tangle that is stuck in my throat, or fingers as the case may be.

I cannot believe that I left my purse in the cart at the Dollar Tree! It's a wonder I did not wreck when I realized it. What if I hadn't remembered and someone had got hold of my purse and this journal? All anyone would have to do is take scissors to that hidden pocket. Our names are in this book. I guess I won't be removing it from the house anymore.

What had happened to take my mind away was Ronni telling me that she is marrying Eric.

Good grief. I must have been blind not to expect this. Ronni has been unpredictable since meeting Eric. Are we all unpredictable and just don't know it?

I am at once thrilled for her and totally bereft. One more person leaving me. She is getting married on a cruise, so I'm not even going to be at her wedding.

Our relationship has definitely taken a turn. Or maybe the relationship never has been what I had thought.

What it seems to me at this moment is that each of us is more alone than we ever realized. People come and go in our lives. Everything in life on this earth is always moving on.

Well, I can't write about all that went on with Jackson on Saturday, beyond saying I went right from believing in us to total doubt with one phone call from *That Woman*. When I saw her name, it was like fire roared up from my toes.

Wait! Why did that one call turn me all topsy-turvy? Am I letting someone I do not even know control me?

It isn't her. It is my own reactions. My own doubt and insecurity.

Or maybe my own good sense.

I'll have to think on that.

One thing all this has me doing is praying. Trials sure do send one running to the Lord. But give thanks for all trials? That is a hard one.

I remember Granny Reba Love saying that if God asks us to do something, we can, no excuses. Possibly she never applied that wisdom to her quitting smoking.

Well, maybe I can give thanks that I am being drawn to God in this trial, and I am getting to know myself better.

I do want to record that I have another party-planning job—a dinner party for Trey's father, E.H. He already has it set, and I'm doing as I did for Trey—embellishing and hosting.

I'm setting up my business on computer, doing a website, business cards. I have to say I am surprised at how much I actually know about getting it all set up in an accounting program. I've kept the household accounts forever and done a lot for the office, too. Another big surprise is how Doreen is helping me. She seems to be happy to help. She actually suggested she come to work for me. I had to make it clear that I am no where near being able to hire anyone. I would never want to hurt her feelings, but I might go stark raving mad if I had to work closely with her every day. She talks and never shuts up.

 But I Still Love You

"I LIKE the changes you made to the website." Doreen's voice floated up from Carley Love's cell phone lying to the right of her notebook computer on the desk in the alcove of her kitchen. Next to that was a plate with with a partially eaten peanut butter and banana sandwich.

"I've worked on this stuff all afternoon," said Carley Love, "but I have made headway. I also assembled goblet lights for Mr. Cumming's dinner party. I lucked onto two cases of glass goblets at the Dollar Tree. You'd never know they came from there. I spoke to Mr. Cumming's secretary today, and I'm keeping everything classy. He has a chef."

"Wow! Take pictures of his house. I want to see it. I'll keep an eye out on the web for a good supplier for glasses. You're goin' to need more. By the way, did the secretary send the money? And you know, you should have gotten a contract. You're goin' to have to draw up a contract."

"I don't know if I should take pictures of the interior of his house. I think that's an invasion of privacy."

"Well, maybe. But maybe you can get permission. Are

you sure you don't want me to go with you tomorrow evenin'? I don't mind breakin' my date. I'd love to break my date," the younger woman added.

"No. That was not the deal with Mr. Cummings. Why did you make the date, if you don't want to go?"

"My cousin suckered me into a blind date, and I wanted to go more than to stay home with Big Mama."

"Uh-huh," was Carley Love's reply. She tilted her ear toward the window. Vehicle headlights flickered into the room. "I have to go, Doreen...I want to add a few more touches to the website tonight."

"Okay...talk to you tomorra'."

Freckles was at the kitchen door, wagging her tail. Carley Love opened the door, then hastily moved to the mirror to check her reflection and fluff her hair before following Freckles out to the porch. She stood at the top of the steps, watching Jackson alight from the driver's seat of his truck. She stiffened as she saw him round the hood and open the passenger door. He pulled out a bag of hanging clothes and a duffle and came along the walkway, speaking to the dog who all but tripped him.

When he reached the bottom of the steps, he stopped and looked up at Carley Love standing in the middle of the entry.

"Good evenin'."

"Good evenin'."

"Uh...I thought I'd move back home. Gordon's daughter is movin' back home, and he needs the room."

She gazed at him. He gazed back.

She said, "Don't you think we should have talked about this?"

He tossed the hanging bag over his shoulder. "This has

been one heck of a busy week, Carle'Love. We haven't seemed to be able to get together enough for talkin', and I think maybe we will if I move back home. It'll save a lot of money over a hotel. And save time, too, and the contractor called me this afternoon, said he's startin' on the house tomorrow. I need to be here to check how it goes."

"Ah-huh." She nodded in understanding. Then, "You could have called to let me know."

"I didn't think it would be a problem."

She opened her mouth and shut it, looked downward and then back at him. "I'm not tryin' to argue. I don't mean it that way. But it seems to me that you can't just decide to come home in the same manner you decided to leave. You could have called. We could have discussed it."

His jaw tighten. He frowned, looked downward, and then up at her again and said, "Okay...how about I stay in the garage loft?" His left eyebrow rose.

Surprise crossed her face, and she glanced at the second story window of the garage.

"Okay."

He shot her a nod, turned, and went to the small door of the garage.

She watched him disappear through the door. She looked upward at the loft window and saw the light come on. Calling Freckles, she returned to the kitchen and shut the door firmly behind her.

She stood a moment, then moved to the desk in the alcove to close her computer. Reaching to turn out the banker's lamp, she paused, and moved her hand to pull papers from a cubbyhole.

She unfolded the papers and scanned them, her eyes lingering on the bold text: The Final Judgement of Divorce.

Closing her eyes, she stood quietly. Next she sat and smoothed the papers flat. Picking up a pen, her hand hovered over the signature line. She lowered her hand for a moment. Then, with a deep breath, she set aside the pen, folded the papers, and returned them to the cubbyhole.

"Well, there's somethin'."

~

FRIDAY, November 17

8:30 p.m.

Jackson has come home in the same manner as he left, just up and doing it without a word to me. I swear he truly did not think to talk to me about this. It is like he is clueless.

Well, he is a *man*, as Ronni pointed out. Perhaps she is right in that the male of our species needs help with relationship.

It seems he had to leave where he was staying with Gordon, and a hotel would be expensive, not to mention he does need to handle the repair on the house. When he said that, I realized I was being clueless—I had been going along, assuming he would handle the repairs, never thought about it at all. And what does that say about me?

I'm excited that he has come home.

There. I said it. I am.

I'm pretty much a mess about it. I think of him there in Granny Myrtle Love's old wrought-iron bed. I love that bed. It was the first bed Jackson and I had in our first own home. A lot of action happened in that bed.

Memories come in a rush. Good mercy, I have to stop them. I get all turned on.

I tried signing the divorce papers again. I couldn't do it.

~

MOONLIGHT FLICKERED AGAINST THE WALL. She lay looking at it and listening to country ballads play softly from the stereo. George Strait singing his country ballad, "You Haven't Left Me Yet."

She cocked her head in a listening manner. In a sudden movement, she threw back the blankets and hurried to the closet, and located a black lace peignoir set hung far to the back. She tugged off her pajamas and slipped on the night-gown and sheer wrapper. She gazed at herself in the mirror, put her fingers to where the neckline dipped low.

Jutting her chin, she slipped her feet into slippers and headed for the door so quickly that the peignoir fluttered out behind her. Freckles partially opened heavy eyes, but remained on her cushion as Carley Love left and flitted through the shadowy rooms to the kitchen.

She strained to peer out the window over the sink. The next instant, she opened the bottom cabinet door, put her foot into the cabinet to boost herself up, and leaned toward the window enough to see the second story window of the garage. A faint light shone there.

Just then the window opened, and Jackson leaned out.

At the sight of him smoking a cigarette, her mouth opened wide, then clamped closed. Dropping to the floor, she stalked to the back door, and jerked it open.

An object sailed down to the walkway and landed with a faint plunk and triggering the motion sensor light. She drew back, but then she craned her neck, squinting, and saw a packet of cigarettes lying on the walkway.

Hearing footsteps thumping on the garage stairs, she quickly shut the kitchen door, grabbing it at the last second to keep it from slamming. She stood to the side and peeked through the blinds of the door window.

She saw Jackson, denim shirt open, step out barefooted and snatch up the packet of cigarettes. He crushed the packet in his hand, opened the lid to the large trash bin sitting beside the garage door, and tossed the pack inside. Then he disappeared back inside the garage.

Carley Love stood very still. Her hand went out and hovered above the doorknob. Next she hurried through the dimness to her bedroom. Yanking off the peignoir, she tossed it aside like a tissue, and threw herself into the bed and pulled the blankets clear to her neck.

George Strait sang out from the stereo about wanting more time. She groped for the remote, turning off the music.

MORNING LIGHT GLOWED through the sheers on the French doors, when she cracked an eyelid. She rolled to her back, eyes slowly fluttering open. She sat up and looked at Freckles' bed cushion. It was empty.

The bedroom door was closed. She sniffed, sighed deeply, and murmured, "Coffee."

She tilted her head. "Sausage? Really?" Her eyebrows rose.

A light knock sounded on the door.

She dropped back to the pillow and closed her eyes, feigning sleep.

The door creaked softly open.

She cracked her eyelids to see Jackson rounding the foot of the bed with stealthy steps, carefully bearing a mug on a saucer.

Her eyes flew open when he reached the side of the bed.

Their gazes met, both surprised.

"Good mornin'," he said, his voice and expression hesitant. "I thought maybe coffee would help you bear the noise and activity that will soon start up. Crew is on the way."

"Thank you," she said, sitting up and raking back her hair.

She considered the mug a moment, as if uncertain, but took it when he extended his arm.

Then, seeing his gaze on her, she looked down at herself and the black negligee, the strap hanging off her shoulder. She jerked up the strap.

Jackson bent to the floor and slowly straightened, bringing the delicate peignoir up with his fingers. A grin tugging his lips, he draped it at the foot of the bed.

Her cheeks bloomed red. She looked down into the coffee.

He said, "I haven't seen you wear that nightgown in a long time." He paused. "Is there some occasion I'm missing?"

"No. Just felt like it. Thank you for the coffee. Is that breakfast I smell?"

"Yep. It's in the oven when you're ready." His eyes remained on her.

She said, not looking at him, "I'm gettin' up. I have to work on preparations for a dinner party tonight. I got another party job."

"Well, good for you. I mean, if that's what you want."

She flicked him a glance, then reached for her phone on

the bedside table, saying, "Thanks for the coffee," her manner as if dismissing him.

He turned to leave, but with suddenness bent down beside her, and whispered in her ear, "You still look terrific in that gown."

His lips lightly kissed her neck, and then he pulled back and gazed into her eyes.

He straightened and left the room.

Carley Love sat with the phone in her hand, staring at it.

The next moment Jackson was back through the door.

"I still love you, Care'lina."

She opened her mouth, closed it, and came out with, "And I still love you, Jackson."

"But?" he said, paused a long second and added, "Can you forgive me?"

"Yes." She swept her hair behind her ear and looked directly at him. "I do forgive you. All resentment is gone. Really, when I consider everything, there's nothing to forgive. Nothin' at all. We both have acted crazy, and you are right that we have had so many good years." She broke off.

"But?" he prompted.

"But just now...for just a second, I wondered how I measure up to her...or if you would think of her when you made love to me. And if you'll leave again one day."

Her voice broke. "And it's more than that. I'm not the same person I was, Jackson. I've grown and changed these months of bein' on my own. I've really begun to be able to be on my own. If we were to get back together, you might find I'm no longer to your liking."

She waited for his response. They studied each other.

The sound of Freckles barking, followed by the ringing of the doorbell cut through the silence.

"They're here," he said and disappear out the door.

THE CREW OF THREE MEN, two young and one older foreman, swarmed into her mother's bedroom, beginning immediately to cut up what was left of the tree trunk and clear the wreckage of the roof and walls. The loud voices and buzzing of saws, pounding of hammers, clatter of boots, and falling timber and sheetrock filled the air.

Carley Love decided her mother's mahogany pineapple-post headboard and footboard should be temporarily stored in the garage loft. "Careful...careful," she hollered to Jackson, as she carried one side of the headboard and he the other.

"If you'd just let me do it," he hollered back.

"You can't get it past the island alone. Oh, let's just sit it down and scoot it."

"Let's just set it all here, and I'll get Royce to help me later," Jackson countered.

"No. I can do it."

Once both the headboard and footboard were deposited in the loft room of the garage, she stood catching her breath and looking around. Her gaze moved over Jackson's clothes hung on wall hooks, his shiny boots and running shoes lined against a wall, and the bed he hadn't made, which still bore the imprint of his body.

Her gaze returned to Jackson to see him watching her. Averting her eyes to the old portable television, she swiped her hand across the top of it, saying, "I'm sorry it's so dusty. I'll get it cleaned up."

"It's okay. I'm just sleepin' here."

Returning to her mother's room in the house, the two of them cleared the final items from the closet, carrying them to pile in the hallway, out of the way of the construction crew's work.

"Well, this old thing can go." Jackson carried the wooden ironing board.

"No! That was Granny Reba Love's and maybe Granny Myrtle's, and I've always loved it." Carley Love grabbed the ironing board and all but hugged it, while Jackson looked at her with raised eyebrows and a chuckle. She carried it off to her bedroom closet.

When she returned to the hallway, she found Jackson crouched beside a box.

He glanced up at her with a grin. "I found my old cowboy guns."

"Oh, Royce's, too," she said with soft pleasure, peering over his shoulder into the box.

Jackson lifted the cracked and worn leather holster. "They don't make 'em like this anymore."

"They didn't even make them like that when Royce was a boy. I don't know how his has survived, bein' vinyl."

"He still had the metal cap guns." He examined one of the pistols. "I bet it'll still work, if we can get caps."

Her gaze lingered on his boyish expression and sudden tears welled up.

He saw her tears. "What is it?"

"Oh, Jackson, you just look so much like Royce. Maybe Royce and Simona will have a boy. He can play with these.

Oh, I miss Royce being a boy...it all went by so fast, and now Mama is gone...everyone is gone."

Jackson stretched out an arm and drew her against him with one hand, setting the box aside with the other, so that he could fully embrace her.

She held to him a moment, then pushed away. "I'm sorry. It's just emptyin' this room."

"I know, honey. It brings so many memories. But they're good ones, most of them."

"Uh-huh." She nodded and her lips worked at a smile but didn't quite make it. "But I always feel that I failed Mama. I wanted so much to make her happy, and it seemed I never quite could. And then you and me..."

"It's not up to you to make the whole world happy, Care'lina. Even if you do a pretty good job of it." He lifted her chin and looked deep into her eyes.

And then he kissed her.

In a motion that was at first hesitant and the next instant ardent, her hands slipped around his neck. She pressed into him and returned his kiss, deeply, hotly.

They drew apart, each gasping for breath.

Just then Jackson's cell phone rang.

Carley Love stiffened and pushed away from him. In a frustrating motion, he drew his phone from his pocket.

"Hello?" His brow furrowed.

Carley Love stood watching him.

"Yeah...okay," he said with a heavy sigh. His gaze came up to meet hers as he spoke. "Yeah...I'm at home, so it'll be about a half hour. Yeah, okay, I understand. I'll take care of it. Don't worry about anything on this end, Gordon," he said, enunciating the name as he looked straight at her.

He clicked off and held the phone screen toward her. "It

was Gordon. I have to go and stand in for him. He's got a problem with his daughter." He pocketed his phone. "He's takin' her to the hospital—it's drugs—and there's a radar malfunction he's workin' on. I have to go."

"Bless their hearts," said Carley Love. "I understand. Go. Don't worry about anything here," she added with a gesture.

"I'll just speak to the foreman. I'll be back as soon as I can."

"I've got that dinner party tonight," she called after his retreating figure.

He cast a nod that he'd heard and disappeared into the bedroom.

She looked at the stack of boxes and items piled in the middle of the hallway and sighed. "Love of Life soap opera."

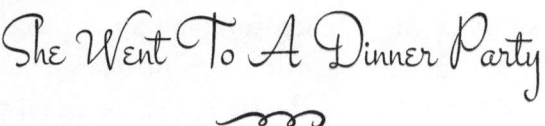

She Went To A Dinner Party

MID-AFTERNOON, with the autumn sun far to the west, she loaded the last box of supplies into the Escalade. The construction foreman's truck pulled to a stop beside her.

"We're done for today, Miz Wells. Everythin' is secure 'til we can return." He scratched his forehead, tipping back his ball cap. "Like I told your husband, I'm not sure 'xactly when that will be. We got a lot of jobs lined up after this storm. But we secured your place all nice and tight. A crew will be by sometime to pick up the debris we piled on the east side of the yard."

She thanked him, and he gave a nod and drove away.

She blew a strand of hair from her face and returned to the house, went to her bathroom, where she leisurely showered and made up her face. While choosing attire for the evening, she carried on a debate with herself and Ronni in her mind.

"I'm not wearin' this one, Ronni," she said, holding the dress with the off the shoulder neckline that she had worn to Trey's open house.

She surveyed three more outfits, muttering, "Probably not jeans. Okay—this one will do well." She chose a burgundy turtleneck cashmere sweater and matching straight sweater skirt, murmuring, "Shapewear required."

She stood at the kitchen sink and ate a piece of toast with jelly and downed a half a cup of black tea. "Well, I rather wish I could break this date, too," she said to Freckles, who stared up, waiting for the last bite of toast. "How did I get myself into this?

"Oh, yes, it was Doreen who got me into it."

With a thoughtful sigh, she murmured, "Carley Love, honey, don't blame your life on someone else. If you hadn't wanted to do it, you could have put your tongue in place and said no. You got carried away by flattery and excitement at the prospect of bein' a party planner."

She frowned in thought as she checked the contents of her small evening handbag for a lipstick. "I'll have to make a list of party services will do and won't do—and one of those might best be to stop havin' whole conversations with myself!"

Then, gazing into the cabinet mirror, she jutted her chin and said, "Girl, you are an intelligent woman to talk to."

She petted Freckles and headed out to the Escalade. As she eased it along the drive, the sun was a bright yellow glow low in the western sky. She turned onto the highway and the glow was behind her, with the autumn sky turning dark velvet ahead of her.

THIRTY MINUTES LATER, Carley Love pulled the Escalade to a stop at a driveway marked by two tall, white brick pillars and a black iron gate that stood open. The very last rays of the setting sun washed it all with a golden glaze.

There was no name, just numbers on one of the pillars. She checked the address with the one written in her notes, turned the wheel, and headed slowly along the ribbon of blacktop that wound up a hill through a meadow and into piney woods. Rounding a wooded corner, she saw a low-sloping, modern-style home, white brick and lots of glass.

She followed the driveway to the rear of the house and parked beside a sporty Toyota and an aging Oldsmobile. She alighted and walked to the glass-paned door and pressed the doorbell to the side of the doorframe. She tilted her ear. Faint opera music floated out.

The door swung open and a slim young man in white shirt and dark slacks stood there. The opera music played behind him—with someone singing along.

The young man took her in with a swift glance and smiled.

She returned the smile, saying, "I'm Carley Love Wells. I'm supposed to..."

"Oh, yes!" A much larger, older man shouldered the younger out of the way. "Miz Simmons called to tell me you were coming. I am Chef Anton...and this is Timon, my assistant. Welcome to my kitchen. Your flowers arrived an hour ago."

The chef was about Carley Love's age, a jovial, good-looking, rotund man, with a baritone voice as rich as that of the singer's coming from the stereo. He indicated the flowers in buckets atop a long stainless steel counter, and then gave a sweeping gesture of his arm. "You may have this much workspace. Don't come any closer to *my* workspace."

"How wonderful of you to share!" She flashed a wide smile. "I promise to take up the least room."

The chef responded with a beautiful and toothy grin of his own and directed the younger man to help her carry in her supplies. That done, the young man showed her the rooms beyond the swinging kitchen door.

She stood blinking in the dining room, taking in the long glass table edged by dark leather chairs and the long dark lacquered buffet against the one white wall. Beyond the dining room, through wide sliding glass doors, stretched a swimming pool. The fading coral rays of the day glinted on the glass and bathed the azure water.

"My goodness," Carley Love said.

"Yes," was the young man's amused response.

She swiftly surveyed the wide hallway and the living areas, all shiny tile and ivory walls and glass, with more dark lacquer pieces and dark leather furniture and a few scattered pieces of abstract art, mostly monochrome, and black and white photographs.

She turned to Timon. "Would you happen to be able to lend me a ladder?"

"Yes, ma'am."

CARLEY LOVE STOOD with her hands on a chair back and looked around with a satisfied expression at what she had accomplished.

Beyond the windows, dark had fallen, enclosing the dining room and swimming pool area. Criss-crossed strings of warm-toned lights glowed above the dining table. China and crystal glimmered below. Goblets of fairy lights buried in blue glass marbles glowed on the table, and more lit goblets were generously scattered throughout the rooms.

Pulling both her cell phone and a small camera from her purse, she took careful close-up photographs of place settings and table decorations. She made adjustments to the two tall, fall-colored bouquets on the long buffet and took two large blue dishes of fragrant white gardenia blossoms to place in the living room. She found the dimming switch and adjusted overhead lights and lamps.

Timon came bearing a rolling tray of hors d'oeuvres. He gestured to one of the plates. "Is this how you wanted the fruit, Miss Carley?"

"Yes...perfect! It looks lovely. Let's set the cart over here, and I'll set a couple of plates on the coffee table."

After arranging the food and dishes, Carley Love surveyed the room once again and glanced in the direction of the dining room.

"I think we're all ready. I'll wait and light the candles at the last minute."

"It looks very nice." Timon inclined his head to indicate the room. "Mr. E.H. likes to have people in when he's here, but none of his parties have ever been decked out like this. 'Course, I don't know what he does at his other places."

"Does he have more than one home?" she asked, then bit her bottom lip.

"Yeah...he's got an apartment up in D.C. and a condo down at Boca Raton." He spoke as he opened the double doors of one of the dark cabinets. Lights within came on, revealing it as liquor storage, with glass and mirror backing gleaming. He pulled out a tray of drinking glasses and set out bottles of liquor. "I'll get the ice."

After considering the bottles of the cabinet a moment,

Carley Love retrieved one of the goblets from the dining room and placed it atop the cabinet where its blue-glowing lights reflected in the finish.

Chef Anton appeared and glanced around. "Very nice... elegant. Mr. E.H. will like...maybe. He doesn't usually get this fancy." A grin lit his face, "I made his favorite tonight, though, beef tenderloin, with cognac butter."

"The aroma is heavenly," she told him.

He smiled widely and retreated to the kitchen, singing with his opera as he went.

Timon, who had come out with the ice in time to hear the chef's comments, said, "Oh, Mr. E.H. is goin' to like what he sees." In long strides he reached the liquor cabinet and set the ice chest in place. He cast her a pointed look, saying, "He'll like it very much," and hurried back through the swinging kitchen door.

Carley Love took a deep breath, walked to the liquor cabinet and gazed thoughtfully at the array of labels— vodka, tequila, bourbon, white rum. Turning, she strode to the kitchen and pushed open the door. "Mr. Anton, may I make a pitcher of sweet tea? We want to offer our guests every option."

The chef gazed at her a moment, then waved her away, saying, "For you, pretty lady. I want you to have what you want. I make excellent tea."

"Carley?"

It was E.H.'s voice. She returned through the kitchen door and met him.

He grinned broadly on sight of her. "I'm sorry to be late." He came toward her, reached to take her hand, and bent to kiss her cheek. He drew back to look at her with admiring eyes. "You are absolutely beautiful. It's very nice, indeed, to come home to see you."

Her gaze met his and skittered away. "Well, thank you." She turned toward the nearby dining room. "I hope what I've done to your house meets with your approval."

He glanced quickly around, nodding. "It does...it is perfect. I think we're in for a pleasurable evenin'." His dark gaze returned to her.

Carley Love smiled shyly, but glanced away.

"Timon!" He called.

The young man came on a trot through the kitchen door and caught the keys his boss tossed to him.

"And tell Anton to shut off that opera." Turning to her, he said, "Carley, darlin', get us some of the good stuff goin' on the stereo. I'll be just a few minutes changing." He hurried away down the hall leading to the other side of the house.

With an expression both hesitant and determined, Carley Love approached the stereo system on the wall shelf. She studied the receiver a moment, then hurried to retrieve her reading glasses from her purse in the dining room. As she did so, she saw a text alert from Jackson. She read: *I know you have changed in these past months. I have changed a whole lot, too. I know what is important in my life. My commitment to you and my family are.*

She slowly replaced the phone into her purse, her lips forming a trembling smile.

Reading glasses perched on her nose, she navigated the stereo, finding a programmed playlist. She tapped the button and Rod Stewart's voice began singing, "Forever young." She hummed as she lit candles.

The doorbell rang. She glanced at the shadowed hallway

to the bedrooms. Setting aside the long-necked lighter, she went to the door. Just before answering, she snatched off her eyeglasses and slipped them behind a nearby table lamp.

A beautiful couple stood on the other side of the door, bathed in the glow of the overhead porch light.

Recognition dawned on Carley Love's face at the same moment as the woman's.

"You?" The woman breezed inside. "Car-ley, right? We met a few weeks ago. You were with Trey...a dinner date."

"Yes. And you are...Karin. Hello, again," Carley Love replied, using her most cordial Southern woman voice and smile. "Welcome. May I take your coat?"

Ignoring Carley Love's outstretched hand, the woman turned and glanced around. "Where's Trey?"

"I'm sorry, he's not here. Please help yourself to hors d'oeuvres. E.H. will be out in a few minutes." Carley Love included the woman's companion in her welcoming smile.

The woman focused a speculative eye on her, saying, "Huh...I know where E.H.'s room is. I'll just pop in to see him," and sashayed away down the hallway, leaving both her date and Carley Love staring after her retreating long legs beneath her short coat.

"Well," Carley Love turned to the woman's companion, a tall, dark, and quite young Adonis, "we've plenty to drink and eat while you wait. Please help yourself."

He regarded her with a mischievous smile and flirty black eyes. He said, "So you know Karin."

"We've met." She extended her hand for a shake. "I'm Carley."

"I gathered," he said, taking her hand, "I'm Gregory... and I'm happy to meet you, Carley." He held on to her hand.

The doorbell rang.

She extricated her hand from his and turned to the door.

Two more of the guests were familiar to her. One was an executive of an oil company and his girlfriend, both of whom she had met at Trey's open house. The man did not reintroduce himself, but his girlfriend, a young beach-type with a friendly manner, said, "I remember you! I'm Brittney."

"I remember you, too, darlin' girl. Very nice to see you, Brittney. Would you like an appetizer or drink?"

"Umm...just a Coke." The younger woman's eyes flitted to her date, who had gone instantly to the drink cabinet.

Carley Love looked over the shelves of the cart Timon had brought. "I don't see any Coke, but we have sweet tea and it looks like Chef Anton made a warm spiced punch. Would you like to try it?"

Brittney nodded, while her gaze again went to her date.

Carley Love handed the young woman a glass mug of amber liquid just as the doorbell rang again. She looked toward the hallway to the bedrooms and saw it still empty. She answered the door, took coats, and hung them in the nearby closet.

Just as she closed the closet door, E.H.'s voice drew her attention. He had come into the room and stood with his arm around Karin's waist, while she hung onto his shoulder, minus her coat, and with one strap of her scanty top slipped off her shoulder.

Greetings were exchanged, along with comments about how great the house looked for the dinner party. "You went all out this time, E.H. What's the occasion?"

He broke away from Karin and came to Carley Love, saying, "This is all Carley's doin'."

He slid his hand to her waist and pulled her close. She smiled at the guests, her gaze touching an instant on Karin's face, and back to E.H., as she eased out of his embrace and offered refreshments.

∾

MALE VOICES ROSE EXCITEDLY at the far end of the dining table. It was the oil executive and another man arguing. Brittney and the other man's date calmed them.

Carley Love looked down the table, her eyes touching on the empty plates and glasses.

"I think it's time for a smoke," said Karin, who cast an odd smile in Carley Love's direction. "I have extra. Anyone want to join me?"

"I'll take one of those." A large, muscular young man rose and stretched his arm across the table.

"I'll get coffee," Carley Love said and pushed from the table.

E.H. rose with her, saying in his low tone, "Good idea, darlin'. Let's have coffee in the livin' room."

He reached her in a long stride and pressed his hand to the small of her back.

She broke away and headed to the kitchen, pushing through the door and calling, "Chef Anton..."

Her voice trailed off as she saw him near the back door slipping into a jacket. "Are you going? I thought...well, I... came for after-dinner coffee."

He nodded and gestured toward a rolling cart, a coffee

urn and tray of mugs sitting atop it. "It's ready. We are done for the evening."

"Oh."

"Mr. E.H. never has us stay." His dark eyes met hers briefly, shifted downward, and he turned to the door. "Goodnight."

"Goodnight." She watched the door close with a click and stared at it for several seconds.

Taking a deep breath, she went to the rolling tray and pushed it ahead of her through the door and out into the wide hall. She saw Karin and the two men at the table in the dining room. Karin was leaning into one of the men. He was not her date Gregory. A haze of smoke swirled around them, and it was as if it snaked out to her in the hall.

She rolled the cart into the living room and served coffee to E.H. and Brittney and another of the women guests, who sat across from E.H. and displayed her ample breasts his way, while her date did his best to impress the older man with his knowledge of yachts.

The oil executive and young man continued their drinking and arguing in the corner.

E.H. took Carley Love by the wrist and tugged her gently to sit on the wide arm of his big chair. His arm came around her hips, while he kept his attention on his guests.

She sat with a fixed pleasant expression on her face. Van Morrison's voice sang out about it being a marvelous night for a moondance.

Her eyes shifted sideways, and she tentatively looked downward, to E.H.'s thumb drawing circles on her thigh. Facing forward, she stared at the flickering candle flame on the nearby table.

The next instant, she jumped to her feet in a manner

that caused her to slosh her coffee. "Excuse me," she said, set the cup and saucer on the coffee table and headed around the chair in the direction of the guest restroom at the beginning of the hallway.

Just then the Adonis, Gregory, and one of the women guests appeared, coming from the direction of the bedrooms arm in arm. Gregory grinned at Carley Love and arched a questioning eyebrow.

She ducked into the restroom and closed the door.

Taking a deep breath, she gazed at her image in the mirror. "So, here you are," she whispered to her reflection. She inhaled deeply and blew out the breath and rolled her eyes skyward. "Dear heart, you have led a sheltered life."

Closing her eyes, she pinched the bridge of her nose for long seconds. Putting both hands on the vanity, she leaned close to the mirror, looking deep into her eyes. She shook her head, bit her bottom lip and again closed her eyes for long seconds, her lips moving with silent words.

Opening her eyes, she shook back her hair and straightened her shoulders.

As she emerged from the restroom, a sound brought her head turning toward a door across the hallway.

The door stood ajar. Faint sounds came from the space, several loud thumps, and a harsh female voice, "I can't!"

Carley Love took a step toward the door, but stopped at the sound of the same tone saying urgently, "Hurry!"

Her eyes widened and she pivoted, returning to the living room with quick steps. "Would anyone like more coffee?" she asked and began cleaning up scattered cups and glasses.

E.H. stretched his arm and took her wrist. "Leave it... Timon will take care of it tomorrow."

"It's part of my job," she said quietly. "And I'm about ready to leave."

She rolled the coffee tray in the direction of the kitchen and left it in the wide hallway, stepping into the now empty dining room. She blew out the candles, pausing to peer closely at the ashes and bits of leavings from the smokes left on a plate. She sniffed with curiosity, wrinkling her nose.

Just then raised voices sounded from the pool area. She saw Brittney and her oil executive at the far end of the pool. The big man pointed his finger at the young woman, who shook her head. He grabbed her arm.

Carley Love frowned and took a hesitant step in the couple's direction. At that moment strong arms came around her waist from behind. Her head jerked around to see it was E.H.

"You don't have to go." He murmured in her ear. She pushed to move out of his arms. He caught her, took her face in his hands, and brought his lips to hers.

Carley Love pushed at his chest. He resisted, then quite suddenly let her go.

"Look, I don't know where you got the idea that I might...but I am not...I'm..." She swallowed and spoke more clearly. "I'm not available for anything beyond organizing and hosting a party. I'm sorry if I gave you any other impression."

He smiled indulgently. "Maybe I could change your mind." He put his hand on the back her head and went to kiss her again.

"No." She avoided his lips.

His response was a cocked eyebrow and bland smile. "Can't blame a guy for tryin'."

"Actually, I can, and I do," she stated. "You are old

enough to know better than this." She gestured with a wave of her arm.

His eyes narrowed. Before he could respond, Brittney's high-pitched, young voice drew their attention.

"No! I won't!"

And she shoved the big man from her and turned toward the dining room, while behind her the man wobbled and fell sideways into the pool, with a loud splash.

"Oh!" Carley Love looked at E.H. "Get him! He might drown!"

"Not deep enough," E.H. responded calmly, yet strode around her toward the pool.

The young Brittney came directly to crumple onto Carley Love's shoulder, sobbing with incomprehensible mumblings. Carley Love, momentarily surprised, put her arms around the woman and made soothing sounds.

Two of the other male guests came from the living room and hurried to the pool area. Carley Love glanced at them, then looked Brittney in the face.

"I'm leaving. Do you want to come with me?"

"Yes, please," the younger woman answered in a hoarse whisper.

Brittney followed Carley Love as if connected by a string. The two women retrieved their purses and made their way to the kitchen, through it, and out the door into the night. They threw themselves into the Escalade. Carley Love was backing the truck even as she strapped the seatbelt. Turning the steering wheel, she headed away from the lights of the house at a fast pace and into deep darkness.

She slowed as she entered the wooded area. The headlights shone on the blacktopped driveway. Beside her, Brittney sniffed and said in a small voice, "Thank you."

"No problem, dear." Carley Love shot her an encouraging smile.

After a moment, the young woman said, "My apartment...it belongs to Tommy."

"Ah, well, you can come home with me tonight, if you would like."

The young woman nodded.

They drove through the dark meadow toward the gate, which was well lit by tall pole lights. The gate was closed.

Carley Love braked. She and Brittney exchanged glances.

"There's a keypad." Brittney pointed.

Carley Love looked in the direction the younger woman indicated. A glowing keypad sat atop a short pole at the right side of the driveway. "Do you happen to know the combination?"

"No."

"Well, let's take a look." She shoved the gear shift into park and got out.

Brittney followed and both women looked over the numbered buttons.

"Maybe it's just the star key," Carley Love pressed it.

Nothing happened. She then tried the number sign. She sighed.

Brittney looked in the direction of the house. "I hope Tommy doesn't come after me."

Carley Love glanced at her, then tried the numbers one, two, three, four. The gates remained closed.

"We'll have to go back. You can stay in the car. I'll go in and have E.H. open the gates."

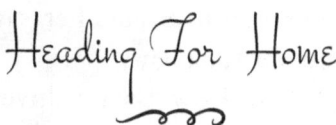

Heading For Home

THE SOUND of an approaching vehicle on the road outside the gates drew both women's attention. Carley Love stopped with her hand on the Escalade door handle.

A pickup truck pulled up on the far side of the iron gates.

Shielding her eyes against the glare of headlights, Carley Love saw the doors open on either side of the truck and two figures alight.

"Carle'Love?"

"Jackson?" She hurried toward the gate. "We don't know the code to open the gate." She saw a second tall figure step to the side. "Trey?"

"Yeah—I got it," Trey called, and seconds later the double gates began swinging open. The men slipped through it as soon as there was room enough.

"Oh, I'm so glad to see you," said Carley Love. "We couldn't figure out how to get out."

"Are you okay?" Jackson took her by the arms and searched her face.

"Yes...yes, I am fine. Just ready to go home." Relief echoed in her voice. She moved her gaze from Jackson to Trey, who had stepped close and whose intense gaze went from her to Brittney. Brittney's face crumpled with tears, and Carley Love put an arm around her, saying, "Brittney is comin' to our house for the night."

Jackson said, "Okay. How 'bout I drive your truck, and Trey can drive mine back?"

"I'll take Brittney with me." Trey reached for the young woman, and she went into the protection of his arm.

Jackson looked at Carley Love, took her hand and led the way to the softly rumbling Escalade and deposited her onto the passenger seat. He shut the door and rounded the hood to slip behind the wheel, instantly putting the vehicle into drive and heading off. Carley Love went right along in the manner of one who is glad to be directed. Neither of them said a word for sometime.

"How did you...what are you and Trey doing here?" Her tone echoed with curiosity, and she tilted her head as she peered at Jackson's profile, his face lit by the silvery glow of the dash lights. All around them was dark countryside.

"Uh, well, Trey and I ran into each other tonight at the Burger Barn." He raked a hand through his hair.

"Oh?" Her eyebrows rose.

"Yeah," Jackson gave a small grin. "We got to talkin', and while we were eatin', Doreen called me, said she couldn't get an answer from you. She said she must have E.H.'s number wrong, because she couldn't get an answer there, either. That's how we found out about you doin' the dinner party for him."

"She must have called after the last time I checked my phone." Carley Love retrieved her phone from her purse and looked at the screen.

"Well, anyway, when Trey heard you were at E.H.'s, he insisted we come out here."

"He did?"

Jackson nodded and shot her a glance. "He said one of E.H.'s parties wasn't *anywhere* you needed to be. He didn't even finish his burger," he added, casting her a questioning glance.

Carley Love breathed deeply. "He is correct." She looked out the windshield at Jackson's truck ahead of them, bathed in the Escalade's headlights.

"Oh, Jackson...I have led such a sheltered life." She chuckled wryly and gave a large sigh. "And you are not alone in foolish decisions."

His eyebrows knotted and his right hand came to lie on her thigh. "Honey, are you sure you are okay? What happened?"

"Oh, probably nothing to E.H. and his guests. But just imagine one of those scenes in the movies where everyone is drinkin' and smokin' pot and swappin' partners."

He shot her a glance and returned his attention out the windshield, while giving a chuckle and saying, "Well, I can imagine pretty well, because that goes on with some people I work with."

She looked at his profile and blinked. "I don't think I need to know," she said.

After a long moment, she said, "I'm fine. Really. And I think that I learned some very good lessons that I needed to learn about runnin' an event planning business...*and* runnin' my life." She nodded decisively. "I learned my limitations and my boundaries."

As she spoke the last, she slipped her hand into his and squeezed. "Thank you for comin' tonight. I appreciate it. I really do."

~

CARLEY LOVE SHOWED Brittney to the guest room and laid out towels for her in the guest bath.

"Everything you may need should be in this basket and there's a robe here on the back of the door. You have a hot shower, and I'll make you a cup of relaxing tea."

"Thank you."

Carley Love enveloped her in a hug. "You can stay here as long as you need to."

"I may need to." Brittney swept away tears and added in a small voice, "I'm not goin' to have a job now."

"You worked for him?"

"Uh-huh." Her gaze shifted to the side.

"Well, you are welcome here as long as necessary, and tomorrow I'll go with you to get your things from your apartment." She cast the young woman an encouraging smile.

Brittney attempted a brave smile and nodded. Then, "He wasn't always like this. I'm really not a complete fool. At first Tommy was so kind. I fell in love with him, and I let myself...get off track with him. And then, well, he got involved with some other people...some big deals. And that led to these people. He just changed." Her fingers came to her lips that trembled. "I never should have..." She broke into sobs.

Carley Love, tears in her own eyes, took the young woman again into her arms. "Bless your sweet heart," she whispered.

~

SHE CLOSED the guest room door and walked through the dimly lit rooms toward the kitchen. The two men's low voices reached her in the dining room.

"I might just punch him," Trey said, and Jackson responded, "An assault charge won't help, Mr. Lawyer."

She entered the kitchen as Trey's lips formed a rueful half grin.

The men, standing next to the counter, turned their heads to her.

"She's okay," she said in response to Trey's anxious expression. "She made a hard decision, but she knows it's right."

"Did she tell you what he wanted—that he wanted to use her to pay a debt?" Trey's jaw went tight.

"She didn't fully explain, but I knew it was bad."

Trey nodded. "Well, I'm done representin' him and his company. He's been askin' me to do stuff that I refused to do. It was only a matter of time before we parted ways." He broke off with a frustrated frown and looked from Jackson to Carley Love. "I have kept stringin' along with Tommy because I wanted to show my dad that I could keep the firm going higher and higher, and the money..." He paused, took a deep breath. "I let tryin' to please my dad and money blind me."

"I get that," Jackson said heavily.

"I think I'm goin' to have to break from my dad, too. Go on my own." His eyes staring downward, he spoke with a sad but firm tone. "We never have seen things the same."

His gaze met theirs. "Eric and I have already talked about it. He saw Tommy straight that first night, the night of the open house. He pegged him a slime-ball and said we could get into trouble with him."

Trey's eyes studied Carley Love. "If I would have known that you were goin' to Dad's tonight, I would have warned you. Did Lila know? I can't believe she didn't say somethin' to you. She knows...or I'm guessin' she knows about Dad's parties. She's known Dad a long time."

"Doreen is the only one who knew where I was. There just wasn't any reason to tell anyone, and so much was going on all around." She put a hand to her forehead.

"Doreen!" Jackson said. "I clean forgot to tell you that the reason Doreen was tryin' to get you was that she's worried about Lila. Somethin' about Norma Fay has quit and Lila is about to have a heart attack."

"Oh, good heavens!" Carley Love reached for her purse and her phone.

"Hold on." Jackson took her by the arm. "There's nothin' to be done at this hour. Doreen and Lila are likely both asleep. Tomorrow will be soon enough." He drew her close and kissed her forehead.

Carley Love let go a breath and relaxed against him.

Trey looked at them and then away. "I need to call it a night, too. Sorry, but I need a ride to pick up my car," he said to Jackson.

Trey kissed Carley Love's cheek as he bid her goodbye.

She hugged him hard. "Thank you...thank you for carin'."

"Tell Brittney I'll check with her tomorrow mornin'. I'll make sure Tommy doesn't bother her in any way," he said as he and Jackson went out the door.

She watched them, her eyes moving from one man's retreating back to the other, before she closed the door.

Lost in thought, she put the kettle on the stove and relaxed into the warm and pleasant atmosphere of kitchen.

"Thank you, Lord. Your tender mercies never end."

SHOWERED and wrapped in a thick robe, hair still wet, she sat curled on the end of the couch in the pool of light from the table lamp. Freckles edged up close to her hip, a fire flickered in the fireplace, and the journal lay open on her lap. She stared into the fire for long minutes as she sipped from the steaming mug. Finally, she sat the mug aside and began to write.

SUNDAY, November 19

12:45 a.m.

Well, what can I say about tonight?

I'm embarrassed, mortified, amazed, humbled and grateful beyond all measure for a million things.

As humbled and embarrassed as I feel, it does seem to me that tonight's experience gave me lessons I could learn no other way.

What did I learn?

That I have a lot to learn.

I think of Granny Reba saying that when we know we don't know everything we are still growing and there's hope.

I sure have limited experience. And I think I am pretty glad of that on a whole.

I sure do assume things that I have no business assuming. And my ego carries me away—is still carrying me away, as I feel this sort of stupid flattery at E.H.'s attention. Oh, Lord, help me.

So grateful that in this moment I know I am no surprise to God.

I've led a sheltered life, and a lot of that thanks to Jackson's protection and provision. God's design for my life.

Now that I have stood in my own shoes of foolish decisions, my heart melts with understanding for what it means to be human.

My heart goes out to E.H. He leads a lonely life, is so lost, and now the thread of relationship with his son is totally severed. But there's a kindness in E.H. It's there. Bless his heart. Help him, Lord.

Mama used to say that there was so much bad in the best of us and so much good in the worst of us. We are all so fallible. And we are all so magnificent.

Well, I did okay tonight, thanks be to God. I did my job, and I learned more of how I want to live. I managed to come through with my dignity intact, and it comes to me suddenly that likely I was there tonight in order to help Brittney.

And Jackson came to help me, as he has always done.

Oh, I was so glad to see him!

Oh, dear Lord, I do still love him.

Scares me, oh, heavens, I'm scared at trying again with him. I don't want to be crushed again.

But, I think, it isn't about trusting him, or trusting myself. It's about trusting You, Lord, isn't it? Trusting that you are always with me and guiding me.

∾

"JACKSON?" Her voice was groggy as she came up from sleep.

"Come on, honey. It's gettin' cold in here. Let's get you to bed." He moved the journal from her lap, dropped it to the floor, and slipped his hands beneath her.

"I've been waitin' for you," she murmured and buried her face in his neck.

He took a deep breath and lifted her, and she tightened her hold around his neck. He strode through the house to the bedroom, closing the door with his foot.

The bedside lamp burned, and the covers on her side were already turned down. With a small grunt, he bent to lay her on the bed.

"Jackson." She kept her arms holding around his neck, her face inches from his.

He looked into her eyes. "You are goin' t' break my back."

Her answer was to bring her lips to his in an eager kiss.

He lost his balance and fell atop her. She gasped and laughed, and he did, too. And then they were looking into each other's eyes.

Her gaze moved to his lips.

Slowly he lowered his head toward her, and she encircled his neck with her arms again, pulling his lips to hers.

Muddling Through

ROYCE CAME through the door into the sunny kitchen, calling, "Mama?"

The room was empty and silent.

Freckles appeared around the corner of the island, and he bent to pet her, saying, "Where is everyone, girl? Their trucks are out there." Then, voice raised, "Mom? Dad?" He glanced into the dining room and strode on into the family room.

Carley Love stirred in the bed, smiling in her sleep. She snuggled toward the heat of Jackson's body.

Suddenly her eyes sprang wide. Her gaze flew to the French doors, the sunlight pouring through the panes.

"Mama?"

At the sound of her son's voice, her head swung toward the door that was partially open.

"Jackson! Jackson, wake up!" She shook him.

"Huh? Wha'..." He opened his eyes, a dazed expression on his face.

"It's Royce!" She yanked the blankets high up to her

neck, snaked out her arm and attempted to cover Jackson completely, too, as he thwarted her efforts by shifting himself up on the pillows and attempted to come fully awake.

"Mama, you in..."

The door swung open and Royce loped through. He stopped and stared at them, his mouth falling open.

The next instant, Royce turned on his heels toward the door, saying, "Sorry." His lips twitched into a grin as he disappeared out the doorway.

Carley Love saw his grin. Fists gripping the blankets, she closed her eyes tight.

Royce's voice came from beyond the door, "Uh, Dad? I need to talk to you about somethin'."

"Sure, son," Jackson responded, his voice still echoing sleep. "Be right there, wait for me in the kitchen."

"Okay." The door closed with a click.

"Oh, my goodness." Carley Love grasped the covering of the blankets as Jackson threw himself out of bed.

"What's wrong?" Jackson asked, as he searched around for his clothes, picking them up where they were strewn on the floor.

Carley Love stared at his bare behind, and turned her head.

"We *are* still married, Carle'Love," Jackson said.

"I just don't want him to think..."

"Think what?" He slipped into his jeans.

She gazed at his firm chest. "That we're back together. I don't want him to get his hopes up."

Jackson regarded her and frowned. "Well, I would say we were pretty well together last night." With that he jerked on his shirt.

"Are we? It was extended drought and raging hormones last night." She fought the sheet to jerk it free from the bed.

"Really?" He left his shirt partially buttoned and snatched up a sock.

She bit her bottom lip and lowered her eyes. "It's just that we haven't settled things between us. We haven't talked about...any of it. I don't know where we're goin'...where you stand."

"Well, I'm standin' right here." He then sat on the edge of the bed to put on his socks.

After a moment, he said, "What do we need to talk about? We both want to get back together. Don't we?" He shot her a raised eyebrow over his shoulder.

"Yes. I do. But...well, I've wondered if you still did." She searched his face, then shifted focus to the sheet she finally succeeded in pulling free.

"I do," he stated. "I think I have showed that. I certainly did last night."

She pressed her lips together and then came out with, "Until the day you left I thought we were together. I thought..." She broke off and wrapped the sheet around her nakedness as she attempted to stand.

"I have seen you naked, Carle'Love."

She rolled her eyes, dropped the sheet and grabbed her robe from the floor, turning her back, saying, "I...I just don't want to get his hopes up, and we flub it all up again." She raked a hand through her hair and felt the floor for her slippers. "I just don't think I can go through a second time."

Jackson hopped on one foot as he tugged on a boot, got the second boot on and straightened to focus sharp eyes on her.

"It sounds to me like you are already expectin' us to break up before we even get started."

Her head came up, her gaze meeting his.

"Look, Care'lina, I don't need to feel like I'm already accused of somethin'."

She opened her mouth, then closed it firmly.

He turned and strode from the room, his boots hitting hard on the wood flooring.

She pivoted and entered the bathroom, grabbed her brush and attacked her hair. She stopped, peered at her image in the wide mirror, and leaned in to stare accusingly at herself.

SHE WATCHED from the living room window to see Jackson and Royce drive away in their respective trucks. Turning, she headed for the kitchen, stopping as she passed the couch to fold the blanket she had used the previous evening. She fluffed the throw pillows, finding a pen beneath one.

She stared at the couch for long seconds, then tossed and scattered the throw pillows she had just put into place, feeling along the cushions, her motions picking up tempo.

"Oh, where is it?"

She lifted the big cushions all along the back of the couch, looked on the floor front and back and beneath the end tables. She got on her knees to look beneath the couch, sticking her arm under and feeling in the darkness there.

"Lookin' for somethin'?" Brittney stood in the kitchen doorway, sleepy-eyed and yawning.

Carley Love, startled, came up with a jerk. "Uh, yes. A

book. I had it here last night." Bending again, she stretched her arm beneath the heavy couch, and brought out a dollar bill, looked at it and tossed it aside.

"Is that it under the footstool?" Brittney came into the room and bent to retrieve the item.

"Oh, yes! That's it." Carley Love reached to take it even before Brittney extended it. "Thank you!"

Holding the journal to her chest, she hurried away to her bedroom, opened the desk drawer and tucked it inside.

DOREEN CAME out the office door as Carley Love pulled the Escalade to a stop next to the younger woman's bright red Mustang.

"Hey, Carley-girl!" Doreen hailed her from the steps and bustled forward on her tall heels. "I'm headin' over to Sunday showin' of the beach house—Lila's havin' me handle it." Her grin spread wide and proud.

"Congratulations. I'm glad for you."

The younger woman came closer and spoke in a confidential tone, despite being in an open parking lot. "It looks like Norma Fay's betrayal is my good fortune."

"Betrayal?"

"Well, like I told you on the phone, Norma Fay says her sister needs her to help take care of her mama, but what I didn't tell you, because Lila was in the office and I didn't want her to hear, is that I'm fairly certain Norma Fay and her sister are goin' in together in real estate up there, and takin' some of our clients, too. You know that Henderson outfit that builds those malls? She's got him to change to Montgomery. I heard her talkin' a couple of times."

"Ah-huh. Lila sounded okay about all of it on the phone when I spoke with her."

"Well, she sure scared me late yesterday. I thought for sure she was havin' a heart attack. I mean, she put her hand to her chest and sank into a chair. That's why I was wantin' to find you. Then I overheard her on the phone to her doctor.

"Now this afternoon she says we'll close all this week for Thanksgiving and will be closed on Sundays for the winter. I've never known her to do that in all the three years I've been with her." Doreen focused curious eyes on Carley Love, who offered, "Well, there's not much business during the winter anyway."

"Yeah, that's true." The younger woman's expression changed from thoughtful to bright questioning. "So the dinner party went well last night...was E.H.'s house fantastic? Did you take pictures? Isn't there an indoor pool?"

"Yes, there's a pool. It's quite grand. I took pictures of the place settings and other decor items I made. But I did not take shots of his house. I think that's private." Her voice trailed off as she glanced toward the office building.

"So, do you think you might do another dinner party for him—or maybe for a guest from last night?"

"Uhm...no, I doubt I'll be doin' any more of those types of dinner parties."

"Really? Why not? You said it went well." Doreen's curious gaze turned sharp. "Did he pay you what was owed?"

Carley Love stepped aside. "I've decided I don't want to do private dinner parties. We'll talk more about it later. I need to get in and see what's what with Lila. She's expectin' me and we don't want to raise her blood pressure."

"Oh, and dear Lord, I can't be late!" The younger woman lifted her tote. "I made up brochures. I'm gettin' good on that computer!"

Wishing her well, Carley Love strode toward the office. At the top step, she focused momentarily on the closed sign hanging on the door, then opened the door and stepped into the vacant lobby, across it, and down the hallway.

Her boss's office door stood open. Lila, at the large desk, cast her a glance. "Hello, Carley. Sit down. Give me a minute." She returned her attention to making notations on the papers in front of her.

Carley Love sat and watched her boss across the wide desk until Lila laid aside her pen. The older woman retrieved her purse and dug into it, bringing out a medicine vial. She shook out a capsule, popped it into her mouth and took a drink from her tall mug.

Lila surveyed her. "Doreen tells me you decorated and hosted a dinner party for E.H. Cummings last night."

"Ah...yes."

"And how did that turn out?" The older woman fixed her with a speculative eye.

Carley Love said, "People ate and had a good time."

"Umm." Lila's lips curved into a small smile. She dug into her purse again and pulled out a packet of cigarettes. With a frown, she returned the packet to her purse, set the purse aside, and focused on Carley Love.

"You've probably been informed by Doreen about Norma Fay leaving us."

"She mentioned it."

"Yes, well, it's really no surprise. John Henderson called me a month ago. I told him to go ahead and no hard feelings. Norma Fay is entitled to do what she wants. And I'm doing just fine without his business. E.H. Cummings and I have entered into a partnership for a development project on property over off the beach expressway.

"And no doubt Doreen has also mentioned my heart acting up. That's all it is. Equally no doubt, Doreen has blown up the entire thing to make it sound like I'm about to keel over."

"More or less. She is truly caring."

Lila gave a nod. "Doreen is that. And I suppose it's to be expected of a woman of eighty to have something start wearing out."

Carley Love's eyes widened. "But at your last birthday we had balloons for seventy..."

Lila cast a dismissing wave, saying, "I know, I know. Turns out that I've lied about my age so much that I pretty much forgot the truth. I had to get out my birth certificate for legalities and am faced with the fact that you can fix up the outside all you want, but the inside is still your real age."

She leaned back in her tall chair and explained in her normal succinct fashion that she would be undergoing tests the following week, was instituting new office hours, and the open house party would be postponed until early spring.

To all of this Carley Love nodded.

Lila then sat forward. "I hope you can help me with a few things." The words came slowly, as if hard to bring forth.

Carley Love replied quickly, "Of course. I'll be glad to help."

Lila passed a paper of typed information across the desk. "I've named you my emergency contact and the executrix of my will, and drawn up a list of important information for you. Bank accounts and things."

Carley Love slowly took the paper and looked at it for long seconds, then raised a questioning gaze at Lila.

"Who else could I entrust with my life?" said the older woman. "My sister is my only relative, and she's a shyster. I can put her in my will but won't trust her with my life. You are the most trustworthy person I know, Carley—and besides, I fully expect to weather this storm. You're also hired as office manager earlier than I'd planned—starting tomorrow."

Long moments passed during which Carley Love gazed at the older woman, glanced at the paper of information, rubbed her forehead, and tapped the toes of her boots.

Lila frowned. "Well?"

Carley Love shifted and faced her boss squarely. "I'm appreciative that you have such a high opinion of me, Lila. I really am. And it is a privilege to help you with your personal affairs and durin' your medical procedures. That's totally familiar territory for me, after all," she added, with a rueful smile.

"But?" Lila's eyebrow arched.

"But...as for steppin' right into the office manager job, I'm going to have to decline. I've changed my mind and realize I can't be takin' on an immediate job."

It was the old woman's turn to stare with wide eyes.

DIRECTING the Escalade down the driveway toward her house, her eyes searched forward and her body tensed. Spying Trey's Lexus in the parking area at the walkway, she tilted her head. She drove past it and into the garage, alighted from the driver's seat, and retrieved grocery sacks from the back seat.

The kitchen door opened at her approach, and Freckles shot out, followed by Trey coming in long strides, saying, "Here, let me help," and reaching to take the sacks.

"Thank you."

"Brittney used your key. Your dog wasn't too sure about me but apparently adores her," he said in a wry tone.

"I've noticed," she replied shooting him a smile. "Brittney is pretty adorable."

Their eyes, filled with silent questions and answers, held until Brittney's sweet voice drew them apart.

"Oh, I'm so glad you came before we left!" Smiling brightly, she came into the room waving a piece of paper. "I was writin' you a message, but now I can tell you in person. I'm goin' to share an apartment with a girlfriend, and Trey will help me get my things and move them there. He's fixed it with Tommy...so Tommy won't bother me." She beamed at Trey.

"I can't thank you anywhere near enough for all your help. And, well, lettin' me stay, and in such comfort. You know, Miss Carley Love, you are comfort itself," she said as she rounded the counter to envelop Carley Love in a heartfelt hug.

Ten minutes later Carley Love waved good-bye from the porch and called, "Now, don't forget about comin' for Thanksgiving dinner."

Trey waved and Brittney blew her kisses.

Returning to the kitchen, she closed the door, and glanced around the room. "Well," she said to Freckles, who swished her tail.

She checked her phone, hesitated long seconds, then typed in a text to Jackson: "I'm home."

As she put away the groceries and tidied the counter, she kept listening for the ping of an answering text.

When the phone rang, she snatched it from the counter, not even checking the screen.

"Hello?" Her voice was expectant.

"Hey, Mama."

"Hi, sweetheart." She breathed deeply. "What's up?"

"I bought a Chevy Suburban today. That was what I needed Dad for, to take a look at it with me." There was laughter in his voice.

Pink tinged her cheeks as she responded, "Ah-huh."

"It's four years old but with really low mileage and great condition. Simona and I are gonna need a family vehicle now, you know."

"Oh, yes. Sounds practical. Are you gettin' rid of your big Smog-Hog then?"

"Oh, no! We'll sell Simona's BMW."

"Ah-huh." She chuckled silently.

"I got the Suburban as a surprise for her. I want to put a big bow on it. Can you make one for me?"

"Yes, of course. I think I have some ribbon on hand that will do."

"Can I get it tonight?" he asked in a hesitant voice. "Simona's comin' back from Atlanta tomorrow."

"Yes, I'll have it for you this evenin'."

"Thanks, Mama!"

She clicked off from the call, murmuring, "I hope Simona likes such surprises and decisions made for her."

Half an hour later, with the sun setting and leaving long shadows, she was in sweat pants and shirt and big fuzzy slippers, hair piled on her head. She sat at the dining table that was littered with rolls of ribbon. She had chosen extra wide glittery silver and gold that she massaged and twisted, forming a giant bow.

At the sound of a text coming on her phone, she jumped. Her hands searched beneath masses of stiff ribbon, located her phone.

Jackson had texted: *I'm working late, but I will be home tonight.*

She stared at the green text letters and bit her bottom lip, her toes wiggling in the fuzzy slippers for a long moment. Then she keyed in *OK,* and hit the send button.

Fifteen minutes later, finished with her sparkling creation, she repacked her bow-making supplies into their cartons, and replaced them into the guest room closet. On her return to the dining room, she stopped at her mother's bedroom, opened the door, turned on the light and looked around at the emptiness. She walked fully into the room and gazed up at the currently patched mess of the ceiling.

"Oh, Mama, this ol' world just keeps on goin' round."

Returning to the kitchen, she fed Freckles, made a sandwich, and ate it at the desk in the alcove, where she worked at the computer and jotted in a notebook.

The long white envelope tucked into the cubby of the desk caught her eye. Hesitantly stretching her hand, she pulled it out and extracted the divorce decree papers inside.

In the yellow glow from the desk lamp, she scanned the typed words. She lifted her gaze and stared at nothing for some minutes. Refolding the papers, she tucked them back into the envelope, opened the top drawer of the desk and slipped the envelope inside, closing the drawer with a hard shove.

She washed her dishes and through the window saw the arrival of a vehicle. A Suburban, faintly cranberry beneath the pole light. Royce alighted from the driver's seat.

She gathered the generous bow and trailing ribbons that she had created and met her son on the walkway.

"Thank you, Mama!" He bent and kissed her cheek.

She smiled broadly. "You're welcome, sweetheart."

She properly admired the vehicle he had bought for his love, assured him that Simona would like it, and then stood watching him drive away until the tail lights were swallowed up by the darkness of the road.

Lingering in the driveway, she turned her eyes upward toward the star-studded velvet sky. She smiled and whispered, "Until we meet in heaven, Mama."

Once more in the house, she made a cup of tea and carried it into the living room, where she started a fire in the fireplace. When it blazed high, she went to her bedroom and returned with her arms full of a pillow, quilt, and journal, and settled on the couch. Freckles jumped up and curled beside her.

~

SUNDAY, November 19

10:15 p.m.

One really never knows what's going to happen in this old world. We only think we do. We probably have to convince ourselves of this in order to stand it. One never knows exactly what one will do, either. We only think we do. That's how we get through.

I made wonderful love with my husband, and then somehow got into a spat with him. I did not intend to do that, don't even fully understand how it happened. And I turned down a full-time job offer from Lila, the one thing I thought only a few days ago that I wanted, and now know for certain is not something I want to take on at this time. I need to pay attention to myself, my life, and my marriage and family.

Lila's expression at my decision was too funny—wish I'd captured it on camera. I suppose turning down her offer was the first time since knowing her that I have said no.

I have always waffled about decisions. Mama said this was because we Love women could see and sympathize with all sides of a situation.

Let me say, though, that when I know in my heart, I *know*. It is as if God shouts.

Right now I know with certainty that I need time and freedom to process all that has gone on in my life. I'm willing to give myself that now. I need to focus on myself and what is right for me going forward.

Jackson is still not home.

He texted that he will be home. He has never said he would do something and not done it—if you don't count our wedding vows.

Well, who hasn't stumbled over those wedding vows?

To have and to hold, to love and to cherish, as long as you both shall live.

Boy, that's a tall order when you look at reality. I don't think I'm alone in standing at the altar with stars and rainbows of romantic love in my eyes. Happily ever after. Quite probably if we knew the day-to-day enormity of what it means to commit to living with another person until death, then no one would ever get married.

I fell down a number of times with the weight of it. I

see that fact so clearly now. The betrayal is in tiny ways. Whenever I got tired and worn with everything and thought maybe I wanted to find someone else. Whenever I believed that I had a right to my anger, or even, truth be known, thought vengeance in tiny, cutting ways, such as turning a cold shoulder to him, complaining of him supposedly in jest, but it really was not. Simply ignoring him.

It is foolish not to take into account the fallibility of human beings, the needs, weaknesses and hurts that we don't even know but that cause us to stumble in ways we wish we would not.

And yet, despite all that has gone on with Jackson and me, last night was the best it has ever been.

Oh, my word, desire comes now with the memory. It sweeps up and makes my heart beat and brings tears, and a smile, and hopeful longing.

That is the preciousness of great love between a man and a woman. That is why we so seek and prize that sort of love.

And let me admit here the amazing fact that there's a lot to be said for sex in the mature years. You know what you are about. And after so many years together, we know each other's bodies. I had not forgotten and neither had he. Oh, how good his skin smells, musky and sweet at the same time. The scent and smoothness of his shoulders, the silkiness of his hair beneath my fingertips. How beautiful, with him.

I've known no other man. A great gift I have been given and have never before realized.

And not once last night did I think of him with that woman. My mind, body, and soul were taken up with loving him and being loved.

But now he has gone off again and not home yet, and the thought of *her* plagues the ragged edges of my mind.

This morning our spat came from our fears. *My* fears started first, and activated Jackson's.

Are all arguments from that, the fear within ourselves?

What would life be like if we humans answered everything with faith?

Well, good luck with that, is what I say. I am not a saint, just an ordinary woman.

I think the basic struggle for my whole life has been that the nature of life on earth is uncertainty. And *my* particular human nature is to crave certainty.

To that I think I hear God whisper: That's why you have Me.

JACKSON STEPPED through the back door just as the mantle clock gently chimed midnight. With exhausted motions, he removed his coat, hung it on the back of a chair, went to the arch of the living room, and saw Carley Love lying on the sofa in the low glow of the table lamp. Freckles, curled at her feet, thumped her tail but did not move. The fire in the fireplace flickered low.

He moved to the refrigerator and looked inside for long seconds, before closing the door. He emptied the contents of his pockets onto the kitchen counter and walked quietly into the living room. With only faint sounds, he crouched and put logs onto the fire and poked them into a blaze.

Crossing to the couch, he gazed down at Carley Love. His hand hovered over her hair, then he withdrew it and shifted to turn out the lamp. The toe of his boot touched something on the floor. He saw a book opened wide.

He bent to pick it up, and in the process, his gaze fell to the open pages, upon the handwriting in blue ink.

The next instant he snapped the book closed and laid it on the end table. He gazed at the cover, bent to peer at the photograph. Switching off the lamp, he crossed the few feet to his recliner, tugged off his boots and stretched himself. He fell instantly asleep.

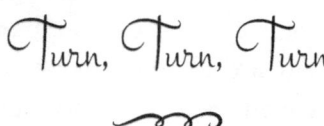

Turn, Turn, Turn

WHEN CARLEY LOVE AWOKE, the window showed faint grey morning. She saw Jackson stretched in the shadows in his chair. Her sleepy eyes rested on him for long minutes.

Freckles pushed against her, and she stroked the dog's head. When she slipped from beneath the quilt, the pen she had been using went flying to the middle of the floor. She retrieved it and spied the journal on the end table. She studied it a long moment, before taking it up and carrying it into the kitchen, to the old desk in the nook.

She let the dog out and made coffee, setting two mugs beside the coffee pot.

She had bacon sizzling and was making biscuits when a ringing phone caused her to jump. She saw Jackson's cell phone on the counter in the midst of dollar bills and change and large ring of keys.

It rang again.

She stepped over and peered at the screen. No name, only a number. She cast the phone a glare, left it to ring, and stepped away to the counter and the business of dumping the biscuit dough onto a floured board. She sighed when the ringing ended.

A minute later, as she pushed the biscuit cutter into the dough, the phone rang again, the sound jarring her hand.

Again she looked at the screen. Same number.

She quickly wiped her hands on a dish cloth and answered.

"This is Jackson's phone. Can I help you?"

There was a space of silence, followed by the line going dead.

"Huh, to you, too." She set the phone to the counter and returned to finish the biscuits.

Just as she popped the iron pan in the oven, the phone rang again, causing her eyes to pop wide.

"Oh, for heavens..." She snatched up the phone and noted the same number. "Hello."

A woman's voice said, "May I speak to Jackson."

Carley Love's answer came instantly. "No, ma'am. He's sleepin' and I'm not wakin' him. Don't call again."

She punched the button ending the call and dropped the phone to the counter.

"Well, Lord?" she murmured. She poured a cup of coffee, and murmured the words in an insistent question again, "Well, Lord?"

Cradling the mug in both hands, she stood gazing out the kitchen window at the golden light beginning to glow on the tops of the trees edging the pasture.

"Smells delicious."

Jackson's voice brought her turning around to see him standing on the other side of the island, scratching his head in a sleepy manner.

With a hint of a smile, he cast her a wink.

A smile twitched her lips, but she averted her eyes to the stove and busied herself with lifting bacon from the pan. "Get your coffee. Do you want eggs?"

"Yes, ma'am...I'd appreciate some," was his reply, his brows knotting with perplexity as he watched her for a moment.

He stepped to the counter, filled the cup that was set out for him with coffee and stood holding it, watching her. She did not look at him.

He stepped beside her and took the pan from her hand. "How 'bout I make the eggs?"

She hesitated, then released the pan to him, took her cup of coffee to the table, sat, and watched him.

Her attention lit on his left hand holding his coffee mug, on the wedding ring she saw there.

"You had a phone call this mornin'," she said.

He shot her a questioning glance.

She said, "I answered."

"Okay. Who was it?" His attention was on breaking an egg into the pan.

"*She* didn't give her name and I didn't ask. I told her I wasn't wakin' you."

"Thank you." His gaze met hers for long seconds.

Silence stretched. He cooked and she finished her coffee.

He brought her a plate with two fried eggs.

"Thank *you*," she said.

"You're welcome."

Minutes later, he brought his own plate of eggs to the table. They sat across from each other, with the first rays of sunlight now falling through the windows and giving a golden wash to the blue plates of eggs and bacon and biscuits, jars of honey and jam, silverware and dark coffee.

Carley Love buttered half a biscuit and lifted it to her lips, paused and said, "Do you have a problem with me answerin' your phone?"

"No. I don't." He forked a heavily honeyed piece of biscuit into his mouth and looked at her as he chewed.

She said, "I don't have a problem with you answerin' mine."

"Okay."

"Did you read my journal?"

"No, I did not," was his instant reply. "I found it on the floor and picked it up."

"Good, 'cause I would have a problem with that."

"Noted," he replied and cut into his eggs.

Jackson complimented the biscuits and bacon, and Carley Love complimented the eggs. Silence stretched again.

Jackson rose to retrieve the coffee pot, returned to fill her cup and then his, and sat back down.

Feeling his eyes on her, she looked up to meet his gaze.

He said, "I have not seen her again. I will not. And I'm takin' steps to make changes." He seemed about to say more but did not.

"Okay," she said.

Silence stretched again. Jackson sat back in his chair. Carley Love replaced the lids onto the jars of honey and jam.

Jackson said, "I'll have to put in longer hours the first of this week, but come Wednesday I'll be here. The construction crew called me yesterday, said they could start work on the house on Wednesday, unless you want them to wait until after Thanksgiving and the weddin'?"

"Wednesday is fine. I don't want to take a chance on it being weeks and weeks to get next in line. And why not one more thing to add to the mix?"

They exchanged wry smiles.

Again silence fell as they drank their coffee.

"Yesterday..." said Carley Love, and "I have..." said Jackson, both speaking at once.

They each stopped.

"You go ahead," said Jackson.

"Well...yesterday Lila offered me the job of office manager startin' right away." She paused for his reaction.

"And?" He glanced at her then averted his gaze to his plate.

"I turned her down. I know I may not get another chance, but the time is just not right for me to commit to it. After all the intense months with Mama, I need rest and time for figuring out my life. I did agree to keep helping her part-time."

He nodded slowly.

"We're winding up some things today and then closin' the offices the entire week. Lila is havin' heart issues, and I've agreed to help her with doctor appointments and things."

"Serious?"

"Serious enough to warrant testing next week. She's downplayin' it, but she has named me her emergency contact and made me the executrix of her will, and even gave me access to her accounts."

"Another old woman to take care of," Jackson said. "You're good at it."

"Well, I don't want to do it for a livin'," she replied, and slowly her grin answered his.

She watched his hand mop his plate with a piece of biscuit and pop it into his mouth, watched him wipe both hands with the checkered napkin, and saw his wedding ring catch the light as he said slowly, "I've been thinkin' to give Royce and Simona a wedding present of the money that came from Dad." He raised an eyebrow to her.

Carley Love opened her mouth, closed it, and reached for her coffee. "I thought we were savin' that for when he has an emergency."

"Getting' married and a baby on the way seems sort of an emergency," he offered.

"It's all normal livin'. An emergency is when he's down to his last dollar."

"Let's let him have it. They can make a good down payment on a house, like Dad did for us."

"Okay," she replied slowly and with a smile of memory. "But don't tell them what to do with it. That's not a gift when you tell them what to do with it."

"Yes, ma'am." He said with a teasing tone. "But they might need guidance," he added seriously.

"As you have said to me, Royce is a grown man. But maybe just save some back, in case they might need it in the future. You never know what is comin'."

He looked at her. She was focused on gathering dirty dishes. She rose and took them to the sink.

He followed, bringing his dishes. "I have to get showered and shove off to work, if I'm goin' to get everything done by Wednesday."

He opened the back door.

"Jackson."

He paused, looked at her.

She turned off the water faucet and grabbed a towel, drying her hands, leaned her hip against the counter. "Why don't you get your things from the garage apartment and use our shower? I imagine our bathroom is a lot more comfortable than that postage stamp one up there."

He searched her face, a tentative smile growing on his lips. "Yes, ma'am, it sure is. I don't know what I was thinkin' when I put that tiny shower in the apartment. Can't hardly turn around in it."

He sprinted out the door, and she stood watching him through the kitchen window as he moved in long, eager strides and disappeared into the garage.

Pivoting from the window, she hurried through the house to the master bath, where she yanked two lacy bras and panties from a hanger in the large shower and dirty towels from the wall rod. She emptied the second sink of her makeup, searched in the tall cabinet and brought out a new bottle of men's gel soap, and set out a fresh towel and washcloth.

Jackson appeared at the opened door, a toiletry case tucked under his arm and a garment bag slung over his shoulder.

"All yours." She slipped passed him in the doorway.

"Uh..." He fixed her with an expression both hopeful and questioning. "Does this mean you are invitin' me to move back in?"

She looked at him from where she opened the closet door. Her eyes darted to the bed and back to him, moving over his face.

"I suppose I invited you back in Saturday night, when I pulled you into the bed with me."

He studied her. "Well, I guess like you said, it was drought and hormones. I just want to make sure of what you mean right now."

"It *was* drought and hormones," she replied and tilted her head. "But I think maybe that says somethin', too."

His eyes questioned hers, and then he smiled.

She turned quickly, and he disappeared into the bathroom, the door closed, and whistling started up from the other side.

CARLEY LOVE WAS DRESSED for going out and in the kitchen, jotting notes into her notebook, when Jackson appeared and in a frustrated voice asked her to help him with his tie.

"A suit and tie?" She stood in front of him and took the ends of the tie dangling around the neck of his crisp shirt. "New dress code?"

"Big-wig meetin' today." He looked to the side.

"Ah-huh...lift your chin."

She finished tying the knot, adjusted it, gave it a pat. "There you go."

"Thanks." He filled his pockets with the change, keys and phone on the counter. Then his eyes straight on hers, he said, "Look, like I said, I'll be late so don't wait supper for me. But I will be home tonight."

She nodded.

In a hesitant motion, he bent and kissed her cheek, and went out the door.

She stepped to the window and saw him stride along the walk way, pulling his cell phone from his pocket and making a call as he went.

At the sight, she folded her arms across herself and gripped her elbows.

Finding My Way Back To You

TUESDAY, November 21

9:15 a.m.

Cornbread in the oven and second cup of coffee in hand. Life is good.

I am so very glad to not be going anywhere today. I need to think and to be, with no demands. Well, demands other than cooking and party prep, which for me are things of comfort. How strange, really. Much is expected of me with the Thanksgiving meal and wedding party. Yet, in these endeavors, I know confidence and even contentment.

Not so with marriage. I've always been insecure there. And I've been too scared of my insecurity to look at it. I've denied it and stuffed it, like a shameful thing. Well, bless my heart. Let me accept God's grace. God's grace fills in what I am not.

Jackson has moved back home, but the together part is harder. Every time he leaves for work, that old insecurity raises up. I think of how one day he just left and didn't come back. And That Woman is there in the back of my mind to pop out when I least want her.

God, please help me. And thank you for the Psalms of comfort I have managed to memorize. Perhaps some day I will manage to be at ease with my best, rather than always wanting to do better than my best, which is of course an impossibility and wrecks confidence all over the place.

The office is closed, and all calls are forwarded to Doreen, and there should not be much of anything come up with the holiday week. Lila is even going out of town. I invited her for Thanksgiving—it was the polite thing—but she said she was going over to Carrabelle Beach. She said an old friend has come down from Chicago with his class A motorhome. His. No mention of a wife. And I'm glad she turned me down. Her being my boss might make socializing awkward.

Speaking of which, Doreen is coming for Thanksgiving and with a date—the guy she had the blind date with. Guess that turned out well for her. His name is Elmore, of all things. She said he's "so fine."

I was up early, even before Jackson, and started cooking. I am planning both turkey and ham, dressing and gravy, of course, mashed potatoes, and I'm using instant. Hardly anyone can tell, and Royce always raves over it. Bought rolls, too. Candied yams, fresh green beans, and Mama's gelled cranberry-pineapple salad, raisin and pumpkin pies.

We'll all just have to roll from the table. But those are the foods that Royce grew up with, and me and Jackson, too, and who knows how far back it goes. Traditions bring us together and hold us all together.

I mean really, would Jackson have left our marriage if his

parents had still been alive? We'd still be traveling to their house for the holidays.

I wonder what everyone would say if I simply ordered the entire Thanksgiving meal from Winn-Dixie? I heard a woman in the checkout line at the grocery store talking about doing that. She said she set herself free. I was amazed to find that the idea sounded a bit tempting.

I looked at my wedding rings again this morning. But I haven't put them back on yet. I don't really know why. So much inside me is a mystery.

A whisper comes: Perhaps my being a mystery at times is another thing to accept.

~

11:45 a.m.

Well, as Mama would say, "Hot-dog!" A delivery man just arrived with three boxes of the party supplies I had left behind Saturday night and given up for lost because I wasn't going back for them. E.H. also sent a card thanking me and praising my efforts for the dinner party. He used the word marvelous, *and* he included a check for the remaining balance!

That man is one to have the last, loud word.

There are millions of people in the world with vastly different ways of living, and none of their choices are my business. The good news is that I don't have to be around them. I pray for E.H. and wish him well, especially for Trey's sake. And I went straight away and addressed a thank you card to him.

I am tickled to have my little light goblets for the wedding celebration on Saturday!

My goodness—this coming Saturday! I've got to get myself together for decorating and hosting and meeting those international in-laws. Oh, thank goodness I do not have to host Simona's parents here at the house!

After this wedding party, I am going to have a breakdown. I will have earned it.

~

3:30 P.M. And a busy day.

Well, a good cup of Darjeeling tea in the afternoon does much for reviving. So does making shiny silvery bows for the party tables, and gazing out the window, and praying, and getting a second wind for the evening.

So does cooking, once you get the rhythm. While I cooked, I danced around the kitchen to bluegrass music. Freckles must think I'm nuts. In no time at all I have the raisin filling ready to make the pie tomorrow, and the cranberry sauce is made, and the jello salad, and the dressing all mixed up. I'm happy in this minute.

I think taking note of when happiness comes would be a good habit to cultivate. So often happiness is there, but it flies by and I forget. I need to make a thankful list of what makes me happy in order to refer to it when troubled times come—a list of blessings to hold on to.

Ronni just now called! A happy thing for my list. She is on her way home. She must have been in that space of North Florida where the cell service is spotty, she kept breaking up, so we couldn't really talk. She said Trey told Eric some about the party at E.H.'s, so they decided to cut their honeymoon short in order for Eric to come back and help Trey with splitting from his father. She asked about the mess of the dinner party, and I told her that I'd have to explain when she comes home.

I don't think I will tell her details, though. It would be professionally poor on my part. And funny thing, I seem to have moved on from it all, and I'm even able to laugh about some of it.

I hear Granny Reba Love: "Isn't life interesting?"

~

WEDNESDAY, November 22

8:45 a.m.

When Jackson got home last night, I was in bed but awake. I had been listening for him to arrive, my brain more or less on fire with wondering if he actually would come home.

When he did, I pretended to be asleep. I was so relieved he was home, but didn't want him to know I was relieved, because then he would know I had been upset.

We are living together but more like polite strangers who can't be themselves. I am afraid to show my doubts, and afraid to show how much I want him. I'm afraid to let my heart want, much less believe. I'm like that saying, "Once burned twice shy."

Yet, it seems like for him we never broke up. None of it haunts him, or doesn't appear to, as it does me. Perhaps that is a basic difference between men and women. Last night Jackson got into bed carefully, as if not to disturb me. I swear as soon as he stretched out, he went to sleep, while I laid there another good half hour listening to him breathe.

Today is warm and smells sweetly of fall. I have the back door open and have been hearing a mourning dove call. Or

I did, until the workmen got here. Making all sorts of noise now, scaring the birds away and causing Freckles to lay on my feet.

Jackson is out there, watching the work and talking to the foreman. When I took out cold drinks for everyone, he told me that he is having the entire roof fortified to help withstand hurricanes.

He is looking out for our future. That's a good sign. He is happy doing this. Maybe if we had decided on home repair and renovation before he left, he would never have gone off and gotten into trouble and me gone crazy.

Muddling through, that's what I'm doing. Trying to find my way back to us—to me—while at the same time I cannot believe in either.

Lord, help my unbelief.

~

9:30 p.m.

Just when I think nothing will surprise me, tonight Jackson went off in the garage with his friend Gordon—for three hours! I do not even know Gordon's last name. The guy showed up, had some boxes of stuff for Jackson, don't know what it was. When I took the trash out, I saw them sitting in lawn chairs in the garage, drinking beers.

Really? And here Jackson and I are trying to rebuild our marriage and have not had a decent conversation other than fifteen minutes about the reinforcing of the roof and new French doors for Mama's room—I suppose it will always be called Mama's room.

When Jackson came in for a bag of pretzels, I asked him if he wanted to invite Gordon to Thanksgiving dinner. He looked at me as if I had lost my mind and said he didn't think so.

The song Mama used to play a lot suddenly pops in my mind: "Where can I go but to the Lord?" I can hear her singing it.

Well, I'm going to bed.

~

THANKSGIVING DAY

5:00 p.m.

I have had the first Thanksgiving in twenty years without Mama. I had not realized how that fact would affect me. I sort of bounced between melancholy at missing her and teary gratitude for all that I had with her. I teared up when setting the table with the old Wells and Downie family china, silver, and crystal. The crystal water glasses date from Big Granny Myrtle Love and possibly her mother. The people who bought and used them first are long gone.

It seems that we are all moving along the river that is life. Just like a river, life passes through mountains and valleys, sometimes smooth as glass and then suddenly, so unexpectedly most of the time, there are the rough rapids, and you have to hold on until you are through them. But it is always flowing on. You can no more stop it than you can the unusual heat here in November.

The weather was so warm today that we had doors open and ceiling fans going. Jackson wanted to close up and turn on the air-conditioning but agreed to my wish not to do so, although when we sat down to eat, he slipped in and turned on the air-conditioning to cool off the dining room— without closing the doors. I did not point out the wastefulness. No one else seemed to take notice, or at least not offense. I don't know Simona's views on energy waste.

~

SHE LOOKED up when Jackson entered the kitchen.

He saw her at the desk in the alcove. "Oh, here you are."

She closed the journal.

He stood uncertainly by the counter. Looking at the opened door, he said, "It's been a really nice day."

"Yes, I've enjoyed it."

"Uh, would you like to walk outside...look at the sunset?"

"That sounds lovely." She rose quickly.

He called Freckles, and the dog shot out ahead of them.

Jackson took Carley Love's hand as they went down the porch steps and kept hold of it as they strolled across the yard toward the pasture.

He said, "It was a great Thanksgiving meal. Thanks." He rubbed his stomach. "I won't need to eat for a week."

"Thank you for helpin'. Your mashed potatoes were greatly appreciated."

"Not much to boilin' water and mixin'." He grinned at her.

"You got the mixin' done just right." She grinned back, paused, and added, "I'm glad we had a tableful. It sort of eased the ache of Mama bein' gone." She added, "Sometimes it's hard to face bein' the last one. That Mama and Granny Reba are gone, and there is no one to remember my history with me."

He nodded. "I've thought a lot of Mom and Dad lately, too."

"I remembered your mama when I made the cranberry sauce. She's who taught me. I wrote the directions down for Simona, so it's passed to another generation."

He cast her a slow smile and squeezed her hand.

They stopped in the pasture to enjoy the golden western sky and the orange ball sun casting long shadows, with deep turquoise above.

"I'm glad Ronni and Eric stopped in," Carley Love said. "I would not have thought them a match but they appear to be wonderfully happy together."

Jackson nodded.

Silence fell again for a long minute, before Jackson said, "Doreen and that Elmore fella seem kinda unlikely, him so tall and her short and wide." He grinned. "I doubt he said five words at dinner."

"I don't think it's his talkin' Doreen appreciates. She says he is like candy to a woman because he is so handsome and yet uncertain and shy."

Silence came again, as the golden horizon deepened to burnt orange.

She said, "It was good to see that Simona is over her sickness enough now that she can enjoy a cup of coffee."

He smiled in agreement.

A breeze passed, blowing tendrils of hair over her forehead. Jackson rocked back on his heels.

He broke the silence with, "It looks like Trey and Brittney may be a couple."

She said, "I don't think there's any maybe about it. She needs him as both a lover and father, and he needs to be needed. He'll grow her up well and be gladly occupied doin' it."

She shifted her gaze to him, brows furrowing in thought as she studied his profile.

His head turned slowly, his eyes coming to hers. They smiled softly at each other, then returned to looking at the sunset that was now only an orange ribbon on the horizon.

"That's it, I guess," he said.

"Yes, another day is done."

They returned hand in hand back to the house, where warm light shone from the windows.

"I love our home," she said with suddenness.

"Yeah, me, too." He paused and said, "You know, you aren't all alone in your memories."

"What?"

"What you said earlier...that there's no one to remember your history with you. I've been with you since you were sixteen. I remember...your dad and your grandparents, and the town where my mother came from...how it was. Not to mention half of our furniture comes from our families. It just sort of makes you remember life back where we came from."

She studied the house. "We've come a long way. And it seems like it passed in a flash."

"I know." His voice echoed with wonder.

"I think that now...I need to live more in the present. Pay attention to where and who I am now." She spoke haltingly, seeking words. "It is as if I've entered a new era of my life."

He nodded. They had reached the porch, and he stopped, looked down at her a moment, then bent and kissed her gently.

When they broke apart, Jackson cleared his throat. "How 'bout we sit out back and have come coffee."

"That sounds lovely," she replied.

Carley Love decided on a cup of hot tea. "There's sweet tea left in the refrigerator, if you'd rather it than coffee."

Jackson opened the refrigerator, reached for the tea pitcher, and pulled it out. He paused, set the pitcher on the counter and then stretched his arm far back into the refrigerator, bringing out the bottle of wine.

Carley Love, turning from the cabinet with a tall glass she had for him, saw him looking at the bottle. "Ronni brought it for me, to help me sleep."

"Uh-huh." He looked from the bottle to her, a smile spreading slowly. "Well, how about we have a glass?" He inclined his head, indicating the stemmed crystal glasses setting on the counter. "We still have these out."

"We don't need to take up drinkin'." She came up straight and tall. "We've already seen what drinkin' can do. Besides, those are water glasses."

"I doubt these glasses will explode if I put wine in them," he drawled, as he poured the dark liquid into a glass and held it up. "See there. And a little glass of this mild wine isn't takin' up drinkin'. It's relaxin', like you said."

"Just so you know, drinkin' alcohol is not the life I want."

"I know that, honey, and I agree. I intend to be goin' to church and being a sober and upright man. But a glass of wine in my own home to celebrate the end of a fine Thanksgivin' day with my beloved wife does not change that."

A grin tugged at her lips. She watched him replace the tea pitcher on the refrigerator shelf, hesitate, and bring forth the leftover pie. "We'll dress it up with raisin pie." His eyes twinkled at her.

"I thought you said you weren't eatin' until next week."

"Sacrilegious to let this fine pie get stale."

"Oh, you are one smooth-talkin' man, Jackson Wells," she said, laughter in her voice.

She looked at the pie as he reached into the drawer for a knife. She said smartly, "Right...and there's enough for me, too." She took the pie plate. "I'll cut."

"If you say so."

She placed the slices of pie onto the fine china dessert plates. He handed her a full glass of wine. She viewed it with a playful questioning eye, and he gave her a wink.

They carried their drinks and pie to the back veranda and sat in the deep chairs. Jackson lit the fireplace and torches. He disappeared inside the house, and shortly country music came softly from the speakers hidden high in the veranda roof—George Strait singing about stumbling through the darkness.

Returning, Jackson sat and raised his glass. "To you—the hostess with the mostest—givin' us all a delicious Thanksgiving meal once again."

She touched her glass lightly against his. "To...us."

"To us," he repeated softly.

She watched him sip and took a tentative sip herself.

He said, "Well, it's not bad at all."

"I guess I really have no idea." She sipped again and cocked her head in thought. "It does have a sweet warmth. But I don't know about cheap blackberry wine and raisin pie together," she said. "I doubt the two would appear on a menu together at any reputable restaurant or gala."

Jackson stretched his legs to prop his boots up on the coffee table, saying, "Maybe not for connoisseurs...but bein' pretty much a country boy, it seems just fine to me."

After long minutes and several sips of wine, she said, "It is relaxin'. Ronni was right about that." She closed her eyes and breathed deeply. "I'm lookin' forward to the wedding party, but I confess, I'll be glad when it is over. I have done enough for a while."

Jackson said, "I'll be around to help with everythin'. I'm off for two weeks, like I said...because I quit my job."

She looked up from her pie. "Quit your job?"

"Yep. I'm no longer workin' for Binson. I've left them. I'll have..."

"You never told me you were thinkin' of that. We didn't discuss it."

"Well, you said I shouldn't be seein'...and anyway, there wasn't any reason to discuss it. I had an opportunity and I took it—the same as you did when you declined Lila's offer of full-time work. I'll have..."

"You can't equate my workin' for Lila with your job. My workin' for Lila doesn't affect you in any real way, but what you do with your job sure affects me. But mostly, when I mentioned you quittin' your job last year, you jumped all over me about it. You thought I was insane to suggest it."

"I disagree. Your workin' for Lila has affected me all along. It changed all our home life. You weren't hardly ever here."

"You said you were fine with me workin'. You said you were proud of me."

"I was...I am. But it did change things around here."

"It gave us extra money. We bought the new living room furniture. I paid for it."

"I don't think in terms of whose money is whose. And we're gettin' all off track. Let me get back to what I'm tryin' to say. I admit that I might have reacted a little poorly last year to your suggestion for me to quit my job, but...

"Poorly is stating it mildly."

"Let me finish. I did think about it, and kept thinking about it, and I came to the conclusion that was what needed to be done."

She opened her mouth to reply, and he held up his hand. She closed her mouth and bit her bottom lip.

He said, "The biggest point is that we are here *now*, and will you just *listen* right now?"

"I am listenin'." She faced him squarely.

"You want to talk about it, well, I'm talkin'."

"Go *ahead*." She gestured with her glass.

"I'll have the next two weeks off, and then I'll start a position with Elliot Contractors. The pay is less..."

"You aren't gonna miss workin' at Binson? You've been there over twenty years."

"Carle'Love, let me explain in my own way."

"Okay. But you've worked there a long time, and I know you have friends there, like Gordon."

His expression turned to surprise. "Gordon isn't so much of a friend."

Her eyebrows rose. "Well, he let you stay at his apartment, and he was here last night for hours of talkin'." She gestured with a sweeping arm. "You talk like that to a stranger?"

"He isn't a stranger, and he isn't what I call a real friend, okay? He just needed to vent. And he is a real talker. He could be a cousin to Doreen. His wife left him and his daughter is messed up, and he's tryin' to figure out a way to change to another company in order to get more money and less hours, so he can help his daughter. You know, the drug treatment."

"Yes, I do," she said concern flitting over her features. She looked from her wiggling toes to him. "The thing is, I don't want to think that somethin' I said caused you to do somethin' you really didn't want to do. Because back then you really acted like you did not want to leave Binson. And if you do what you really don't want to do, you'll just end up resentin' me...and we'll be right back where we were." Her tone dropped to a whisper with the last.

He observed her a moment, then said, "I've told you that you did not cause me to do anythin'. I never really resented you, Carle'Love. I love you. The change now is from thinkin' about it all these months. And you were right about me not seein' Ani...well...you were right that I needed to cut ties.

"And I wasn't ever really against leavin' Binson. I just couldn't see where else I could go. I couldn't see a whole lot of things," he added in a thoughtful tone. "I wasn't mad at you all those months ago when you suggested I quit. You just happened to be in the way of my anger at myself."

She opened her mouth to speak, closed it and nodded.

"Look, I came around to realizin' that I've wanted to leave Binson for some time. I haven't liked the direction the company has taken since Thomas Binson stepped down two years ago. I didn't want to face that, because it meant I would have to go find something else, and at my age that's not so easy. I felt boxed in, honey, stuck and not likin' my life.

"I finally realized, though, that I had to take the chance. And that I had to step out on faith and just go ahead and quit, so I did. And it turned out that I got a chance with Elliot."

His tone rose with excitement. "It wasn't two hours after turnin' in my resignation that Carter Elliot heard I was quittin' Binson and called me. Right out of the blue. I'll be workin' in a totally different building, with totally different personnel." His happy eyes met hers.

"Am I supposed to say somethin' now?"

"Yes."

She brought out a smile. "Well. You seem happy with the idea, so I'm happy for you. What will you be doin' with the new company?"

"Pretty much the same thing that I have been doin'— workin' with government personnel to keep the radars up. The pay is a little less, but so are the hours, and I won't be on call. And they've promised, in writing, promotion to headin' my own team within a year. There's real chance for advancement and good retirement, too."

"Well, if you're sure."

"I'm sure."

"Then," She lifted her crystal glass, "a toast to success in your wonderful new job."

He raised his glass to hers. They each drank and sat for a moment gazing into the fire that flickered low and steady.

"The wine *does* make one nicely relaxed." She gave a large sigh of contentment.

He grinned at her.

The mellow voice of country singer Keith Urban floated out, singing of the grace of God.

Jackson got up, took her by the hand and swept her into his arms, dancing her seductively across the veranda.

When the song ended, she rested her head in the hollow of his shoulder. His hand came up, stroked her hair.

"I love you," he said, his voice resonant with emotion, "and I won't ever let a day go by where I don't show you how much I do, and how much I value what we have."

She pulled back to look into his eyes. "I love you, Jackson. I always have...and I always will." And she brought her lips to his.

They kissed long and deeply, while Rascal Flatts sang from the stereo about the blessed broken road.

Drawing apart, slowly, they gazed at each other as if in a daze.

"I'll take care of the fire and lock up," Jackson said, and reached for the remote control to silence the music.

He turned to the fireplace and Carley Love moved to gather the few dishes, taking them into the kitchen sink.

She then hurried through the house to the bedroom, where she retrieved the ring box from her bedside chest. She slipped the rings onto her finger and clasped her right hand over them for a long second, before rising to retrieve the black lace gown from the closet and disappear into the bathroom.

When she reemerged she saw Jackson removing his shirt. She stood waiting for him to turn and see her.

When he did, his eyes jumped and a smile spread over his face. She smiled in return.

Carley Love slipped into bed. Jackson came and sat beside her.

"You are more beautiful now than the day I married you," he said.

A shadow passed over her face, and she opened her

mouth to reply, but he silenced her with a kiss. He parted from her only long enough to turn out the lamp.

LATER, as they lay in each other's arms, they spoke in the drowsy whispers of sleep talk. They murmured about being grandparents, but not feeling like grandparents, about their guests that day, and what their parents might have said about this thing and that thing.

They fell silent. Carley Love's cheek lay against Jackson's warm chest. She listened to the rhythmic beating of his heart.

Just then Jackson tightened his arms around her and whispered, "I'm sure glad to be home with you."

"I'm glad you are home," came her ardent whispered reply.

She gazed at the silver moon-glow on the distant wall, contentment on her face.

Vows

CARLEY LOVE WORE a Marchesa designer cocktail dress with long sleeves and a cut-out back and flowing tea-length skirt that Simona had brought back from her latest modeling job in Atlanta. Simona was hesitant with the gift, afraid of offending, but Carley Love delighted not only in the beautiful dress but that her daughter-in-law already knew her so well. The fit and style of the dress suited her perfectly. She felt she floated along on her heels, even while carrying two large and somewhat heavy cardboard boxes.

She peered around the boxes as she approached the glass double doors of the condominium and frowned. For an instant, she attempted to balance the boxes with one hand in order to open the door with the other. The boxes wobbled, and she quickly took hold of them, and looked around for a space in which to set them. There did not appear to be one.

Just then the doors opened from the other side, and Royce and Simona exited.

"Oh, good, you two! I wasn't certain how I was going to get inside. Here, Royce, take one of these boxes."

"Everything is looking so lovely in the hall," Simona said. "Thank you! We're just goin' to go pick up my father from the airport. I've got to get my things...I'll meet you at the car, Royce." She spoke as she slipped passed and dashed off.

Carley Love turned her eyes to Royce, who walked beside her. "Okay, what is it? What's the problem?"

"What?"

"Well, I believe Simona was upset. She didn't look at me, and she always kisses my cheek, and you are scowling."

He cast her a hesitant look and ended up coming out with, "We had a fight about sellin' her BMW."

"Ah." They entered the event room, went to a table and set the boxes on it. "Look, I'm not goin' to butt in...but I guess I will, since we are in a time crunch. In less than two hours now, we're havin' a party to celebrate yours and Simona's union, so it would be best that you both are actually together in body and heart. The long and short of it is, what means the most to you—your big truck or Simona?" She fixed him with a questioning eye.

"Of course it's Simona, Mom. But she doesn't understand how much of my blood and sweat I've put into that truck. I built that truck, Mama. From the ground up. It's a custom, one of a kind."

She gazed at him. "Honey, I hear you. That truck is a work of art. You love it, unlike the BMW, which is utility." She continued, humor lacing her tone, "But what memory do you want to put on the wall? That truck? Or you and Simona happy with your children?"

She paused deliberately, then stated, "In any case, the

decision doesn't have to be resolved right now. Lettin'
Simona know you love her more than your truck *does*."

"I do love her more than my truck," he stated.

"And that needs to be the most important factor for
you at any moment...and that's the only way either of you
will enjoy this party. And it is too late to cancel it," she
added.

"I know, Mama." He shook his head with a rueful smile
and kissed her cheek. Then he strode away, breaking into a
jog toward the door.

She set about arranging the candles on the tables already
covered with crisp white linen cloths.

Minutes later Jackson arrived with several of Royce's
friends trailing behind him and hauling a trolley of chairs.
"Your gardenias, extra chairs, and your crew have arrived,"
he said, lifting the box he carried.

"I saw Royce and Simona outside," he told her as she
investigated the box's contents.

"Had they made up?"

Surprise crossed his face. "They looked pretty made up
to me. They were kissin'."

"Good," she said with relief. "I promised myself I would
stay out of their business, but your wife just butted in."

He laughed. "My mother did plenty of buttin' in, too.
Isn't that your job?" He began rolling up his sleeves. "We
have lucked out with the warm weather."

"Not luck. Simona and I prayed. Oh, these gardenias
smell heavenly!" She smiled happily at him. "Thank you for
pickin' them up. Get water in those pitchers, if you would.
I'm gonna float some blossoms in Granny's blue hobnail
compotes. Oh, and have them scatter the extra chairs along
that wall," she added, gesturing at the young men who were

at the moment boisterously playing as they tossed chairs and opened them.

"Yes, ma'am."

He strode away to do as she bid and returned with the pitchers of water for her flowers and a cold bottle of water for himself. "Good idea, the big ice chests." He gestured toward two tall red ice chests on legs with wheels.

"They are a gift from Dwight Fellows Construction, one of Royce's biggest customers. Dwight, the younger, is a good friend. And the coolers came filled, too."

"All-right!"

"There's also two types of fruit punch—Royce and Simona made that choice with no input from me." She lifted her palms in innocence. "Royce said some of his friends might BYOB, but he and Simona were supporting Simona's father, who it turns out is a recovering alcoholic."

"Well, then, sounds good."

"In addition, the caterer will be providing gluten-free and vegan offerings—labelled—and absolutely no shellfish, nuts, or strawberries, as at least two children and one adult are highly allergic." She looked at him with round eyes. "I have emergency on speed dial."

"You've got it covered, Miss Party-planner."

"I hope so. How did the original twenty-five close family and friends turn into seventy-five plus?"

"Probably because your son and daughter-in-law kept invitin' everyone they bumped into." He drank deeply of his water, then winked. "And it bein' free food and casual."

"I told the caterer eighty, and I sure hope we don't go over. This room will be crowded with that, and we'll either be carryin' home leftovers or runnin' out. Runnin' out is fine, actually, people won't linger. Oh, there's the caterer now."

She hurried to place the sky-blue dishes of gardenias on the tables, calling over her shoulder to Jackson to please get the ladder and help to string the lights over the dance floor.

～

CARLEY LOVE and Jackson met at the punch bowl. Jackson leaned close to be heard, while filling two glasses.

"I think your attendee estimate is close, and thank goodness the air-conditioning works well."

"How's Simona's father?"

"He's an engineer," he replied with a wide grin.

"Ah...a lot in common?"

"We both know some of the same people up in D.C." His expression registered surprise.

She smilingly said, "There are no coincidences." Then— "Oh, my goodness—that must be Simona's mother at last! She *is* beautiful," she said, glanced down and smoothed her dress, then hurried away to greet the woman.

～

THE GUESTS BEGAN to move outside to the beach where Royce and Simona were to repeat their vows in front of a minister with the setting sun behind them. A pile of shoes grew on the patio outside the doors.

"Wait!" Carley Love called, and, shaking off her heels, padded quickly across the cool sand to give Simona the bouquet of gardenias. "And this for your hair."

On sight of the hair wreath Carley Love had created

with gardenias, Simona's face lit with delight. She bent, and Carley Love went up on tiptoe to fasten the wreath combs into the younger woman's abundant hair.

"They smell so good." Simona's voice echoed with joy.

"There. You are beautiful, darling girl."

"It's crooked," said Simona's mother, appearing beside them and reaching out easily from her equally tall height to adjust the wreath. "It's...well, that will have to do."

Simona's smile faltered. She shifted her eyes to Royce, who gazed at her adoringly. A full smile returning, she stepped beside him and took his hand.

With the peaceful sound of surf in the distance and the sun blessing the scene with final ethereal coral rays, the young couple stood in front of the minister and said vows they had composed, Simona from memory, Royce using notes written on his palm.

"Trey helped him do that," whispered Brittney.

Trey murmured, "He wasn't supposed to be so obvious about it, though." His voice was loud enough that faint chuckles floated through the crowd.

Royce finished his vows and said to the audience, "Well, I want to get it just right."

"Good start!" called a male voice, and laughter rippled.

The minister, a petite woman wearing a grey pantsuit with a white clergy stole draped around her neck, raised her hands to quiet everyone.

She smiled at the couple. "God bless and keep you in love with each other. Go and serve God and your neighbor in all that you do." She turned her gaze to the audience. "You all, Simona and Royce's friends and family, bear witness to their love and commitment. Support them with your love and prayers. The grace of the Lord Jesus Christ and the love of God and the communion of the Holy Spirit be with you all."

A shout went up and everyone clapped and rushed to gather around the couple. Royce was heard saying, "Well, I think maybe now, after sayin' I do twice, I feel really married."

People began making their way back inside.

Doreen, who still wore her platform heels and steadied herself by holding tightly to Elmore, said, "Well, I'm glad they are already married, because I'm not certain how legal this would be with that woman minister."

Walking close behind, Brittney said, "What's wrong with a woman minister? My mother has one at her church."

"No doubt," was Doreen's flat reply. "Aside from citin' the Word, I think this minister may have obtained her pastor license from one of those online places that sells 'em."

"What's wrong with that? Is it legal?" Brittney turned anxious eyes up to Trey.

"I imagine so," he replied in a noncommittal manner. Then he added in his attorney tone, "Just as much as a civil wedding, if all the filings are done correctly."

A thoughtful expression swept his face. "I'm pretty sure I can perform a marriage ceremony as a notary. I can file the paperwork."

"Oh, that is awesome!" Brittney gave a jump as she held on to him and gazed at him as if he had hung the moon.

Carley Love and Jackson grinned at each other and in wordless agreement moved on quickly to leave the debate behind. Inside, music began to play—the song "I Do Cherish You." People made room as Royce and Simona swept onto the dance floor. He wore his boots and she was still barefoot, so they were closer in height. They had eyes only for each other as they moved in dreamy unison.

Moments later, Simona tossed the bouquet. It flew in an arc across a table into Carley Love's hands that instinctively went up to catch it with a startled "Oh!"

She looked down at the bouquet, and when she looked up, she saw Jackson standing some feet away, smiling at her.

The music changed to the upbeat rhythm of "How Forever Feels," and Royce strode to Carley Love and swept her, barefoot and laughing, onto the dance floor to join Simona and her father waltzing around.

At the end of the music, Royce led his mother back to her table and kissed her cheek. "Thanks, Mom."

She touched his face tenderly and watched him with pride as many congratulated him.

Ronni and Eric were at the table. "Sorry we're late," said Ronni, handing Carley Love a glass of punch. "But we got here in time to see the ceremony. It was really precious." She looked around and observed, "How many of these people here are Baptists dancin'?"

Carley Love laughed.

"What's the joke?" Eric asked.

Doreen put in, "Baptists can only dance with one foot."

Startled, Eric scanned the crowd on the dance floor. "Really?"

Ronni said, "Honey, she's jokin'. Y'all have mercy on him. He's northern Lutheran and has married a southern Catholic, so he's confused. I'll explain all of our denominations to you when we get home, sweetheart."

Doreen rose, taking Elmore with her, telling him, "Forget you are Baptist for a bit and dance with me."

He looked perplexed and was heard to say, "Why wouldn't I dance?"

Carley Love watched them take the floor and allowed her gaze to flow over the crowd in the habitual manner of a hostess searching for needs. Her gaze rested on Royce dancing with Simona's mother and Simona dancing with her mother's date, and a small boy and girl just beyond them holding hands and swaying to the music. Her smile broadened. She noted Simona's father and Royce's friend, Dwight, in deep conversation, and Jackson and Trey, heads bent together. Her gaze rested on the two men, and she cocked her head, as if she could possibly hear them. Trey nodded and grinned. Ronni and Eric danced into her line of sight and her attention followed them, warmth sweeping her expression.

Moments later she spied Simona's chic mother coming toward her.

"I want to thank you for invitin' us. It has been a lovely party," the woman said in her cultured Southern accent.

Carley Love's eyes widened. "Why, thank you. But...are you leavin'?"

"Yes. We've booked over in Destin for a few days." The woman's companion appeared and draped a cashmere wrap around her shoulders. "Thank you again. It's been delightful to meet Simona's husband and family."

"I am very glad to have met you, too. I hope you will visit often."

Carley Love was about to say more, but the couple walked away, the aloof elegant woman secure in the shelter of her companion's arm.

"Was that Simona's mother?" Ronni asked, coming off the dance floor with Eric.

"Yes...and her boyfriend. Actually, I'm assuming that's her boyfriend. We barely had any conversation." She paused. "Do you know, I think this is the first time she has met Royce."

"Well," Ronni offered, letting the word stand a moment before adding brightly, "We see where Simona got her beauty, and that Royce has a lot to look forward to."

THE CATERER DEPARTED, followed half an hour later by the last of the guests—Gordon, who Jackson had ended up inviting, Dwight and his date, and Simona's father. Simona and Royce, Trey and Brittney, Ronni and Eric danced on, slowly. The DJ, who propped himself back in the chair with his feet on the table, played timeless, intimate love ballads.

Doreen had taken charge of boxing up decorations, instructing Elmore in how to help. Elmore could reach the strings of lights without a ladder.

Jackson took Carley Love's hand. "Walk outside with me and see the moonlight on the water."

"I need to help Doreen...and it's gettin' cold."

"She's got it under control. Here." He pulled a table cloth off a table and wrapped it around her shoulders.

She chuckled and put her hand into his. At the door she slipped off her heels. "Oh, my gosh, the sand is chilly!"

He wrapped his arm around her. They walked to the firmer damp sand and admired the moonlight glimmering on the water.

He said, "Well, Care'lina, our boy is makin' his own nest now."

"Yes." A pause. "He has made a good choice in Simona."

"He has...as I did." He smiled down at her for a long moment.

"Me, too," she said, looking up into his eyes.

They turned their faces to the dark and rippling waves glimmering beneath moonbeams.

Jackson said, "If you had it to do over, would you marry me again?"

She opened her mouth but hesitated, gazing in thought before answering.

"Yes," she said to him. "Marryin' you was the best decision of my life. I have so very much because I married you."

She leaned into him and added in a low tone, "I got your parents with you—as you got Mama," she said with a chuckle.

He smiled thoughtfully.

"Do you remember me sayin' the other night that Trey would grow Brittney up?"

"I do."

"I realize now that you did that for me. I was such a child when I married you. Oh, I know we both were. But I really was, Jackson. You've always been more mature than I in many ways. Granted, not in *every* way."

She tapped him pointedly with her elbow. "But I never had much of a father. I didn't even know him. I never missed him when he died, because he had disappeared into himself. *You* became in large part that father I never had.

"You've been my lover, my husband, my father, and I'm grateful for all you have given me. You've grown me up, Jackson."

She turned her eyes to his profile, as he looked thoughtfully down at the sand and then out at the glimmering water.

She added softly, "Neither of us are perfect, and expectations can be a heavy load to bear. But in truth, you have been a very good husband to me, Jackson."

His head came round, his gaze to meet hers. "I'm glad you feel that way." His tone was hoarse. "I have also grown up a lot in the past year, that's for sure. And I'm grateful to you, Care'lina. So very grateful."

He hugged her to him, kissed her hair, and squeezed his eyes closed. A tear escaped and slipped down his cheek.

He murmured, his voice choked, "We've had a really good life. I'm grateful you want me to come back and to start again."

"I see it more as we are continuin' on." Her voice became choked, too. "I think we have grown together and can't be split."

"I think you're right."

He held her and breathed deeply, then pulled back to look into her face. The salty breeze teased tendrils of her moonlit hair.

"What would you say to us renewin' our vows?" His tone was hesitant but his eyes unwavering.

"Well...I think that's a lovely idea."

"Good." He beamed at her, then strode out on the sand, tugging her along. "Trey will hear us renew our vows."

"What?"

"I already spoke to him about it."

"Trey? Oh...I don't know. I'm pretty worn...and we're all tired. And this is Royce and Simona's day."

"Honey, Royce and Simona had their day. And you look fine...you look beautiful. And everyone waited so they could join in."

"You arranged it all already?"

"Yep."

"Oh." She took that in, halting him and looking at the brightly lit windows before them. "But...I would like to do it beautifully...not in a room half-decorated and scattered with discarded plastic dishes."

"We'll do it right here in the moonlight on the beach."

He waited.

"Does Trey know the wording? I don't know what all to say." She hesitated but her eyes began to sparkle.

"It doesn't have to be fancy. And you always know what to say."

"Not always." Caution again.

He regarded her with a decidedly hopeful expression.

"Oh, okay! After all, I'm in a designer dress!" She breathed deeply and the two of them, hand in hand, strode toward the building.

Trey came to the opened door before they reached it. "So is it a go?"

"Yes." Jackson's face spread with a wide smile.

Carley Love's eyes went to Royce and Simona. They grinned and she grinned back.

"Trey made notes on his palm," said Brittney with her bubbly excitement. "I didn't think I'd get to see him officiate a weddin' so soon."

"You do know they are already married, right?" Ronni spoke as if to bring the younger woman back to earth. "Both couples tonight are already married."

Carley Love and Jackson shared a chuckle, their eyes lingering on each other.

"Oh, my word, on the sand again?" Doreen regarded the beach with dismay.

Elmore, without a word, scooped her up into his arms and carried her.

They gathered in the silvery moonlight on the flat damp sand, with the gentle surf giving a rhythmic welcome. Ronni helped Carley Love tie the white table cloth artfully around her shoulders, leaving her hands free, one to hold Jackson's hand and the other to hold the gardenia bouquet that Simona had thought to bring.

Everyone got quiet and Trey held his palm this way and that toward the moonlight, squinting at it.

"Wait! Trey, you stand here." Carley Love repositioned him with his back to the moon, and Jackson and herself with the moon like a gentle spotlight on them.

"There, that's better." She shook back her hair and beamed at Jackson.

Trey again lifted his hand and squinted at it.

Eric said, "You're an attorney. You can talk without notes."

"Right. We've come here to witness and celebrate the re-commitment of Carley Love and Jackson as husband and wife. Carley Love and Jackson are truly gifts to each other. Lord, please hear and bless their vows to one another."

He said, "Jackson."

Jackson looked at Carley Love. He opened his mouth, closed it, took a breath, and finally spoke.

"Care'lina Love Wells, I thank you for all the years that we've been together. I'm grateful you married me to begin with, and that you are willin' to keep on with me. I'm sorry for the times I let you down."

A shadow passed over his face, and he paused, his eyes intent on hers. "I promise to love and cherish you always...

to not take you for granted, even when our hair turns grey. Or, I guess grey-er."

He smiled tenderly and seemed to lean into her. "I will do my best to be the leader God calls me to be..." his tone picked up tempo, "...will be slow to anger and quick to listen...and always let you know where I am, so that you don't have to wonder, ever. I'll never let a day go by that I don't let you know my love, through good times and tough times. I will be faithful to you alone...until God calls me home."

As Jackson spoke, Carley Love's eyes, fixed on his face, began to shimmer.

Trey prodded, "Carley?"

She cleared her throat. "Jackson Paul Wells, I thank you for marryin' me all those years ago and givin' me a secure home, takin' care of me as you have. I, too, am sorry for the times I've let you down."

She paused, moonlight glimmering on unshed tears. "In the years to come I will do my best to love you, accept you, to honor and respect you, and to listen, and let you lead— and to trust God when I can't understand," she said ardently. "And to forgive, even as I am forgiven," she added with trembling lips.

She would have continued, but Jackson cupped her face with his hands and kissed her deeply.

When he released her, she said, "I promise, forever and ever, amen."

Their friends began clapping.

Trey said in his official voice. "God bless your union." His voice returned to normal as he added, "And we are all sure glad to see you back together."

"Amen!" shouted Royce and Ronni at once.

"Oh, that was just so beau-ti-ful." Brittney broke out in sobs and fell upon Trey's chest.

Immediately everyone turned to head up the beach to the building, agreeing that the sand and air had become much too cold, although Eric informed them that it was sixty-two degrees, and Ronni told him that he was not in the North anymore.

Jackson held Carley Love's hand and kept back, letting the others go on ahead. When they did approach the open doors, he said, "They're playin' our song."

"Our song?" She cocked her ear to listen.

Randy Travis' voice floated out, singing "Forever and Ever, Amen."

"You planned this, too?" she said in breathless wonder.

Jackson smiled broadly and hurried her onto the dance floor, took her in his arms and guided her smoothly, as he sang the song in her ear.

When the music ended, he whispered, "Forever, I promise, Care'lina."

She laid her head into the hollow of his shoulder, where it fit just right.

Two and a half years later

SHE SAT at her desk in the bedroom. The glow of sunlight filtered through the open French doors, along with the heat and indistinct voices from the backyard pool. Hearing childish laughter erupt, she smiled as she spread open her journal to a new blank page and took up her blue ink pen.

FRIDAY, June 10, 2009
    1:15 p.m.
    I am home and gratified to have seen Mama buried with her people back in North Carolina, where she belongs—with Granny Reba Love and Granny Myrtle Love, and as it turns out, six other Love women in the cemetery!
    I still can't get over that Daddy is buried in his family's Crocker section right across the cemetery driveway. If I knew that, I had forgotten. Mama and Daddy's headstones gaze at each other across a cinder drive. There's some sort of cosmic meaning in that.
    A tiny bit of Mama's ashes rest in a keepsake box on my desk. I can almost hear her saying, "It's about time."
    Isn't everything? is what I say.
    The past two weeks have been a wonderful getaway—a memorable trip to the places of our beginnings. "The blood's country," Jackson calls it. Somehow we needed to go back, to take a look at life lessons, and at blessings. And both a saying thank-you and farewell to where we started.
    Jackson and I agreed that we wanted to get home for

our anniversary today. We have made it to celebrating thirty-eight years. A miracle of grace.

I keep looking at Jackson. He has more grey at his temples but plenty of dark brown hair yet, his eyes more iridescent blue than ever. He took up going to the gym with Royce some time back, and my word, he has the neck and shoulders of a man in his prime. I figured I needed to do something to keep up, but the gym with Simona was beyond me. I chose walking with Freckles two or three miles a day, and since summer I swim most days.

I hear Simona bringing the children inside from the pool for afternoon nap. It is lovely that Simona and Royce seem to like spending time with us. Both of them have proven to be amazing all the way around. The only worry those two have given us was when they decided to buy a yacht rather than a house with the wedding gift money. I told Jackson that we could not interfere. You can't tell people what to do with the gift you give them.

And the questionable situation turned out for good, as most do. Royce and Simona enjoyed the yacht for a memorable honeymoon, and afterward used the money from the sale of it at a profit to purchase their first house. Simona no longer models, but she still has connections that provide her with Ferragamo shoes and Saint Laurent outfits, which she wears when listening to country music and growing her garden and pureeing baby food.

Ronni often says to me these days, Anything can happen, anything can be. She got that from Eric. He is perpetually upbeat with positive sayings. Trey says it can drive him nuts, but Ronni has greatly needed his boosting ways since the devastating loss of her daughter's baby the past February.

While Jackson and I were away, Doreen became Lila's office manager. I am ever so glad that I never stepped into that position. Doreen is truly a managerial person. She really was a lifesaver of help on what turned out to be a monstrous party I took on for the hospital fund-raiser. I'm still tending to get myself into such deep and wide situations, but I no longer fear my tendency. God always sends help.

I do have more confidence—and Doreen and I are becoming such good friends. I wish she would marry Elmore. Maybe if I start planning a wedding party for her, that will do the trick.

Tonight will be the first time to see Trey and Brittney for several months—since their anniversary dinner party in March. I marvel at them, am so proud of both of them for taking care of E.H. as they have since his stroke. It has required a lot of forgiveness on Trey's part and travel for them both back and forth to Miami. We spoke to Trey on the phone during our trip, and he said E.H. is making great progress and that he has a girlfriend! A nurse from the hospital. I'll have to ask Brittney tonight. That young woman is the dearest heart.

Just think, three years ago at this time Jackson and I were broken up. Our marriage and our very selves shattered and lost beyond all reason.

But God—the two most important words in the Bible. Never reckon without God.

I remember how afraid I always have been of heartache. I thought I could not survive. It was the fear itself that kept me bound. Today I see that brokenness is part and parcel of everyday life. The brokenness is used as the means to bring us closer to God, to love and joy.

Oh, dear Father, thank you for what has been mended and made new—for the times that love flows smooth and sparkling. I know with humans this is not a constant and that disappointment and discord often break us wide open. And then it is that we can see and hear what we could not. Help me to remember that fact in the rough times. Help me to hold on to love, to trust it to carry me always.

~

THE BEDROOM DOOR creaked as it swung inward and Jackson strode into the room, removing his shirt as he came.

"Sorry to interrupt, but I need a clean shirt. Your grandson and I shared ice cream before his nap," he said as he headed to the closet. "Are you 'bout ready? Trey and Brittney just arrived. And Gordon is comin' up the drive."

"Gordon." She laughed.

"Yeah," He tossed her a sheepish grin. "I guess he's one of us all now."

Their eyes met in the mirror above the desk, and smiles slowly bloomed on their faces.

She rose and went to him, wrapping her arms around his neck and her fingernails stroking his silky hair.

"Happy anniversary," he said, his eyes caressing her face and his hands her hips.

"Happy anniversary," she replied.

He kissed her fully, until they were both breathless.

"I guess we have to go out to our own party." He frowned a playful frown.

"Yes," and she added with a flirtatious eye, "But there is tonight."

Stepping to the desk, she closed the journal and deposited it into the bottom deep drawer, atop of the many already there.

Her gaze rested upon the stack of books just before she closed the drawer. With her fingers still on the drawer front, her gaze flitted to the small rosewood box on the desktop and lingered on the gold embossing: June Marie Love Murray Crocker.

She breathed deeply, saw her image in the mirror, and then Jackson behind her.

She turned, saying, "Let's go, handsome. It's *our* party."

He put his arm around her and pulled her close as they left the room.

Acknowledgments

I am deeply grateful for advice, discussions, boosting, and general hand-holding during the writing journey of this book from writer friends Mary Ann McSweeny and Cait London, and from all the dear readers of my blog, who sent encouragement at just the time I needed it. Thank you all!

Love,

CurtissAnn

About the Author

Told with a strong Southern voice, Curtiss Ann Matlock's touching and warm-hearted stories portray the grace, grit, and human comedy of men and women striving to live and love well in small-town America. Her novels have placed on the *USA TODAY* best-seller lists and received numerous awards, among them two National Readers' Choice Awards, and three nominations for the *Romance Writers of America's* prestigious RITA Award.

Please connect with her at <u>curtissannmatlock.com</u>.

Also by Curtiss Ann Matlock

Lost Highways, Valentine Series Book #1

Sweet Dreams at the Goodnight Motel, Valentine Series Book #6

Little Town, Great Big Life, Valentine Series Book #8

Miracle On I-40, a Christmas Romance

Book Club Discussion Questions

1. What did you like about *According to Carley Love*?
2. What are your impressions of Carley Love? Of Jackson?
3. What did you think of their situation, and of how they handled it? How do you think you would handle the situation?
4. Was there any one line or passage that stood out to you?
5. What feelings/emotions does this novel bring up for you?
6. Do you have a favorite character, or a character with whom you identify? Why?
7. If the book were adapted to a movie, what actors would you see in the main character roles?
8. What would you say are the main themes from the book?
9. Have you read other books by Curtiss Ann Matlock? If so, how does this one compare?

10. Did you know anything about *According to Carley Love* before you read it? Were you surprised by any of it?